WILDLING'S CLAIM

Book Four

Salvaggio's Light

An Epic Contemporary Romance Serial

By C. L. Cattano

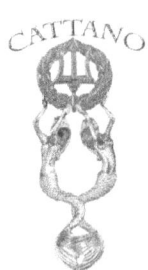

VAGARY PUBLISHING

Wildling's Claim
Book Four
Salvaggio's Light

A Vagary Publishing Book
Copyright © 2017 by C. L. Cattano

Cover Art, Title Page Art and Typesetting Copyright © 2017 by Chynsia Hinesley

Published by:

VAGARY PUBLISHING

www.vagarypublishing.com
inquiry@vagarypublishing.com

Rogena Mitchell-Jones, Independent Literary Editor
RMJ Manuscript Services LLC *www.rogenamitchell.com*

ISBN: 978-0-9980906-9-6
First Edition

WARNING

It is suggested readers of this story be adults over the age of eighteen.

This dramatic romance series has many scenes describing sex as well as intense emotional scenes and acts of violence.

This is a serial story with themes that flow from one book into another with lots of twists and turns. Reading this series from the beginning is highly suggested, or the reader may not be able to follow all of the story lines.

Go to the Salvaggio's Light Facebook page to join other readers who are talking about the series.
www.facebook.com/SalvaggiosLight/

Join the C L Cattano mailing list and check out my website at www.clcattano.com.

Acknowledgments

THANK YOU TO everyone who made it to the fourth book with me! Things have been happening so fast and I want to thank everyone involved for helping me keep things organized and on schedule. Thank you to all the readers who have bought the books and are waiting for the next one to come out. I appreciate your encouraging emails and I hope your patience is rewarded with this book…but don't get too complacent! Thank you to my great editor, Rogena, for all her hard work and helping me 'keep it together' with all the edits and changes. Finally, to my significant other, Marie, thank you for letting me have my ego moments, few though they are, and having the patience to live with me – and all the women in this story.

Dedication

For Marie — who is truly my scrumptious love.

Salvaggio's Light

An Epic Contemporary Romance Serial

Shattered Paradise
Blue Inferno
Secrets & Rivalry
Wildling's Claim
Sowers of Discord*
Fire of Wrath*

Coming Soon

From a small spark
Great flame hath risen.
—Dante Alighieri, *The Divine Comedy*

1

Aphrodite... I beg you with reproaches and harms
Do not beat down, O Lady, my soul...
And you, O blessed one, smiling with your immortal countenance
Asked who hurt me and for whom now do I cry out.
And what do I want to happen most in my crazy heart.

"Whom then dost wish sweet persuasion to bring to you, dearest?
Who Sappho hurts you?
And if she flees, soon she will follow,
And if she does not take gifts, she will give,
If she does not love, she will love despite herself."

Come to me now, the harsh worry
Let loose, what my heart wants to be done, do it!
And you yourself be my battle-ally.

~Sappho

Two days later...

IN THE KITCHEN at Rafe Salvaggio's house, Abby Van Falkov was pleased everyone showed up as planned for the dinner party she had arranged. Letty and Julia were helping with the food and, thankfully, Rafe was staying out of everyone's way. Gathering the silverware to take out to Jude and help set up the table, Abby hoped Eden appreciated what she was doing for her. She was still upset over what had happened Saturday when Eden found out Rafe had gone to New York without telling anyone. Despite her displeasure with Eden, she was determined tonight would go over well.

A light rain began to fall outside as Jude started putting out the dishes. Jude ran over to the sliding door. "Abby," Jude called into the house, "I guess we need to put everything in the dining room. It's starting to rain," she said and went back to restack the plates.

Abby popped her head out the door and looked unhappily up at the sky. "Okay. Just let me find a tablecloth for the dining table. Where's Rafe?"

"She and Flynn are putting up patio furniture and stuff because the wind is picking up out here too," said Jude as she brought in the plates.

Abby looked at Eden who was on the living room floor playing with Bronte. "Eden, will you help me find a tablecloth?"

"Sure," answered Eden with a smile. The fact she was at Rafe's house made her happy. She got up and headed for the built-in cupboard in the dining room. "They're in here." She opened a drawer, pulled out a tablecloth, and helped Abby put it on the table. "Anything else I can help with?"

"If you could help Jude set the table, it would help a lot. Thanks," she said and headed into the kitchen.

When Abby walked into the kitchen, Letty cornered her. "Abby," Letty whispered, "I thought you said they were trying to work things out again. Why's Rafe outside and Eden inside?"

"I'm not sure," said Abby, flustered, "but they'll both be inside now because it's raining out there."

"I don't know," said Julia who was stirring a pan on the stove, "Rafe is very stubborn. She might decide to eat out in the rain."

"Julia, you're not being helpful," hissed Abby. "Do you want me to banish you tonight like I did Stacey?"

"You banished Stacey?" asked Letty with a laugh, amused by Abby's antics.

"She did," said Julia as she scooped a small spoonful of food and tasted one of the dishes she was cooking. "Abby doesn't think Stacey has been exactly helpful because she apparently keeps saying things to Eden and making her uncomfortable. Granted, some of the things she says hit close to home."

"But they aren't helpful when they're trying to work things out," said Abby with clenched teeth. "She just has no tact," continued Abby as she frowned, "so I told her she should stay home and make a dinner out of her latex and alien masks or something."

"Where's your side-kick Erica tonight?" asked Letty as she finished making the salad.

"It's 'Wet Wednesday' so she's getting interviews and video for the blog tonight. It should be hot!" said Abby with a wink, happy with the subject change.

"Aww... Wet Wednesday was tonight?" asked Julia upset she was missing the party and all the women.

Laughing and shaking her head, Letty cleaned off the countertop. "You two are something else," she said with a chuckle.

Julia looked in the oven. "Okay," she said satisfied with what she saw, "it looks like we're ready. Start taking things to the table, and I'll bring this out straight away."

Abby walked into the dining room carrying two platters of food to the table. "It's dinner time. Jude, go tell Rafe and Flynn to get in here."

"I'll get Bronte's chair," Eden said and then went to get the chair from the side porch where Rafe kept it when Bronte wasn't at the house.

Flynn came inside, rain covered and dripping. "It's starting to really come down out there."

Rafe stepped in behind Flynn and began wiping water off her arms. "Thanks for helping me get things put away, Flynn. I'll get some towels."

"Everything smells good," said Jude as she sat at the table eying the food.

Abby followed Rafe who was on her way to get towels. "Rafe, what are you doing?" she whispered.

"I'm drying off," she said as she got a towel from her bathroom and dried off before making her way to her closet to change her shirt.

"Why do you do those things?" Abby tried to ask softly in her frustration. "You know what I'm talking about. Why'd you spend all your time outside while Eden was inside?"

Rafe walked around Abby to take a towel to Flynn. "Why'd she spend so much time inside while I was outside?"

"You're driving me crazy!" Abby said. She stomped her foot and then kept following her.

Rafe found Flynn and handed the towel to him as she smiled at Abby. "Come with me." She led Abby to the table. "Sit here." She sat down next to Abby and smiled at her. "Now you can tell me each time I do something you think is wrong," she whispered. She looked over the table at the food. "Everything looks good. Letty, sit next to me. Where's Ephraim?"

"He's got a private event he's catering tonight," she said as she sat down.

"Here, Eden," said Abby and started to get up, "Why don't you sit here?"

"It's okay, Abby," said Eden anxiously. She looked at Rafe, and Rafe avoided her gaze. "I'll sit down here. Bronte's chair will fit better."

Abby leaned over to Rafe. "What is going on?" she whispered harshly.

"We're having dinner." Rafe smiled back at her then looked around at the group. "Where's Stacey?"

"She's working on a Latex project tonight." Julia snickered as she looked at Abby. "Right, Abby?"

"Right," said Abby as she gave Julia a blazing look. "And Erica is on assignment. So, tell everyone about your thingy at work, Rafe."

"Sure," said Rafe as everyone filled their plates and began eating. "We won the Jackson-Goyer Grant." She smiled proudly as everyone congratulated her. "So there will be a small board member party next Friday. You should all come. The press release should be in the Sunday's art section and will announce the bigger celebration happening later. They'll probably do another story for the paper then too." She turned to look at Letty. "By the way, Letty, I gave your number to the coordinator and told her about The Kiki Bistro. I hope you get the booking."

"Thanks," said Letty excited. "Maybe you can give me the coordinator's number, and I can call her tomorrow."

"Sure, no problem." Rafe smiled at Letty, proud of her cousin and how well she and her husband were doing with their business. "You're really on top of things. I'm so proud of you."

"Where's the board member party?" asked Flynn and took a bite of his food.

"In the Conservatory Gallery," said Rafe turning her attention to him. "You can see some of my photography while you're there. I put a photo of you in, Jude."

"I'm honored," said Jude with a slight bow of her head. "We'll definitely be there."

"Wow, the Jackson-Goyer," Julia said impressed, "half a million dollars impressive!"

"I know. It's incredible," said Rafe. "I got Clarice to sign off on my priority projects before I left to make sure the board didn't appropriate everything to other projects before I got back. We'll soon have state of the art equipment and labs in all of our digital art departments."

"That's my girl!" said Letty proudly.

Abby looked over at Eden, who was helping Bronte with her dinner. She decided to try to pull Eden into the conversation. "So, Eden, how are things going for you at work?" asked Abby loudly.

Eden looked up to see everyone at the table looking at her. Everyone except Rafe, who was looking down at her food. "Things are going fine," she said anxiously. "Nothing as exciting as winning a half a million dollars, though." She hesitated and then looked at Rafe. "Oh, Rafe, I have those business cards for the students we talked with the other night."

"Thanks. I know they'll appreciate them," said Rafe as she continued to concentrate on her plate.

Julia looked at Rafe and smiled. She knew what would get her attention. "So, Eden, you were telling me how you're trying to land a new biography on Louise Nevelson, aren't you?"

"I'm just going to some meetings right now." Eden smiled weakly.

Rafe's head had popped up at the mention of the artist Louise Nevelson. She did research on her in college and was drawn to her art. Her father hated it. He complained how most of her work was only one color, and it was not marble or stone. 'Just junk,' he had said. But to Rafe, it was an interesting break from the formal techniques she had grown up seeing in the Uffizi Gallery in Italy.

She looked over at Eden impressed. "I hope you get it. She was a real piece of work. Her life and art are so incredible."

Eden looked away from Rafe's gray-blue eyes, which were blazing with a passion for the subject, and blushed. "When I saw the book, I remembered when we went and looked at her work in New York and some of the things you told me. The writer did a lot of good research and talked to a lot of people about her." She looked back at Rafe, and she was looking at her plate again. "It's really good," she said softly, unsure if she should continue. "I hope we get it too," she ended and turned her attention back to Bronte.

"Yes, the client I met at the studio told me they were working on some kind of zombie trilogy and a TV series about the undead," Julia said trying to save the conversation. "I'm sure I couldn't tell you the difference between a zombie and the undead!" She laughed and shook her head.

"Julia," said Flynn shyly, "I think they're basically the same thing."

"They are?" Julia covered her mouth as she laughed. "Shit! I think I work with some of them!"

Rafe gave a small laugh. "Julia, you should try to get into catering something with Ephraim. You're a really good cook. Sometimes I miss you living here." She sighed because it was still hard coming home to an empty house at times.

"I've thought about doing something like catering before," said the silver-haired woman, happy for the compliment. "But I don't know if I'd like the hours."

Eden looked over at Rafe. For the first time in a long time, she was actually aware of how sad Rafe looked, and it shocked her. She remembered Rafe talking about a poem she knew by heart called 'Alone.' Eden wondered if Rafe was feeling alone again and it was why she remembered the poem. "I'm sure Julia misses you too, Rafe. You should have her come over and cook for you again. Or, if you want, I can come over and cook for you sometime," she offered tentatively.

"Great idea, Eden," approved Abby. "You should totally do it. Right, Rafe?"

"I'll think about it," said Rafe politely. She put down her fork and took a sip of wine. "What are your plans for us this evening, Abby?"

2

AFTER DINNER HAD concluded, Julia Hawthorn brought out the desserts and after dinner treats. She took them upstairs to the small kitchen in the entertainment room, and Jude brought up the alcohol. Abby pulled out her box of party games and put it on the game table while others helped clear the table and put away food downstairs before making their way up.

Letty pulled a game out of the box and read the title. "I don't think this game is fair to everyone in the room," she said with a laugh as she looked at the game.

"What is it?" Jude asked and looked at the game Letty was holding. "'Who's Done that Sexual Position?' Really, Abby?" Jude laughed and looked at Abby as if she had lost her mind. "Why'd you bring this game?"

Abby grabbed the game from Jude's hands. "I always bring it. We never play it, but I still always bring it," she said with a wink.

"Abby, you bring it because you know you'll win," said Rafe and smiled at her knowingly. "I remember about eight years ago or so, you saying you were going to try every one of those positions so there would be at least one game you could always win," she said as she stood next to Letty. "You were funny then, and you're funny now."

"Watch it, Salvaggio," exclaimed Abby. "I seem to remember someone else who did very well playing the game at one time." Rafe ignored her and walked into the small kitchenette they used to keep drinks and snacks for the theater room.

Letty chuckled. "I think it's time to see what else is in here." She looked inside the game box again. "Abby, didn't you bring any normal games?"

Jude began reading the game boxes enthusiastically for everyone to hear. "Sexionary—a sexual version of Pictionary, Twister." She gave Abby a look. "I don't think so. Trivial Pursuit: The Deluxe Sex Pack? Sexopoly?" Jude shook her head. "Abby, what were you thinking?"

"Sorry," Abby blushed. "I guess I just picked up the wrong box of games."

Rafe returned from the small kitchen. "Here," she said and dropped a couple of small boxes on the table. "A couple of nice regular decks of cards," she quipped and smiled at Abby. There was no way she was going to let Abby talk anyone into playing one of her sex games tonight.

"Now you're talking," said Letty as she grinned. "Let's play a nice game of poker."

Abby looked at Jude. "Don't say it, Jude!"

Okay, okay," Jude laughed determined to sneak in jokes about poker later just for Abby.

"Everyone, bring your drinks, pull out your money, and gather 'round cuz I'm dealing the first hand," said Letty as she shuffled the cards.

3

UPSTAIRS IN THE entertainment and theater room of Rafe Salvaggio's house, Bronte had fallen asleep on the couch, and the group of friends had been playing poker and enjoying each other's company for almost two hours. Jude, Rafe, and Eden had won the most hands, and their piles of money testified to the fact. The last hand went to Jude.

"Deal me out this hand, Letty," Abby said as she stood up. "I have to pee. Too much wine!" She rushed to the bathroom.

"Thanks for sharing, Abby," Julia called after her.

"I need to stretch," said Rafe as she stood up.

Outside, a loud rumbling filled the air, and the house shook and moaned from the thunder.

"What was that?" grumbled Rafe as she walked over to the balcony doors and looked outside. "It's getting worse out there," said Rafe. "The rain is coming down hard. Look at all the lightning. Maybe we should start to wrap this up."

"It's not even ten o'clock, and I want the chance to win some of my money back," complained Julia.

Flynn went over to look out the door with Rafe. "Maybe we should turn on the radio or something," he suggested. "It looks like a major storm."

"I'll turn on the one down in the kitchen," offered Eden as she gathered empty bottles and started to walk downstairs to the kitchen.

"I'll come with you," said Letty as she followed her with some empty plates.

Opening the balcony doors, Rafe looked outside at the roaring rain and heard more thunder rumbling in the distance. "I'm glad we got all the patio stuff put away."

"I hope Stacey's okay," said Jude as she went to stand with Rafe and Flynn by the balcony door.

Letty rushed back up from the kitchen. "They're telling everyone to stay inside and off the roads," she reported. "There are extremely high winds, and the rain is coming down in sheets in places, and there is zero visibility on the roads."

"What's going on?" asked Abby as she returned from the restroom and found Rafe closing the balcony doors and everyone heading downstairs.

"Looks like the party's over," said Rafe as she picked up the sleeping Bronte then ushered Abby down the stairs. Rafe put Bronte in the crib in her room, and then she found everyone gathered in the kitchen and dining room looking out the patio doors.

"We need to go," said Julia. "This storm's getting worse and headed this way. If we don't leave now, we may not be able to make it home."

"No, no," Letty said with authority. "You girls can't leave now. It's already too late." She looked over at Rafe. "Rafe, they'll have to stay the night."

"We can make it home, Letty," said Abby waving off her concern.

"I'm sure we can make it," Julia said confidently.

"Rafe, tell them they have to stay," demanded Letty. "Eden and Bronte too." Rafe looked toward the kitchen where Eden was listening to the radio. "Rafe, tell them," Letty said firmly.

Rafe looked uncomfortably at her friends then out the patio door as the lightning flashed. "Letty's right. You all should just stay," she said with concern as the rain started coming down harder.

"I'm going to check on Stacey," said Jude. "I think I can make it one house over without a problem.

"Me too," said Flynn. They headed out the door for home.

Rafe and Letty watched from the patio door trying to make sure they made it, but there was hardly any visibility.

"So, how are you set up for blankets and stuff?" asked Letty as Rafe closed the door.

"We should be okay," said Rafe and quickly left to get them as Eden came back into the dining room.

"Why is she acting so weird?" Abby whispered to Letty.

"I don't know," said Letty. "It's like she's ready to bolt in an instant." She turned to Eden. "You and B have to stay the night. It's too bad out there to drive home," she informed her as she went to the living room followed closely by Abby.

"What?" Eden stammered as she followed Letty. "Oh, I don't know," she said as Rafe came in with some blankets and tossed them on the couch.

"So how's this going to work out?" asked Abby looking around. "Where are we going to sleep?"

Rafe looked toward Eden then at Abby. "Letty can sleep in the living room," she said quickly. "You and Julia can have the couches upstairs, and Eden and Bronte the guest room, I guess. I can move Bronte's crib in there. Or, Abby, you could stay with Eden if she wants you to sleep in there with her and B Girl."

"I'll be okay upstairs with Julia," said Abby puzzled at why Rafe would suggest she stay in with Eden.

"Okay, you guys figure it out," she said and started upstairs to clean off the game table and take the bottles and glasses down to the main kitchen.

Letty followed Rafe upstairs because she could see how uncomfortable Rafe was acting. "What's going on Rafe?" she asked as she helped clean up.

"I just," Rafe hesitated, "nothing. Nothing's going on," she said and carried the things she had gathered back downstairs with Letty following closely.

"Cugina, there's something going on. I can tell," said Letty as they brought everything to the kitchen.

"I just wasn't expecting to have company spend the night," Rafe claimed. "It's fine. I'm going to move Bronte's bed." She walked out of the kitchen and straight to her room to get Bronte and to move her crib.

4

IT WAS TWO in the morning, and Rafe Salvaggio was lying awake in her room listening to the rain. A nightmare had brought her out of her restless sleep, and the fear of having those dreams again would not allow her to sleep. The house had been quiet for a long time, but later in the night, Rafe heard an unfamiliar noise. She got up quietly and unlocked her bedroom door to check the house and investigate the sound.

Walking silently through the house, she checked upstairs then went back down and saw Letty asleep in the living room. She checked the doors and windows and found nothing wrong. At the guest room, she quietly and carefully opened the door and looked inside.

"Oh, shit! Eden!" she blurted as she ran to the crib and caught Bronte as she was trying to climb over the side rail. "What are you doing up, little one?" she whispered as she held her close.

Rafe looked over at Eden and saw she hadn't woke up. "Eden?" she said softly. She walked over to the bed and touched Eden on her shoulder. "Eden." She didn't wake, and Rafe noticed the sleeping pills on the nightstand. "I guess Mommy needed some help sleeping tonight. Let's go rock," she cooed to Bronte.

She took Bronte and sat in the rocking chair beside the bed, and she rocked her. "I guess we'll have to look into getting you a trundle bed, little climber. Then you don't have as far to fall. Want me to sing you a song?" Rafe patted Bronte on her back as she lay against her shoulder and snuggled. "I'll sing you the Sleeping Beauty song. She's always been my favorite princess story." She looked over at Eden. "Your Mommy reminds me of her right now. I always wanted to be the one to kiss Sleeping Beauty and make her wake up, and then she would look at me and fall in love with me forever." She tore her eyes away from Eden. "Okay, are you ready for the song?" Rafe began to sing the song in Italian quietly. *"So chi sei,"*[1] she began and sang the song through softly as they rocked.

Rafe looked down at Bronte when she finished. "Still awake? What am I going to do with you?" She chuckled. She kissed her and rocked her some more as she watched Eden sleep. After a while, she got up and put Bronte in the bed next to Eden.

"Eden," she said just above a whisper. "Eden, wake up, Bronte's awake." She got no response. "Mommy's got some really good sleeping pills," she said to the baby.

Rafe climbed onto the bed, placing Bronte between them. She rubbed the baby's back to soothe her as she looked at Eden and sighed. She just didn't understand why Eden was doing all of this to their family, to herself. She pushed back a lock of golden hair from Eden's face. She knew she had hurt Eden and made a lot of mistakes, but she never stopped being there for her or loving her. She hated being so close to her, but at the same time, so far away.

---

[1] I know who you are...

Rafe looked down at Bronte's shining eyes as the baby turned over onto her back. "You need to close those eyes, little girl," Rafe whispered. Bronte smiled at her, and Rafe saw Eden in her face. "You are going to be as beautiful as your mommy," she said and looked at Eden again. She could see she was dreaming and wondered what—or who—she was dreaming about. "Eden," she whispered. "I really did think you were starting to love me again. I want to believe you don't love him, I really do." She was hesitant to believe her, though. The problem was the other day, Eden insisted she wasn't seeing him anymore. And there was the lie. She had to have seen him because she said she talked to him. So she did see him. How many more lies was she going to try to make her believe? Rafe wondered if she asked those questions aloud, would Eden punish her and take Bronte away?

Rafe rubbed her hand over Bronte hoping to sooth her and continued to watch Eden sleep. So many things ran through her mind as she looked at her. "Eden, I don't want you to hurt again," she whispered in torment, hoping saying things out loud might help her think things through. "If you do love him, I want you to be happy with him. I don't want you to sacrifice yourself just to punish me. I just wish I could turn all of those lies into love for us... because I do love you." She was tempted to kiss Eden on her lips but stopped herself, knowing it was not only wrong to take what was not hers, but also, it would only hurt herself. "My sleeping beauty, if only a kiss really would make you wake up and love me again." Rafe looked down at Bronte whose eyes were still shining brightly. "Come on, B Girl.

Let's go for a walk around the house." She got up, walked out of the room with Bronte in her arms, and closed the door quietly.

"There you are," whispered Letty when she saw Rafe come out of the guest room. "What were you doing in there?"

Rafe turned so Letty could see Bronte. "I was just trying to get Bronte back to sleep," she whispered. "Eden took some sleeping pills, and I couldn't wake her up. I hope it was okay for her to take those with her Xanax. Bronte was climbing over the edge of the crib."

"Don't worry. She let me know she was taking them. It's why I'm up checking on the baby. Eden wouldn't take them if it weren't okay," Letty assured her and held her hands out to Bronte. "Give her to me," she said and took Bronte as she reached for her. "You go back to bed. I'll take care of her. I know you have an early day tomorrow."

Rafe kissed Bronte and Letty on their cheeks. "Thank you, Letty. You're the best," she whispered.

"Don't you forget it, either." Letty chuckled as she smiled and watched Rafe walk back to her bedroom. "Little one, your two mommies gotta get their acts together."

5

WORKING OUTSIDE IN her backyard, Rafe Salvaggio was cleaning up debris the storm had strewn around the pool and yard. After dragging poolside furniture back out to set it up again, she began working on getting the biggest pieces of debris out of the pool until the pool girl could come to clean up the rest. She piled the last of the large debris from the pool by the fence and looked up to see Julia walking into the yard.

"Ah, the pitfalls of home ownership," Julia feigned sympathy. "You have to do everything yourself."

Rafe smiled as she dipped leaves out of the pool. "Right. I have to do everything including taking in stray English women."

"I'm one hundred percent American, and you know it! Don't let the boarding school accent fool you." She laughed at their old joke. "You're in a better mood. Was it seeing four women in your pajamas this morning?"

"No," Rafe said with a laugh. "It's how I now have four sets of pajamas back in my drawer."

"Well, you finish your cleanup, and I'll get the wine," said Julia and headed into the house while Rafe put away the pool skimmer. When Julia came back out, she carried a bottle of wine and two glasses and set everything on the table between the loungers. "So, how was work," asked Julia as Rafe came back over from the other side of the pool. "Daddy called and said to congratulate you. Apparently, your name came up about the grant at one of his club dinners. He was disappointed you didn't go see him."

"Work was fine." Rafe laughed because she knew Julia hated being a messenger. "I should have," she said softly. "Tell him I said thank you."

"Anyway, I guess you know why I'm here." Julia smiled as she poured the wine. "The same reason Abby sends me over all the time. I don't know why she won't just let me call you. She insists I come over personally."

"I know why you're here, and the answer is the same," said Rafe. "I don't want to go out tonight. She wants you to come over personally because she thinks it'll annoy me more."

"Does it?" asked Julia as she sat down on one of the pool loungers and handed Rafe her wine.

Rafe settled into the lounger next to Julia and smiled. "No. I think I'm actually beginning to enjoy turning you down just to see Abby's reaction the next time I see her." She laughed mischievously.

"So, what excuse do I give her this time?" Julia asked cheerfully.

"Tell her I'm studying alchemy tonight, and I'm trying to turn lead into gold," said Rafe. She winked as she took a sip of her wine.

"The thing is," said Julia, "I know you're telling her exactly what you're doing, but I can't figure out your riddles. You're so cryptic." She sipped her wine then looked over at Rafe. "You know she's over inviting Eden to come with us."

"Well, I hope she gets her to go out with her," Rafe said encouragingly. "She could probably benefit from a little fun." She also thought the more time they could keep Eden from spending with Jake, the better. Maybe spending time with them would make Eden change her mind about everything.

"What are you doing, Rafe?" Julia asked somberly. "What are you letting Eden do to you? Last night, you were acting like you were walking on hot coals. You were losing to Eden on purpose when we played poker," she said and saw Rafe getting ready to deny the fact. "Yes, I noticed, and I think everyone else did too. Then when Letty made you tell everyone they had to stay over, you bolted into your room right after you put Bronte's bed in the guest room."

"Julia, I have some really tough decisions to make," Rafe paused, "about everything. Eden is wearing me down, the injunction is wearing me down, the fucking amendments and accusations are wearing me down, and you and Abby think I should be out partying. I'm not sure what I'm doing right now."

"Why are you still putting yourself through this?" Julia asked concerned. "Maybe it's time you made a change in your life. If Eden isn't giving you what you need, you should find someone who will." Julia knew she had to be careful or Rafe would say she was just being jealous again. It irked Julia when Rafe would accuse her of jealousy, but she also knew, to a certain extent, Rafe was right. After all these years, Julia still felt she and Rafe should try to be together. Right now, though, she mostly missed her old friend and the fun they were just beginning to have again.

"I know this may sound crazy to you, but I have to try. It's Eden," Rafe said as if this should explain everything. "There is just something inside me, and I'm just unable to let go of her. Even Greer saw it."

"So this is the reason you're not seeing Greer anymore? Maybe you should consider going back to Greer," Julia said, unable to believe she was seriously making the suggestion. It just proved how much Julia truly cared for Rafe. "I know I thought Greer was too old for you, and I know it sounds terrible, and I do like Eden but..." She paused hating to see her friend in crisis. "Rafe, you're miserable. At least, with Greer, you had some happiness, and you laughed more."

"I do love Greer," Rafe admitted. "I don't know," she paused, "it's hard to explain. I love Greer, but it's not the same as with Eden."

"Do you think it's because Greer is more," she hesitated, "mature? She's probably not interested in having children."

"No," Rafe laughed at Julia's reasoning. "Her age has nothing to do with it. If I were with her, I could have the babies. It's just with Greer, I can be apart from her and feel fine," she explained. "With Eden," she shook her head, "it's so hard to be apart from her. It's like part of me is missing."

Julia looked at Rafe in wonder. "I had no idea you would even consider having children."

"Yes, I'm a mystery," said Rafe and laughed wryly. "If Eden hadn't wanted to have our baby so much, I would have had her." They sat silently for a while and sipped their wine.

Julia couldn't imagine Rafe pregnant and breastfeeding like Eden had done. It was strange enough seeing her take care of Bronte. She couldn't reconcile the wild, danger seeking, and partner in crime with motherhood in her mind. She also couldn't understand why, after all this time, she still couldn't let go of Eden. "Is it possible your want of Eden is just co-dependency?" Julia theorized. "If it is, then instead of promising to spend time with her, maybe you should promise yourself to spend time away from her. Maybe it'll clear your head so you can get on with your life."

"No. No, I've been apart from her," Rafe stressed. "It hasn't worked. Even now, while we're spending some time together and seeing each other for Bronte, I still feel miles apart from her. I don't know if we're meant to be together or not, but I can't go on with the rest of my life without knowing for certain."

Julia frowned and looked into her half empty glass. In her mind, they weren't meant for each other, especially after all this time and the things Eden had done. "I always wondered if you were with her because you thought you had to take care of her," Julia admitted. "You'd always get so mad when I complained about her anxiety issues. If her problems are why you think you should be with her," Julia shook her head, "you shouldn't burden yourself with someone who makes your life harder."

Rafe looked at Julia with a frown and then leaned back in her chair. "She's not a burden," she said firmly. "I wasn't with her just to take care of her. I was with her because I love her."

Julia looked past Rafe. "Speaking of Eden," she nodded to the back gate, "it looks like Abby has convinced her to go out, and they are now descending upon you."

"Great." Rafe sighed and looked at Julia. "No telling Eden or Abby anything I said. You know how Abby blabs everything. *Lo giuri?*"[2]

"I swear," Julia said as she held up her hand then crossed her heart quickly like they had done when they were kids. She would also keep her feelings about Rafe and her opinions to herself, as she had done in their youth, until she was sure they would be well received, if ever.

Abby came in through the gate then walked up and stood over Rafe. "Hey, Salvaggio," she said as she smiled down at her. "Shouldn't you be getting ready to go out?"

---

[2] You promise?

"Hi, Abby," she said with a smirk because Abby only called her by her last name when she was either annoyed or wanted to be pushy. She looked up at Eden. "Hello, Eden." She looked back at Abby. "I can't go out tonight."

"Yeah, she's doing alchemy tonight," interjected Julia, "something about turning lead into gold."

"Nice delivery," said Rafe sarcastically to Julia.

"Whatever." Abby rolled her eyes. "Eden needs to talk to you. Privately." Abby gave Rafe a look confirming she wouldn't take no for an answer.

Rafe looked at Abby with a frown because now it was clear the use of her last name was because she had come to be pushy.

"See if you can convince her to come out with us, Eden," said Abby with a nod. "Come on, Julia. Let's go see if Jude's home." She dragged Julia out of the back yard with her as Julia tried not to spill her wine.

Eden sat next to Rafe nervously. "Hi," she said softly.

"Hi," Rafe answered guardedly.

"I know I'm breaking the 'someone else has to be there rule' but," she hesitated nervously, "I just need to talk to you privately." Rafe looked at her and nodded then looked away. "I just..." she began cautiously, "I just wanted to tell you I'm sorry about Sunday night. I pushed you after telling you so many things at once and I," she stammered, "I just wanted to say, I'm sorry. I know you need time to think about everything, and I understand. I do want you. I really do, you know..." She let her words trail off. She looked at Rafe and hoped she could feel the love in her words.

"Okay," Rafe whispered, "thank you." She looked into Eden's eyes searching for the woman she thought she knew. "Eden, I've changed a lot over the past year or so since we've been apart. I may have changed in ways…" she shook her head, "in ways you can't accept. If you find it's true, I understand if you can't be with me. I just hope when you realize you don't want to be with me, you'll let me stay in Bronte's life."

Eden touched Rafe's hand then pulled back quickly. "Sorry," she said and looked down worried. "It," she cleared her throat, "it sounds like you're giving me a back door to walk out of. Are you?"

Rafe leaned away from her. "I'm just telling you, if we do try to get back together, things won't be the same as they were before," said Rafe somberly. "I'm telling you the changes in me may not be good changes for you."

"Are you happy with the changes?" asked Eden.

"Yes, I am," Rafe answered and looked at her penetratingly.

Eden looked away from Rafe's gaze. "I'm not really the same either, you know."

"I know," Rafe said sadly but did not ask her if she was happy with the changes. She didn't want to do anything to cause her to have to lie.

"You do?" asked Eden and watched Rafe nod. "Are you okay with the changes in me?"

Rafe looked at her in misery. She didn't know how to answer her question. "I don't know."

"Oh." Eden sighed as she nodded understanding Rafe was still processing the things she had told her on Sunday. "Do you still want to spend time with me?"

"Yes, I still want to spend time with you," Rafe confirmed. "I promised I would. I just don't want to go out tonight."

"You don't have to go," Eden reassured her. She looked at Rafe and wanted to touch her. "Rafe," she asked cautiously, "will you please let me touch you?" Rafe looked at her sadly and nodded her head. Eden put her hand on Rafe's face and caressed it. "I want to tell you how I feel. I know you don't want to hear it from me right now. I just hope you believe what I told you." She touched Rafe's lips, and Rafe closed her eyes. "I hope you can let me tell you soon."

6

ALONE AGAIN IN her backyard, Rafe Salvaggio was picking up more broken branches and debris, only this time she was after the smaller pieces. She was going over in her mind the conversation she'd had with Eden and all the things she was doing and saying. It was hard to understand why Jake was standing by watching her do them. The more she thought about it, the angrier it made her. She had to put some kind of plan into action, but first, she needed to make a few changes in her strategy.

"Want some help?" a voice came from behind her.

Rafe turned around and smiled at Flynn. "Sure, thanks," she said. "You can help me with our project in the garage again too."

"Okay," said Flynn happily. "So, do you want to do another strategy game tonight?"

Rafe laughed. "You're really getting into it, aren't you?"

"I just like listening to you talk about it," Flynn admitted shyly. "I want to be able to think like you."

"Well, it's easy to think about what you could do, but actually doing it is hard," Rafe confessed.

"I don't know," said Flynn as he shrugged. "If someone's really my enemy, and I didn't like him, I don't think I'd have a problem. So give me another scenario."

Rafe nodded and motioned for him to follow her to the garage as she thought of a scenario. "Remember the very first scenario we talked about?" she asked as she flipped on the garage lights.

"The island with the traitor and the possible killer?" Flynn recalled, and Rafe nodded. "I remember."

"Okay," she began, "you've been on the island for a while, and one day, your supposed killer offers to make a sacrifice for you. He offers to do something for you his countryman shouldn't let him do."

"What?" Flynn asked.

"He offers to hide you and not let them capture you when they're rescued. The traitor knows about it but doesn't do anything about it. Do you take the offer, or is it a trap? Why would the traitor allow it? They could both be court marshaled or executed if it was found out." She pulled out the pieces she had been working on and placed them on the workbench.

"Maybe the traitor plans to turn you both in," Flynn guessed. "Maybe he wants to get rid of both of you." He looked at what Rafe had put on the workbench. "Wow. You finished the carving. I can't even tell you just made it. It's amazing."

Rafe laughed at Flynn's surprise. "I did do this sort of thing for a living for a long time, you know, but just on houses and buildings. This is ready for us to reattach it to the chase. After the glue is dry, we can add the final finish. Then I can send it out to the upholsterer. It's one part of restoration I like to leave to a really good upholsterer to make sure it's perfect.

"I guess I just didn't realize what you did before," he said. "Abby told me you did buildings and stuff but not things like this." He helped Rafe take the pieces to the chase frame, and Rafe started gluing and clamping them together.

Rafe thought about Flynn's answer to her question as she applied glue to the wood. "You may be right about the traitor wanting to get rid of them both, but why?" she asked. "Did you ever figure out how to get them apart?"

"No," Flynn admitted as he held a piece of the wood in place for her.

"I think it's time to figure it out," Rafe mused. "Sometimes, in war, you just have to face the enemy, take the pain, and leave the intrigue behind."

7

ON FRIDAY AFTERNOON, Rafe Salvaggio walked into a small bar not far from campus. She looked around letting her eyes adjust to the low light and then smiled at the bartender as she ordered an Absolut martini. The bartender sat the martini in front of her, and Rafe took a small sip. She smiled and nodded to the bartender then paid him for the drink, including a nice tip.

The door to the bar opened letting in the daylight. Rafe saw the person she was waiting for as they walked in, looked around, and then headed toward her and the bar.

"Jake, thank you for meeting me," Rafe said gravely as Jake offered his hand to shake. She didn't take his hand. She was not there to be nice. "Let's sit." She led him to an empty table, and they sat down. "I would offer you a martini, but it's my understanding you don't drink." Rafe smiled tolerantly.

"So, what did you want to talk to me about?" Jake asked perturbed with her rebuff and wanting to get straight to the point of their meeting. He was hoping Rafe was going to ask him more about Eden's plan so he could reinforce what he already had in place. It was always nice when the work practically took care of itself, especially when it came in a package as beautiful as Rafe. It wasn't the first time he had wished she was the one assigned to him on this mission rather than Eden.

"You didn't tell Eden we were meeting, did you?" Rafe asked sternly.

"Of course not," Jake confirmed reassuringly to show her he was on her side.

"Well, good." Rafe gave him a disarming smile. "I just wanted to thank you for opening my eyes about her." She leaned back and took a sip of her martini. "So, what did she tell you about Sunday night?"

Unsure about what Rafe was talking about, he took a chance guessing whatever happened had to have been bad, or she wouldn't be here. "She didn't say very much, but she seemed," he paused debating his choice of words, "upset. What happened?"

Rafe ignored his question. "Did you tell her you told me everything?" she asked pointedly.

Jake looked at her but remained guarded. "What do you mean?"

"I mean, did you tell her you told me about her plan for getting me out of her life," Rafe outlined for him.

"No, no, I wouldn't..." Jake paused shaking his head.

"But you did talk to her about me," she stated. "About the fact you told me she was still in love with you?"

Jake realized this was about Eden's visit to his apartment but wasn't sure what they said to each other and didn't want to make a mistake.

"I," he nodded, "I may have let it slip."

"Why are you betraying her? Why did you tell me all of this?" she asked curiously.

"I told you," Jake said earnestly, "I don't agree with what she's doing or how far she is willing to go to hurt you. I would hope someone would do the same for me if I were in your situation."

Rafe looked at him and raised her eyebrow. "Why are you letting her do this?" she asked insistently.

"I don't know what you mean," he said and leaned back in his chair.

"I mean, Jake, why are you letting her do the things she's doing?" Rafe clarified. "Don't you love her?"

"I do love her, but I can't control her," said Jake holding his hands up as if he were helpless. "She's very determined to do this to you."

"I guess she is," mused Rafe and took another sip of her drink. "Did you know she was willing to prostitute herself to get what she wants?"

"I don't know what you're talking about," Jake said baffled.

"So," Rafe paused and frowned, "you didn't know she was willing to sleep with me to make sure her plan worked?"

Jake looked up in surprise at this information but recovered. "Like I said, Eden is very determined."

"So, you're okay with it?" Rafe asked calmly. "You're okay if she and I had sex?"

"Of course, I'm not okay with it, but I can't stop her," he insisted trying to hide the fact he was flustered and afraid of what this might mean to his superiors.

Rafe took a breath and leaned back in her chair. She looked over the table at Jake. Eden and the others had told her all about Jake and how tolerant he was with Eden's past relationship with her and how he was taking good care of Eden. From their descriptions, she thought he was a sacricolist—a devout believer—who believed in the turning of the cheek, being in a monogamous relationship, and all the other rules and parables for the pious taught by their chosen moral guide. This was one of the many reasons she could never be part of religion, organized or not. They were all infected with too many sciolists pretending to have great knowledge and were filled with an illogical doctrine, contradicting to itself, or just plain harmful to people. Lessons learned in life, and throughout her education in art, architecture, and cultural histories enforced her opinions on the subject. Theology always seemed to be something used to control someone or something.

She couldn't believe, based on what she knew, Jake would allow Eden to go down a path of self-destruction willingly. Especially if he really was a reverent man professing his love for Eden. Maybe he just didn't want to see her go back into a relationship with a woman, or maybe he was just not as devout as he led people to believe. Or, like many, maybe he was only using religion as a crutch for something else. Whatever it was, his beliefs were not of any help to Eden.

"You don't really love her, do you? You can't," she said contemplatively. "If you did, you'd find a way to keep her from doing this to herself," she insisted feeling her anger rise because Eden deserved better than this man.

Jake scoffed. "I don't control Eden like you did. She really is her own person since she's not under your constant control. I love her, but I don't own her. This isn't exactly the dark ages anymore." He laughed nervously as he tried to remember things he could use to make her back off and stay away from Eden.

Rafe copied his laugh mockingly. "This has nothing to do with control or owning someone," Rafe explained. "It has to do with protecting her from making a mistake and hurting herself."

"What can I do about it?" Jake shrugged and shook his head hoping she would make a suggestion working to his benefit and dig him out of the hole he had found himself.

"Obviously," said Rafe smiling condescendingly, "you can't do anything about it. So it means it's up to me."

Jake realized he was losing control of the conversation. "What are you going to do?" he asked as he looked at her warily.

"I'm just going to have to take her away from you," she declared feigning concern.

Jake thought quickly about how to regain the upper hand. "Rafe, no, you can't. She's out to destroy you, and she loves me," he said and pointed to himself for emphasis.

"Are you sure?" Rafe asked and calmly took a drink. "She says she wants to tell me she loves me. Maybe she's changed her mind." She sat her glass back on the table. "You know, I really don't think you love her at all. I just don't think you're up for the job."

"Oh, I'm up for the job," Jake said getting angry. "I've been up for it since before she was even out of your bed. Did she tell you we fucked in your room? We were in your bed the whole time you were gone on one of your 'business trips,'" he spat and made air quotes with his fingers. "We were fucking before she even moved out of the house." He could see his words were causing the desired effect, and Rafe was getting angry. "She probably just wants to give you a little reminder fuck so she can use it to hurt you," he seethed wanting his words to cause her pain so she would take her anger out on Eden and make her even more vulnerable.

Rafe held tightly onto the stem of her glass fighting back her temper. She could see she was right about him being one of those pious pretenders who were out to fool everyone with his mendacity.

"Everyone is entitled to a mistake, and you were hers," she said stonily.

"She hasn't made a mistake," Jake said with an arrogant laugh. "I thought you were supposed to be smart." He took a deep breath and let it out slowly. "I really don't understand how you could want someone who's such a burden to you and who doesn't even like you. She's only doing these things to hurt you. Can't you see? It's the only reason she's staying close to you," he insisted mockingly.

Rafe looked at him as she took a sip of her drink giving her time to think. This was the second person who said Eden had been a burden to her. She didn't know why anyone would think she thought Eden was a burden. If Eden were, Rafe wouldn't be sitting in this bar across from someone she loathed.

"There's really no need for her to do the things she's doing to take herself and Bronte out of my life and hurt me," said Rafe, deciding to ignore his remarks. She put her glass down carefully wondering if she would discover Jake and Eden were actually meant to be together. "You could have taken her far away long ago and kept her from hurting herself. I think she might be fooling you. Maybe she really does love me and not you, and this is why she's trying to stay close to me."

"Rafe, you're acting like you are delusional," argued Jake knowing she was probably right. He had tried to get Eden to move, but she was always fighting him about it. "What on earth would she use me for? Maybe to make you jealous, but she could use anyone...a woman, even. She wants to be with me. She wants to hurt you. And it's why she's staying close to you. You really think you can make her feel something that isn't there?"

"Yes, I do," said Rafe assertively. She looked at Jake and saw he was about to make another argument and cut him off. "You believe in all this superstitious mumbo jumbo so maybe I can use some to help you understand." She looked at him and his blank face. "I'm a Scorpio. A Scorpio doesn't just go around telling everyone they love them. When I say it, I mean it. But you probably don't know anything about the true meaning of love, either."

Jake shook his head in dismay. "So, you're justifying sleeping with her when you know she's just doing it to get what she wants," Jake contended. "You're not treating her any better than what you're accusing me of, Rafe."

"You really don't get it do you?" She leaned forward and looked at him speaking with confidence. "I don't care about what mistakes she's made. I've never felt like she was any kind of burden. I'm in love with her," she proclaimed and looked at him with passionate fury in her eyes. "Every time I see her or smell her, or even just think about her, my brain produces so much dopamine I get this intense high I just don't ever want to lose. No one else even comes close to making me feel the same way. I know it won't stop happening because it has been going on for me since the first time I laid eyes on her. Being without her feels like I'm going through some kind of painful drug withdrawal. But it's even more than chemical. It's like she is part of me. I need her with me. She's the other half of my soul. I'm just not complete without her in my life," she explained passionately.

"So she's an addiction and a toy for sex," he countered. "This proves if anyone is trying to hurt Eden, it's you because you can't let go. Nothing you've said proves what you feel is love. Needing someone to get a high only makes you seem more pitiful. Maybe she understands your weakness, and it's why this is all so easy for her." He looked at her with a concerned frown. "Addictions are what lead people into the darkness, Rafe. Don't do this to yourself."

"No, you're wrong," said Rafe with a smile not wanting to give him the satisfaction of seeing how tortured she really felt about the possibility of hurting Eden. "This is not an addiction, and it really doesn't have a lot to do with sex. I know what I feel is much deeper. I know what I feel is love for her. And it's why, if she wants me too, I'll sleep with her. Because I love her. But," she said and looked at him unwaveringly, "I won't allow her to sleep with you if she decides to have sex with me."

Jake looked at her with a furrowed brow. "What are you saying?"

"I'm saying if we aren't meant to be together, it won't be from a lack of trying on my part. I'm saying you won't be seeing Eden anymore, Jake." Rafe smiled and ate her olive.

"You can't keep her from seeing me," Jake protested. "You can't force her to not see me."

Rafe pointed at him with her toothpick. "Yes, I can, and I will."

"So you're going to take the chance of losing everything, of losing Bronte for good?" Jake asked in disbelief. "You're going to let her do all the things she has planned to hurt you?"

"Yes," Rafe admitted. "I'm going to give Eden everything she wants, even if it means losing everything for myself later. As I see it, I have nothing really to lose and everything to gain."

Looking at the determination on Rafe's face, Jake knew he had to come up with something to make her change her mind or, at the very least, have more doubts about Eden. He shook his head then tactically unleashed the anger he was feeling, using words he hoped would cut her deep enough so his mission would be saved.

"If you do this, you'll not only be hurting yourself, you'll be playing right into her hands," he began evenly. "Every time you let her tell you she loves you, it will be a lie. Every time she tells you she wants you to fuck her, it will be a means to an end." He leaned toward her. "Every time you fuck her, it will be me she's thinking about," he said, pointing to himself and letting his anger seethe. "Anytime she has a chance to get away from you, she'll be with me. Any chance I have to see her and fuck her, I will—gladly. She loves telling me the things she does to you! She loves fucking me after hurting you! And you know what?" he asked scornfully as he leaned back in his chair. "I'm beginning to understand why she's doing this to you. She knows exactly how you feel and about your obsessive addiction, but you, you know nothing about her anymore. I'll let her do this because I love her, and I know she loves me. I know it because it's my name she calls out in her dreams at night. It's me she calls to talk with and tell all about her victories of getting even with you for everything you did to her." He smiled smugly. "I have nothing to worry about when it comes to you, no matter what happens between you and Eden."

Every muscle in Rafe's body was tensed and ready to spring over the table to destroy Jake. It took everything in her to keep the expression on her face neutral and not reveal the anger erupting inside her at his words. She couldn't believe Eden had turned into the woman he described. She didn't want to accept the possibility of her own actions being the reason Eden had changed so drastically. If she really had done this to Eden, just maybe, Rafe would deserve everything Eden might do to her in return. She didn't understand how he could let her turn into the person he described and be fine with it.

She took the last calming sip of her martini. She decided not to address Jake's cutting words because, at this point, arguing with him was pointless. She came in with the intent of making Jake back off, and she intended to stick with her plan and not allow him to distract her by his desperate attempt to keep Eden in his life. She had her own desperation to worry about. She cleared her throat to speak.

"I think the only reason I haven't done this before was I really did believe she was in love with you, and I wanted her to be happy," she said as she pushed her martini glass away.

"She is in love with me, Rafe," Jake asserted angrily.

"But you don't love her," Rafe said sadly, "and it will eventually lead to her being unhappy."

"I do love her," Jake claimed. "I keep telling you I love her, but you just won't listen to reason! Don't be foolish. Her plan is working out perfectly for her, and now you're handing everything to her. If you do this, she'll file the restraining order, and then it's all over for you." He looked at her with mock sympathy. "I thought you at least wanted to save your relationship with Bronte."

"Don't worry." Rafe reached over and patted his hand as if he were a child. "I have a good lawyer who I have a lot of faith in and, if I succeed with Eden, I'll have everything I want, and she'll have everything she wants too. Because, since the court date keeps being pushed back, by the time the final court date comes up, she'll be in love with me again."

"You're making a mistake, Rafe," Jake insisted.

"No, you will be making a mistake if you don't walk away," she said with animosity. "Do you understand me? Stay away from her. Avoid her at all costs starting today. Don't see her and don't call her. Just disappear." She looked fiercely at Jake. "Don't fuck with me!"

Jake stared back at her speechless as she got up and gave him a slight smile. He couldn't believe she hadn't backed down after everything he had told her. She was so fucking stubborn.

"It was good talking with you, Jake. I hope we don't have to see each other again." Rafe turned and walked out of the bar without looking back.

Jake watched Rafe walk away as he went into a panic.

"Shit!"

He pulled out his phone and called his contact. "Hello, we have a problem. Rafe just challenged me for Eden. I don't know what I'm going to do. It's not as if I've been keeping in contact with her. I didn't think I'd have to. I know this has never happened before. It's not my fault. I made sure to paint the situation to our benefit. Rafe may think about things and change her mind. You just better make sure we can win in court. I'll try to get more on her and see what I can do about splitting them up again if they get together. I know the child takes priority. I don't know what I'm going to do! Okay, okay, if the reverend wants to meet with me, I'll come, but see if you can stall the meeting until I can figure out how to take care of this."

He hung up. "Shit! Shit! Shit!"

8

FRIDAY EVENING, THE board member party for the Jackson-Goyer Grant was in full swing at the Conservatory Gallery. The gallery was filled with board members, alumni, and instructors, as well as a few students and friends. Food and non-alcoholic drinks were flowing freely. Part of the gallery exhibit was a collection of photographs taken by students, and since Rafe was auditing the class, it included several of the photos she had taken, as well.

Eden Kingsley was walking through the gallery with her glass of sparkling grape juice when she stopped in front of the photograph of Rafe with 'Greer's Claim' painted on her body. She looked at the photograph with trepidation.

"Isn't it amazing?" asked a voice behind her.

Eden turned and saw Carolyn along with the other students she had met at the bistro a few weeks ago. "It's nice," Eden said hesitantly.

"I hear it's going to a New York Exhibit with Greer Noble's work next year," said Janell. "Did you see the ones Dean Salvaggio took of Professor Noble? Wow!"

"I asked if I could put it up on the web page," said Carolyn as she looked at the photograph, "but she said I'd have to wait a while before she could to do it."

"By the way, thanks for the business cards," Emily said enthusiastically. "Dean Salvaggio actually came and found us to give them to us. She's so cool!" She laughed, and the other girls joined her.

Eden smiled at their admiration of Rafe. "You're welcome. I hope you get the opportunity to do an internship."

"She is so hot," gushed Carolyn as she looked at the photos. "Professor Noble is too. I didn't know they were dating. You're so lucky you used to be with her!"

"Yeah," said Eden and looked down trying not to show her discomfort.

"Look! There's Professor Moss," Emily pointed. "Let's go say hi."

"See you later, Ms. Kingsley," Carolyn called back as they walked away.

"Bye," Eden said knowing they didn't hear her. Eden looked back at the photo of Rafe and the mark Greer had made on her body. She noticed the framed words beside it 'Greer's Claim over Rafe,' and she felt the beginning of anxiety building inside her.

Greer loves Rafe.

She tried to put the anxiety aside, but she couldn't help wondering if Rafe would decide, in the end, to go to her.

Rafe saw Eden standing in front of the photograph of Greer. Her conversation with Jake was still fresh in her mind. She decided it was a good time to give Eden hope the plan she made with Jake for punishing her and getting her out of her life still might work. She walked up behind Eden and put her hand on her back. "Don't worry," Rafe whispered in her ear, "the claim was only temporary." She turned and walked away to greet more guests as Eden turned and watched her, still feeling Rafe's warm touch on her back.

9

SATURDAY MORNING, WHILE Eden Kingsley was feeding Bronte, Abby was having coffee and a pilfered piece of Eden's toast. Abby had come over early to talk to Eden before she took Bronte to her art lesson. Abby had an unwavering need to know. It was pricked last night at the Gallery, and she was following her instincts. Eden had left the party early last night right after Rafe said something to her, and Abby needed to know what had happened.

"So," Abby started cautiously, "what did you think of Rafe's pictures last night? I saw you were looking at them."

"They were nice," Eden said absently as she put more egg on Bronte's plate. "They were really good."

"Sooo," Abby dragged out the word as she peeled the crust off her toast. "What'd she say to you?"

"What?" asked Eden as she handed Bronte a small piece of strawberry.

"Rafe," Abby said louder to get Eden's attention. "I saw her come up to you and say something while you were looking at the risqué picture of her. What'd she say?"

Eden looked at Abby and smiled. "She said, 'Don't worry, the claim was only temporary,' then she just walked away." She thoughtfully took a bite of her toast. "I think she was trying to tell me she's not going to go back to Greer and she still wants to try."

"Really?" asked Abby surprised.

"Abby, I need to talk to her again," Eden said with her eyes shining with hope. "I want to do this right, and I don't want to break the rule again. You know the one where someone else has to be there. Will you come with me?"

"I don't know," said Abby hesitantly. "I already took a chance doing it once. You're not going to hurt her again, are you? I don't want to be part of it if you are."

"I've never wanted to hurt her," insisted Eden. "I just want to see if she'll let me tell her how I feel and see if she wants to try spending more time together again."

"I think she will. I know she loves you," said Abby encouragingly.

"I'm glad you think so." Eden sighed. "Abby, I know this is asking a lot, but if she does want to talk, and she's willing to be alone with me," she paused, "would you mind taking Bronte to her art lesson?"

"Sure." Abby smiled. "And if you guys need more time," she gave Eden a wink, "I can take her to Letty later."

10

STILL IN HER LOUNGE pants and a tank top, Rafe Salvaggio was sitting back on the couch reading student essays she needed to grade. As she furiously wrote a comment on the paper she had just read, there was a knock at the door. She got up, agitated by the interruption, and went to answer the door, still holding the paper she had just graded in her fist.

Rafe yanked open the door and frowned. "Abby. This really isn't a good time. I'm grading papers right now," she growled.

Abby walked inside anyway and headed for the living room. "Eden's outside," she announced. "She wants to talk with you. Alone. I think you should talk to her."

Rafe looked out the door and saw Eden with Bronte. She sighed as she waved her in and then followed Abby back into the living room.

Abby sat on the couch and looked at the papers Rafe had been grading. "So you're one of those red pen teachers," she observed.

Rafe and grabbed the paper Abby was holding and put it back in the graded pile. "I'm not in a good mood right now Abby. Having to read these papers is pissing me off."

Abby picked up another paper and read Rafe's comments. "Rafe, you can't say this to a student! You wrote 'You should drop this class and retake it when you have time to come to class.' Was it really so bad?"

"It was bad," Rafe said as she crossed her arms with her gray-blue eyes flashing angrily. "The sad thing is it's not the worst of them. Look at this one." She handed Abby a paper.

Abby read Rafe's comments. "Whoa, Rafe. 'If you are going to quote me, cite me. You should get an F for the plagiarism, but I'll give you a D because you at least listened to something in class.' Jesus, Rafe! Cruel much?"

Eden walked inside as Rafe went into her passionate rage. "Hi," was all she managed to get out.

"You think the comment is bad?" asked Rafe fuming. "For this one, I really want to just write to the parents and tell them to keep their kid at home and invest the money they would spend on her education into real estate! They'll get a much better return on their money over the next four years. Listen to this. It's supposed to be a comparison of the two Davids done by Donatello and Bernini. The girl writes, 'Donatello's David looks a bit like a girl, but Bernini's David is hot.' What the hell kind of comparison is that? I can't believe she would think this shit is acceptable!" she roared and threw the paper on the couch with the others.

"Isn't this a freshman general education class?" asked Abby waving off Rafe's anger.

"What the hell does being a freshman have to do with anything?" Rafe asked bewildered and angry.

"Well," replied Abby with a shrug, "it's their first year, and it's just a class they have to take to graduate." She paused. "They just want to pass."

"They just want to pass?" asked Rafe incredulous. "Abby, what the hell are you talking about? Freshmen should be working twice as hard as everyone else to build up their GPA, so when they take the really hard classes as juniors and seniors, they can afford to get a lower grade and not compromise their ability to graduate!"

Abby rolled her eyes. "And I suppose you had a great GPA?"

Rafe looked at Abby and stood up straight in angry pride. "When I graduated from my undergraduate program, I had the equivalent of an American 4.50 GPA.

"No way. It's not even possible! GPAs just go to 4.0," Abby said in disbelief.

"For your information, I got straight A's in college and took some Honors Program courses, and they increased my undergraduate GPA. I was able to graduate in three years. Also, I helped with several clubs and organizations and attended study abroad programs."

"Not everyone has a rich father to hand them everything," Abby said, her snarkiness showing.

Rafe looked at her incensed. "For your information, my papa never gave anyone anything! I was required to work for him in his Milano office. I did it all and started college a year earlier than everyone else in my class because my father moved me to Italy and insisted I start college. He arranged it so I could take the entrance test when I got there, and when I passed, he set me up in a flat and left me there to succeed or fail. I never took a class to just pass!"

Abby laughed and shook her head. "Aren't you little miss over achiever," she said smarmily. "I should have known when Greer told me you were a doctor. Why didn't you ever tell me you were a doctor?" she asked jealously.

"I just didn't," said Rafe annoyed Abby wasn't really listening. "I was lucky I found my passion early. I went on for my graduate work, which I had to do in three different languages by the way, and I started my restoration business. Because I had already been working in my chosen profession for years, they accepted me into my doctoral program quickly. I worked hard in school and built my restoration business at the same time," she informed her hotly.

"But still, Rafe, these kids aren't you," said Abby as she perused a student paper. "Why don't you go by Doctor Salvaggio?"

Rafe grabbed the paper Abby was holding from her and ignored her question. "You're right. They aren't me. Obviously, their parents didn't care enough about them to send them to schools where they could learn how to think before entering college!"

"Just because you got an Ivy League education doesn't make you better than everyone else," Abby said indifferently.

Rafe scoffed. "Do you even know what Ivy League means?"

"Sure," she said with a smirk. "Some hoity-toity school for rich kids."

Rafe shook her head at Abby's cluelessness. "Abby," she began her lecture with eyes blazing, "you obviously don't have a clue what Ivy League means, and I didn't go to one of those schools. But the schools I did go to were what I needed for the career I dreamed of having." She watched Abby roll her eyes, and her anger flared. "Do you really think I would be where I am today if my father hadn't made sure I got the best education available? As a gay woman, I already have a minimum of two strikes against me. I was dropped into an American private school when I had just turned fourteen and had to learn an entirely new way of life than what I had in Italy. My education helps, but it doesn't even the playing field. The rest is up to me and depends on the effort I put forth. My father insisted I get top grades, and I had to work for him to learn his business. My grades prove I'll put forth effort in any task given to me to any organization or person who looks at them. Any parent, no matter their race, gender, income level, or background, who sits back and doesn't take an active role in encouraging their child to put effort into everything they do, and in providing the best education possible for their child, especially their daughters, is a fool. They are setting their child up for a harder life! *Non capisco che cosa è errato con la gente là fuori!*[3]

"Rafe, you're over reacting," said Abby calmly. "Calm down. It's just a freshman GE class, and no one understands what you're saying when you do your Italy talk."

"Abby, you don't get it, do you? No class is just a class." Rafe tried to get her to understand. "Every grade you make shows up on your transcript and will tell anyone who looks at it exactly what type of asset or liability you will be to their

---

[3] I don't understand what is wrong with people out there!

company or organization!" She threw the paper she was holding onto the table.

Abby picked up the paper Rafe had thrown down and looked at it. "You gave her an Fx? Is Fx even a grade?"

"It's what she deserves. I didn't give her a solid F because at least she turned in the paper," Rafe growled and took a deep breath ignoring Abby's other question. "I can't do this anymore right now. I'll have to start grading again tomorrow. Otherwise, they may all get an F." She sat in her place on the couch, the heat of anger rolling over her, and put her hand to her temple to try to rub away the headache she felt threatening.

"I don't think Fx is even an American grade," Abby said with confusion as she looked at the paper and not letting Rafe's anger faze her. "I think if you give them an F, it's just an F, but still," she insisted. "Harsh." She looked up at Eden who had just been standing at the edge of the living room holding Bronte and watching them argue. "Good luck talking to her, Eden. Do you want to do it another time?"

"Abby, stop," Rafe said annoyed. "I'll be fine."

Eden broke out of her trance at the beauty of Rafe in her Salvaggio rage. "No, it's okay," she said. "I agree with Rafe. It's important to try to do well in all your classes."

"See," said Rafe smugly. "Thank you, Eden."

Abby got up and took Bronte from Eden. "We'll be right outside so you two can talk. Try not to fail them all, Rafe. They're only freshmen," she reminded her as she hurried outside before Rafe could rebut.

"She is so without a clue!" Rafe complained as she rubbed the tense muscles in her neck. "But," Rafe sighed, "she may be right about the grade. I probably need to look at the grading scale again. I was just mad and wrote an Italian grade by mistake." She looked up at Eden. "I may not be any good to talk to right now, after all." She picked up all the papers off the couch and put them in a stack on the coffee table.

"You want me to fix you a drink?" offered Eden. "Maybe it'll soothe your nerves."

"Sure, okay," Rafe said and laid her head back on the couch.

Eden went into the kitchen to mix Rafe a screwdriver and took it to her. "Here you go." She sat down next to her.

"Thanks," she said and took a sip then looked at Eden. "I'm sorry. I just can't relax."

"I'd offer to rub your back but," Eden paused, "I don't know if we're there yet."

Rafe laughed. "We aren't there, but I don't think we'll do much talking while I'm in this state." She sat her drink down and turned her back to Eden. "Go ahead, rub. I remember you used to give pretty good neck rubs."

Eden looked at Rafe's tank top covered back in front of her and couldn't believe she was about to touch her again. She moved up onto her knees on the couch so she could get to Rafe's neck and shoulders better. She reached out tentatively then gently pushed Rafe's dark hair away from her neck.

She stroked her fingers down the sides of her neck feeling the sensation of her smooth skin against her fingertips. As Eden moved her fingers back up Rafe's neck, she made small circular motions, working the tense muscles gently but firmly.

She felt Rafe flinch as she touched an especially tender part of her neck, and she instinctually eased her touch.

From Rafe's neck, Eden moved her hands across her shoulders gripping them and kneading them with her fingers and thumbs as she moved out from and then back to her neck. She could feel Rafe's muscles responding, and as Rafe leaned her head back, Eden felt her hair touch her face. She breathed in Rafe's scent and closed her eyes for a moment. Moving her hands to Rafe's shoulder blades, she pushed forward on her back, and Rafe tilted her head down again, revealing the arch of her bare neck. Eden moved one hand fluidly back to Rafe's neck using her fingers to gently manipulate the tense muscles while she used the heel of her other hand to work the muscles along the sides of her spine and her lower back.

As Eden moved her hand up Rafe's back, Rafe sat up straight arching her lower back, pushing her shoulders back and leaning into Eden's hands. Rafe rolled her shoulders and Eden could feel some of the tension leaving as she turned her attention back to the shoulders. Using the tips of her fingers, Eden walked them back and forth across Rafe's shoulders to massage the smaller knots in her muscles. Rafe took a deep breath releasing more tension from her body and leaned back slightly against Eden.

Eden lightened her touch as she ran her hands gently across Rafe's smooth skin and over her soft shirt. Moving from Rafe's shoulders, she ran her hands over and down her arms and back up again, and she couldn't help but notice the difference in the tone and firmness of her now well-etched arms. Everything about her body was so much more defined than she remembered. She continued running her hands over her back then down her spine and back up to her neck, keeping her touch light and smooth. She could feel Rafe's skin warming under her hands and her muscles responding and relaxing under her touch.

"Eden, it feels so good," whispered Rafe.

"I'm glad," said Eden as she pulled Rafe back against her.

She gently rubbed down the sides of Rafe's neck and then forward to just below her collarbone, massaging the tender muscles there, and then returning to her neck and shoulders. Rafe leaned her head forward and revealed her neck again. Eden closed her eyes because the temptation to kiss her neck was becoming too hard to resist.

The feel of her warm skin, her scent and the sight of her bare skin was making Eden's senses reel. She moved her hands from Rafe's neck back to her shoulders and massaged them gently.

"Rafe," she said hesitantly. Rafe moaned a response, and Eden placed a hesitant kiss on Rafe's neck. She heard Rafe take a deep, jagged breath from the sensation. "You smell so good," Eden told her softly. She placed her head against the back of Rafe's neck as she continued to run her hands down her back and arms.

Rafe leaned to one side, so Eden's head rested on her shoulder. "You're making me feel so relaxed," Rafe whispered in her ear.

Eden turned her head and found herself looking into Rafe's brilliant gray-blue eyes. "I want you," she breathed and placed her mouth against Rafe's, kissing her deeply.

As Eden kissed her, Rafe turned her body around to face her. She looked up at her, taking hold of Eden's shirt, and pulled her closer.

"You want me?" she asked quietly.

"Yes," said Eden softly. She then leaned down and kissed her again—and again—then she ran her hands over Rafe's hair and body.

"Eden," Rafe breathed between kisses, "Eden."

Eden felt the familiar warmth making its way through her body as she kissed Rafe. "I want you, Rafe, please," she breathed.

Rafe's hands were still gripping Eden's shirt as she put her head against Eden's head and smiled sadly. She pushed Eden back gently as she pulled herself away from Eden and stood up. "No," she managed to say. "I think we should talk."

Eden looked at Rafe with surprise, "Wh—" she started, "What?"

Rafe cleared her mind and raised her eyebrows. "I said, I think we should talk."

"I," Eden began, not understanding why Rafe had stopped, "I don't understand. I thought—"

"I know what you thought," Rafe said, cutting her off. "Eden, you can't do this to yourself." She shook her head and frowned. "I just won't allow it. I love you, and I don't want you to do something you may regret."

"I really don't know what you're talking about," said Eden, a bit disoriented, but elated Rafe had said she loved her. "I'm not doing anything with you I'll regret."

The memory of Jake's words about the reasons Eden wanted to have sex with her echoed through her mind. The fact Eden wouldn't regret hurting her cut deeply into her heart.

"Eden, you really need to think about what you're doing," Rafe said earnestly. "I just don't want you to be with me for the wrong reasons."

"I don't understand," said Eden confused and getting upset. "I told you I want you. You said to tell you what I want. Why is it you can be with everyone else but not with me?"

Rafe looked at Eden with pain in her eyes. "I don't want to treat you like everyone else. I do want you to tell me what you want. I want you to tell me the truth. Do you really want me to give you my heart, or are you just doing this to use me and hurt me?"

"I don't understand what truth you want me to tell you," said Eden as she looked away from Rafe and whispered, "I don't want to hurt you."

Rafe looked intently at Eden and saw there were tears forming in her eyes. She knelt down in front of the couch where Eden was still on her knees. She put her arms around Eden's waist and placed her head on Eden's chest. "Okay, I didn't mean to make you cry. But, for now, I'll just hold you, and if you want, you can tell me how you feel. It's something I need to hear from you."

Eden stroked Rafe's hair, and a tear fell from her eye. "Rafe," she said and pulled Rafe up then lay back on the couch with her. She wrapped her arms around her then kissed her. "I've been waiting for you to let me tell you how I feel. I'm glad you're ready." She kissed her again and stroked her hair and face. "I love you, Rafe. I don't love anyone else. Do you believe me?"

Rafe hugged Eden tight then loosened her hold and whispered, "I want to." But she couldn't help wondering if those words were really a lie and just a means to an end.

"Rafe, whatever Jake said to you," she started and felt Rafe go rigid.

"Please, don't talk about him right now," Rafe whispered.

"Okay," Eden nodded as she kissed Rafe's face and mouth. "I won't," she kissed her again, "I love you, I love you," she kissed her, "I love you," she kissed her again, "I want you," she breathed, "I love you,"

"I love you too," Rafe whispered as she felt Eden kiss her again. She tasted the kiss on her mouth then she buried her face in Eden's neck and inhaled her scent. The smell of her filled her senses and made her feel like she was floating. Her heart beat hard against her chest as she whispered, "I love you so much."

11

RAFE SALVAGGIO WAS sitting up and watching Eden nap on her couch. Abby had been happy to take Bronte to her art lesson and would be back with her any minute. Rafe sighed as she thought about earlier. She knew it may have been a bad idea, but she wanted just one last peaceful moment with Eden, in case it might never happen again. Waking up with Eden lying next to her again was worth it, even if it wasn't real. She reached out and moved a stray piece of hair away from Eden's face. She would have to talk to her about Jake soon.

Jake was her other big problem. Was he going to do what she told him and disappear, or did she piss him off enough he would do something about Eden and take her and Bronte away? Will Eden be gone soon after they talk about Jake, or will she stay? She could do nothing but give those possibilities time to happen. Rafe looked up at the sound of knocking on the patio door.

Putting her hand on Eden, she shook her gently. "Abby's back with Bronte," she said when Eden opened her eyes. Rafe got up and went over to let them inside with Eden close behind.

Abby handed off a messy Bronte to Eden. "Here's your girl."

"Thanks, Abby," Eden smiled as she took Bronte then looked over at Rafe. "Maybe we can stay, and I can make dinner," she suggested then turned to take Bronte to the guest bathroom to clean her up.

"Maybe," Rafe said uneasily wondering if she should regret the kissing earlier.

Abby smacked Rafe lightly on her arm. "I saw her in here practically seducing you. You're not making things easy for her."

"She wasn't seducing me. She was giving me a back rub," said Rafe hotly.

"I saw you guys kissing," Abby teased.

"I'll bet you saw us stop too," Rafe said annoyed with her snooping.

"And start again!" Abby laughed at Rafe's discomfort. It wasn't every day she was able to see Rafe in this state. "So, you think she is still on the fence? You don't think there's something between you?"

"Something like that," Rafe said guardedly, "and there *is* definitely *something* between us."

Abby rolled her eyes. "Let her stay."

Rafe looked at Abby with a sad smile tinged with a slight amount of unease. "Do you want to stay? Sit down, and I'll fix you a drink." She left Abby in the living room and headed to the kitchen.

When Bronte was clean, Eden brought her back into the living room and looked around for Rafe. She looked at Abby who pointed to the kitchen. She whispered to Abby, "Will you take her to Letty? I talked with her while I was in the bathroom, and she told me if I needed her to, she'd keep her tonight. I'm going to see if Rafe will let me stay."

"Sure," agreed Abby. "I'll stay for a while to see if you can convince her. She's supposedly making me a drink, but she's taking her sweet time. I was just about to go in there."

Eden sat down on the couch next to Abby and let Bronte play on the floor. "Maybe you can help me convince her."

"You guys are doing okay, aren't you?" asked Abby since Rafe was not a fount of information and had practically abandoned her. "I saw you kissing earlier."

"I think so." Eden nodded. "I just—" She smiled hopefully. "I want to stay longer."

Abby looked seriously at Eden. "I'll help, Eden, but I won't push Rafe too hard."

Rafe walked in with a tray of drinks and a small snack plate before Eden could respond. "What are you girls whispering about?" she asked as she sat the tray on the coffee table.

"It's about time." Abby picked up a drink from the tray and sat back on the couch. "I was just saying how Letty told me she wished she could see more of Bronte and was asking Eden if I could take Little B over to see her Zia Letty."

Rafe looked from Abby to Eden and thought she knew exactly what they were discussing. It wasn't like Abby could keep her nose out of anything. She picked up her drink and sat opposite Abby in one of the chairs. "Maybe I should call and make sure it's okay with Letty first."

Abby shot Rafe a look. "I talked to her already, and it's fine. So now Eden can make dinner for you two, and you can spend more time together."

Eden gave Bronte a piece of fruit from the tray then looked at Rafe hopefully. "It sounds nice to me. What do you think?"

Rafe looked into her glass. "I think I need more ice." She got up and walked into the kitchen.

Abby motioned for Eden to stay and followed Rafe. "Things are going well. You should let her stay."

"Abby, we're making some progress, but I don't want her getting the wrong idea about where things are going right now."

"Don't keep pushing her away," Abby implored. "You'll never get the answers you need if you keep pushing."

"You're right," agreed Rafe sadly. "Maybe I should be trying to keep her close," she mumbled to herself.

"Great!" Abby exclaimed. "I'll have Eden get Bronte's things together, and I'll take her to Letty."

Rafe watched Abby scamper away wishing she hadn't heard her and wondering if she would regret her words.

12

SINCE THERE WAS nothing in Rafe Salvaggio's house not frozen or canned or was basically useless on its own, Eden ordered Chinese food for dinner. They made a run to pick it up along with a trip to the liquor store for some plum wine. After eating in silence, for the most part, they took their plum wine out to the patio to enjoy it in the night air. They stretched out and were relaxing in a couple of the loungers. After a long silence, Rafe looked at Eden and decided it was time.

"Eden," said Rafe cautiously, "I think we need to talk about Jake now."

Eden looked at her plum wine nervously, unsure of how much she would have to reveal tonight. "Okay," she said as she sat up and readied herself.

"You tell me you're not in love with him," began Rafe as she looked at her sadly, "but he told me you are." She paused for a moment. "Why?"

Eden toyed with the stem of her wine glass. "I don't know. Maybe he's upset about how I broke it off with him. I did do it rather suddenly,"

"Maybe?" asked Rafe stunned at the vague answer. "It seems like he would have been over it by now if you really weren't seeing him all this time," she mused. "Why did you break up with him?"

"I wasn't seeing him," Eden began. "I haven't been seeing him," she stammered. "He just," she hesitated, "he isn't," she stumbled, "wasn't the person I thought he was."

The hollow and nonsensical answer irritated Rafe, and she stood up and paced the patio. "What do you mean?" She rounded on Eden. "You have seen him if you talked to him about me." She began to fume. "Don't lie to me!"

"I only... I only saw him," Eden swallowed, "just once. It's when he told me." She looked at Rafe fretfully. "He told me what he said to you." Eden could see Rafe's anger was surfacing, and it was making her anxious. "I guess I just made a big mistake with him," she blurted out.

"What else did he tell you?" asked Rafe, not liking the broken answers Eden was giving her. "Did he tell you the other things he said to me?"

Eden sat her glass down and rubbed the back of her neck where a bead of sweat was forming. "He said..." she looked away, "he told you Bronte and I would... we would be better off with him. You know it's not true, Rafe." She looked back at her with pleading eyes. "You are Bronte's mother. I would never take her away from you," she swore. "And I don't want to be without you."

"Thank you for those words," said Rafe feeling a hopeless emptiness. Eden's words sounded hollow because those threats had been repeated so many times. She looked into her eyes trenchantly. "Is there anything else about him I need to know or anything he might have told you? Or is there anything at all you want to tell me?"

Flicking her eyes to the side and back again Eden jutted out her chin slightly in an involuntary defensive tick. "Anything else?" she repeated and forced a quick, nervous artificial laugh. "Of course not. Why would you think there was something else?"

Rafe noted Eden's telltale sign she was lying and sighed. "I just wanted to make sure there was nothing more you need to tell me," she said with a sad vacivity threatening to overflow with anger.

"No," said Eden as she clutched her hands together so they wouldn't shake. "No, there's nothing I can think of right now. Nothing."

"I've got to tell you," Rafe said as she shook her head with false insouciance. She knew there was definitely more than she was telling. "It really seems, I don't know, convenient I guess, how you find out Jake told me those things, and now you say you love me. I think you're lying and there's more." She watched Eden's eyes widen in surprise. "You couldn't tell me you loved me last Friday, but now, suddenly you can. Seems like a very abrupt change of heart to me. When did Jake talk to you?"

"He," she hesitated. "He told me over a month ago," she said quietly, unsure if she should tell her what happened while she was in New York when she had come over and found her gone.

Rafe looked at her in shock, and she felt an incendiary rage run through her body. "You have got to be fucking kidding me!" she yelled. "I don't believe this! Over a fucking month ago? You've known for a fucking month he said those things to me? Why—" She clenched her fists in anger and gritted her teeth to try to control herself because she thought she knew the answer to her own question. "Why the hell would you wait so fucking long to tell me he lied?"

"I was," Eden cowered, her voice trembling along with her body. "I was trying to figure things out. I wanted to be sure about things."

Rafe turned and paced in front of Eden. Rafe was beside herself and inflamed with anger. "I don't understand. I don't know if I believe you. What exactly did you have to be sure of or to figure out before you could say something?" she roared in anger. "Even if you fucking hated me, you could have told me he lied out of—" She fought to be able to even speak. "Oh, I don't know... maybe out of courtesy!"

"You're right, you're right!" Eden shook with fear at the level of Rafe's anger. "I should have told you sooner. I'm sorry. It's just you were so hard to talk to. You wouldn't answer my calls, and when we did spend time together, we never got the chance to talk." She looked at Rafe worriedly and agonizing at the difference in her anger toward her and the impassioned anger she had displayed earlier with Abby. "Maybe I should have written you a note," she said as she reflected on her therapist's words. "Would you have believed it?"

"From where I am right now..." she said looking at her with disbelief. "No, I wouldn't. I can't tell you how I would have fucking reacted a month ago!" she said hotly and becoming more incensed as she thought about everything happening to her. "You could have just left it in one of your fucking pathetic voice mails! 'Rafe, I need to see you so I can figure out my feelings for you. I need to know if I can love you again,'" she quoted Eden, "'by the way, Jake is a fucking liar, but I still just might love him too!'" It was clear Eden really was lying to her, and it was becoming harder to control her anger. She doubted she found out Jake talked with her over a month ago. Eden probably found out sometime while she was in New York. It was after Rafe returned from New York when Eden started acting differently toward her. She took a deep breath then crossed her arms. "When was the last time you saw him?" she asked evenly, holding back the rage on the edge of eruption.

Tears were dripping down Eden's cheeks as sat on the edge of her lounger. "I don't love him!" she yelled back at her. "The last time I saw him was when he told me what he said to you." Eden watched as Rafe closed her eyes and sighed. She then uncrossed her arms and clenched her hands into fists. "Do you believe me?" she asked desperately. "Do you believe I don't love him? Do you believe me when I say I love you? Do you believe me when I tell you I haven't seen him since then?" she asked through her tears.

Rafe opened her eyes remembering Jake had said he saw her Sunday night. "No, I don't," she said in frustration. She turned away from Eden and rubbed her temples against the pain developing as she tried to calm herself. She took a deep breath and faced Eden again. "Did you fuck him in our bed?"

Eden quickly looked away and put her tear covered face in her hands and didn't answer because she knew what she had done was ineffable. She was caught up in the romance of everything and didn't think about where they were until Jake pointed it out later. She hated Jake for telling Rafe what they had done.

"You did," Rafe choked. "You have no respect for me at all, do you?" Her voice went calm and cold, contrasting with the burning rage in her eyes as she stood over Eden looking at her with revulsion. "You could have fucked him anywhere you wanted, and you chose to defile our bed!" Rafe could only think Eden had imagined it was condign for the dalliance in New York. "I know," she clenched her jaw in anger then continued, "I know I really fucked up, but even I didn't do anything so low. Why the fuck do you want me, Eden?" she screamed her question over her. She then turned away with her fists clenched, her body tensed, her eyes watering, and was unable to look at Eden because Jake hadn't lied.

"I'm sorry, I'm sorry!" cried Eden shaking with fear and sorrow. "I made a mistake," she sobbed, "a terrible mistake! Everything I've done without you has been a mistake! Being without you is a mistake!" She stood and put her hand on Rafe's back. "You have to believe me, I love you!" she cried desperately.

"Mistake," Rafe whispered softly. "It was no mistake." Her voice level rose in anger. "You knew what you were doing!" She turned, so Eden's hand came off her back, and they were facing each other. "Tell me why the fuck you want me!" she screamed again because Eden was evading the question. In frustration, Rafe turned away from her sick with pain.

"It was a mistake!" Eden screamed back at Rafe as her own anger was building. "I want you because," she hesitated thinking of all the reasons she wanted her, "because I love you, Rafe!"

Taking note of Eden's hesitation, Rafe turned back slowly and purposely to confront Eden, and she spat out her words. "You want me because you love me?" She laughed sickly. "Will this love for me you've suddenly found last until tomorrow? Will it go away as soon as I give you what you want and fuck you?"

"Stop it, Rafe!" shrieked Eden incensed by Rafe's words and smacked her hard across the face. "I'm freaking telling you I love you! I never stopped loving you! You have to believe me!" she screamed. She stopped and realized in horror what she had done. She looked up from her hand and into Rafe's burning molten gray-blue eyes.

"Right, okay," Rafe said softly as she put her hand to her face and smiled. "I see," she growled and grabbed hold of Eden's shoulders and kissed her deeply then pushed her, so she sat down on the lounger. "Is it what you want?" she asked hotly. "Is it? One last fuck! Well, my answer is no!" she roared.

"No!" cried Eden holding herself and shaking. "It's not what I want! Rafe, I'm sorry." She sobbed. "Please, believe me. I lo—"

"Why do I have to believe you?" Rafe angrily cut her off. "By my count, it's Jake with at least four or five definite truths, if not more, and Eden none!" she spat. "Because you have told me nothing!"

Eden looked up into Rafe's angry face in misery. "Because I love you! Jake lied about it! I swear I'm telling you the truth!"

Furious, Rafe spoke menacingly, "Eden, tell me why I should believe you. Tell me something to give me no choice but to believe you! Tell me!" she demanded in a fury.

Eden was terrified and didn't want to tell Rafe anything while she was so angry because she was afraid anything she might say wrong would make her leave for good. "I can't talk to you! I can't talk to you like this! You're scaring me, and I can't think!" Her body shook, and her face was covered with tears.

"It's okay," Rafe said coldly as Eden looked up at her warily. "I understand you really do still love him and you two are going away and taking Bronte out of my life!"

Eden looked at Rafe in horror and shook her head. "No." She gasped. "No!" Rafe just stared at her in a silent fury. "It's a lie, Rafe." She choked. "It's a lie!"

Rafe shook her head cynically not believing her. "Tell me who I should really believe, Eden. Jake who, as far as I know, has no reason to lie to me, or you, who supposedly waited a month to tell me he lied! Why the hell are you still here?" she screamed, then turned and walked back into the house. Hearing all the lies coming out of Eden made her think maybe she had made a mistake. Maybe Jake was right. By continuing to let herself love Eden, and doing all of this, she was only hurting herself.

"I'm here because it's not true!" Eden yelled as she followed Rafe inside the house. "I'm here because I do love you!"

Rafe turned to face her angrily. "Tell me why I should believe you!" she begged, wanting her to just tell the truth, any truth.

"I want to tell you things," said Eden as she wiped tears from her face, "everything. You have to believe me. I just, I just can't do it like this. I need you to give me time! I need you to have some patience with me instead of pressuring me and yelling at me! I love you. Please, Rafe," she said softly. "I love you. I'm not going to stop. Please believe me," she begged and swallowed hard, "I don't love him. I love you, and it's the truth!"

"Why do you love me?" asked Rafe as she looked painfully into her eyes.

Eden was floored by the question. So many things jumped into her mind making it so she was unable to answer before Rafe continued.

"Eden, I think I'm running short on both time and patience, so I need—"

The front door flung open and was followed by screeching words. "What the hell is going on?" Abby shouted as she barged inside with Jude close behind. "It sounds like fucking world war three over here!"

Jude looked from Eden to Rafe. "I'm sorry." She cringed at Rafe's deadly look. "I was worried."

"What the hell are you doing, Rafe?" yelled Abby, and Rafe turned and glared at her. "I leave for a while, and when I come back to hang out with Jude, she tells me you're pushing Eden around and hurting her!"

"Abby, stop!" cried Eden and went to Abby before she got too far into the house. "Please don't! Please, you have to go!"

Jude looked at Rafe then at Eden. "I saw her push you, Eden," she said as she looked at Rafe. "You came inside, and I thought," she hesitated and grimaced, "I thought things were getting physical in here."

"You should come with us, Eden," insisted Abby. She turned and frowned at Rafe. "You can't let her hurt you!"

Rafe looked at Abby with indignation. "Fuck you, Abby! Why the fuck am I always the monster?"

Eden hugged Abby to her and whispered to her, "Please, go. I don't want her to shut me out," she begged. "Please, don't make her angrier than she already is!"

Abby bristled as she looked at Rafe. "Eden, if you won't leave, maybe we should stay to make sure nothing happens."

"Why don't you both just get the hell out and take Eden with you!" Rafe growled and started toward her room.

"No!" Eden gasped and ran after Rafe then blocked her bedroom door. "Please, Rafe, don't!" She caught her breath. "Don't shut me out. I swear I'm telling you the truth! Abby!" she cried out. "Abby, please leave!"

"Get out of my way!" Rafe said menacingly.

"No!" cried Eden frantically. "Please, Rafe! Don't!"

Rafe stared Eden down, her demeanor and eyes full of rage and frustration. "Are you going to tell me the truth?"

"I am telling you the truth!" Eden swore desperately.

"You're not telling me anything!" Rafe raged. "You're evading! You're repeating the same things over and over!"

"Rafe," Abby intruded, "Eden wouldn't lie! If she says she loves you, then she does!"

Rafe spun and turned her fury on Abby. "She loves me?" Rafe repeated. "Oh, right. She's loved me since Sunday night! But do you want to know the first thing she told me? She didn't tell me she loved me," she seethed, "she told me she wanted me! She only told me she loved me after I said no! Maybe she thought it would get her what she wanted! She's just doing this to hurt me and punish me!"

"Rafe," Eden said softly and paled, "you can't," she shook her head, "you can't believe what you're saying!"

"What the fuck are you talking about, Rafe?" asked Abby in confusion because she knew nothing about Sunday night.

"She wants me, and she loves me," fumed Rafe, "but she can't answer some very simple questions or tell me anything true!" She looked at Eden in anger. "Why don't you fill her in, Eden? You obviously still can't talk to *me* honestly! Maybe Abby will believe all your lies!" She stepped past Abby and went to the living room.

"Rafe, you're not talking—you're yelling!" Eden pointed out. She looked at Abby. "Abby. Abby, please go!" She looked at Jude desperately. "Please, both of you go!"

"All of you go!" Rafe yelled as she sat back on the couch in exhausted fury, fighting the painful pressure in her chest and head, causing a vermillion darkness around her vision.

Eden looked at Abby and Jude pleadingly then nodded toward the door. She walked into the living room. "I'm not leaving."

"Come on, Abby," Jude said quietly. "We'll be next door," she said as she pulled Abby by the arm and steered her out.

Eden stepped in front of Rafe who was leaning over with her head in her hands. "Rafe," Eden said softly, trying to de-escalate the situation. "I..." she stammered. "I've been screwing this whole thing up, I know. You're right. I should have told you Jake lied right away. I should have told you I loved you first," she said as tears ran down her face. "I was just so relieved you came back. I thought you left me forever. I had so many things to tell you," she paused and wiped her tears, "but it was hard for me." Rafe didn't move, and Eden knelt down in front of her and could feel the body heat caused by Rafe's anger wash over her. "Please, let me start again." She took Rafe's warm face in her hands and looked into her anger stained eyes. "I love you. I've always loved you. I'm not going to stop loving you."

"Why won't you answer my questions?" Rafe whispered. "Why won't you tell me the truth? Something to make me believe you," she said in torment.

"I will," Eden said and laid her head on Rafe's knee. "I just need time." She looked up at her anxiously. "I need you to be patient with me. I don't want to lose you, Rafe. I love you. Will you please believe me and give me those things?"

Rafe took a deep breath, swallowing back the sick feeling in her stomach because this was going nowhere. When she could open her hands again, she stroked Eden's hair and spoke calmly. "I have a request," she said calmly. "I'm not going to make you promise because I don't want you to have to lie to me any more than you already have." She felt Eden give a startled shake, but she remained silent. Rafe was sure Eden's silence must mean she understood she could no longer protest the truth. "My request is for you to stay away from Jake. Don't see him or talk to him again," she took a calming breath, "and you don't fuck him." She saw Eden start to speak, and she put her fingers on her lips. "This is what I need from you if I'm going to even begin to believe you."

Relief flooded through Eden because she knew this was what she wanted, too. "I won't see or talk to him," she promised. "I don't want to see him or talk to him. I don't want to be with him, babe."

A bead of sweat flowed from Rafe's hairline and spilled down her cheek as her body burned with frustration and want for Eden, but her heart just couldn't go there yet. "Eden, I need you to answer my questions and make me believe you. I need you to tell me the truth. Until you can, the rules are still the same. You have to tell me what you want, and I'm not yours yet."

"Okay," Eden agreed and looked up at Rafe worried, "but you still love me, don't you?" She watched as Rafe nodded yes. "Thank you," she said as a wave of relief flooded over her again.

"Okay, I'm glad we talked about this," Rafe said as she took a deep breath steeling herself and her heart. Now she just wanted the conversation to end and to be alone.

Eden looked at Rafe, surprised and confused Rafe was ending the conversation. "So... so, are we okay?" she asked anxiously.

"I hope we will be," Rafe said in exhaustion.

"Can I," Eden started cautiously as she wiped the tears from her face, "can I stay here tonight?"

Rafe shook her head wondering why Eden was asking this after what they had just gone through. "No," she said firmly, "I'm not ready."

"I mean just to sleep," she clarified with a smile. She stood up from the floor and then sat close to Rafe on the couch. Not wanting to set her off again, Eden took her warm hand carefully and kissed it. "Maybe," she said softly, "maybe I can just," she ran her hand down Rafe's back, "hold you for a while again." She looked into Rafe's eyes. "You have to believe me, I love you."

Rafe closed her eyes and turned her head away. She took a deep breath and felt her head spin as white flashes burst under her eyelids, and she snapped her eyes open to recover. She needed to be alone, but she felt Eden's hand move over her back again and knew she would have to let her stay. She challenged Jake for a reason. She had to know the truth, and even if he was right, she still loved her. "I'd like you to hold me again," she conceded, "for a little while." She felt Eden lean in, then push her hair aside, kissing her on the cheek. "Eden?"

"Yeah, babe," Eden answered as she kissed her warm face again.

She turned her head and looked sorrowfully at Eden. "I want to believe you. I love you, and I do want you. I just want it to be right."

Her heart was pounding with the hope Rafe would believe her. Eden gently pushed Rafe back on the couch and spoke softly between the wary kisses. "I'm so glad you love me." She placed her lips on Rafe's face and eyes, kissing her intimately, wanting to take her doubts away. "I'm so glad you want me. Whenever you're ready, it'll be right. I love you," she whispered as she felt Rafe's body begin to relax. "I don't want anyone else but you. I want you to believe me. I love you."

"I hear you." Rafe breathed raggedly as she let her anger go. "You're telling me just what I need to hear. Thank you," she said softly, "but tonight..." Her words fell away.

"I know," Eden whispered back to her. "I'll just hold you for a while, and kiss you." She wrapped herself around Rafe and carefully caressed and kissed her warm face and mouth.

Rafe gave in to her need for Eden's kisses. "And kiss me," she yielded.

13

IT HAD BEEN a beautiful Sunday morning. Eden Kingsley was feeling good she was able to spend time with Rafe yesterday and ended up sleeping over. She was relieved, even though it was hard and scary at times, she was able to talk to Rafe and tell her Jake had lied. She just needed more time to tell her the rest, as soon as she figured out what Rafe meant when she asked for the truth. She told her she loved her, but Rafe kept asking for the truth, so it was clear there must be something else Jake had told her or she knew about somehow.

After leaving Rafe's house, Eden picked up Bronte from Letty and took her out to the park to run the path and get some time in the sun. After their run, they played on the swings and the slide for a while and then headed home for lunch. Bronte was finally down for her nap, and Eden was picking up toys when there was a knock at the door.

She walked over to answer the door happily. "Hi, Flynn. Come on in," she said smiling.

"Thanks. I thought I'd come by to see if you need help with anything or if you wanted to talk," said Flynn as he followed Eden into her kitchen. "I heard about last night from Jude and Abby."

Eden got drinks out of the refrigerator, and they sat at the table. "Last night was scary. I don't know if she'll ever really believe me. Freaking Jake!"

"Did you tell her?" he asked with hopeful concern.

"No," Eden said shaking her head. "I couldn't." She looked at Flynn with the shadow of fear in her eyes. "She was so angry. I couldn't risk telling her then. She was already so, *so* mad at me." Eden leaned her head into her shaking hands. In all the time they had been apart, Rafe had never yelled or showed her anger. She supposed she should have expected it since everyone had said she was angry. Maybe she even deserved to be on the receiving end of Rafe's wrath. It was still hard to take, and she was just glad it was over. Hopefully, they could move forward now.

"I went to Rafe's house before I came over," Flynn said and took a drink of his beer. "She was grading papers."

"She's home?" asked Eden in surprise. "She wasn't there when I woke up this morning."

"I think she was out running," Flynn guessed. "I think she's still mad, and I think she's going to flunk every student in her class."

Eden sighed remembering Rafe's lecture about grades yesterday. "I don't think she would flunk her students unless they deserve it." She couldn't help the smile on her face.

"What's the smile for?" asked Flynn returning the smile.

"Rafe," she said with a grin. "Yesterday, when I walked in her house, I couldn't even speak. I just looked at her."

"What was she doing?"

Eden laughed. "She was in a Salvaggio rage," she said with a lot of animation. "She was magnificent. I just looked at her flashing eyes and listened to her go on passionately about getting good grades in college. She even had an outburst in Italian. Something I haven't seen in a while." She chuckled. "I just kept thinking, when did it become such a burden to see her and hear her be passionate about something?" Tears filled her eyes. "I don't know what was wrong with me."

"There's nothing wrong with you, Eden," Flynn said sympathetically.

"Says you and Cathcart," quipped Eden wiping her tears. "He says I just needed to recognize my fears, face them, and work through them. He said my fears turned things I once admired in her into reasons to be unsure and angry or unhappy with her."

Flynn looked at her with concern again. "But you're sure of things now, right?"

"I am," she said confidently. "I love her so much. I just feel like I've wasted so much time and caused her so much pain. I hope she doesn't decide too much time has gone by for us to be able to work things out."

"And hope she doesn't believe the things Jake said to her," Flynn said crossly.

"I wish I knew what else Jake told her," Eden said in frustration. "She just kept demanding I tell her the truth. I wish I knew what truth she wants. "I," she hesitated, "I haven't told her about seeing Cathcart. I think Abby might have, though. I haven't told her about my fears or about the anger and why I was having problems. And I haven't told her about Michael and some other things." She looked nervously at Flynn. "Do you think that's what she's talking about?"

"I don't know," Flynn said as he picked at his fingernail. "I don't think Jake even knows about it all."

"I don't either," said Eden feeling the anxiety building inside her. "I don't want to tell her everything at once and make her hate me again," she paused fretfully, "but what if it's one of those things? If I don't say something, she may never trust me and may decide not to try with me again." She took a calming drink of her beer. "What if it's about the information we have about Jake and the fact all this started because of me and my stupid cyber sex? What if I tell her about those things and it just makes everything bad again?" She paled as she remembered Rafe's anger. "She was so angry when we talked about Jake. I really screwed up, and I don't know what to do. I don't want to make another mistake."

"Are you going to talk to Cathcart about it?" Flynn asked, hoping she would.

"Some of it," Eden assured him with a nod. "Not the Jake part, though. I still need to talk to him more about Rafe."

14

HAPPY FOR A change, Eden Kingsley had arrived for her regular Monday evening six o'clock appointment at Dr. Cathcart's office. She walked into the office and sat lightly on the couch smiling. Cathcart observed Eden as she sat down and could see a big change in her from their last session.

"You seem happy," Cathcart said as he welcomed her with a smile. "Did something good happen last week?"

Eden smiled and nodded. "I did what you said, and you were right," she told him. "Rafe just needed time. She still needs some, but I think things are going to be good for us again. This weekend was," she began hesitantly, "it was good."

"It doesn't seem like it took her long to start coming around," Cathcart observed. "Do you want to talk about what happened?"

"I gave her space," Eden reported. "I had to go to a dinner party at her house, and I left her alone and just spoke to her about general things. Nothing about relationships," she assured him. "Then Thursday, Abby invited me to go out, and we went to Rafe's house. I told Abby I wanted to talk to Rafe in private, and she got Rafe to agree. Then, I just apologized to her," she said and smiled. "I told her I hoped she could let me tell her how I felt soon. I told her I understood she needed time."

"Very good. What did she say?" asked Cathcart.

"She just looked at me. Then she told me she had changed," Eden said starting to get anxious about what all she wanted to tell him. "I think she was giving me an opening to walk away if I changed my mind. But I'm not changing my mind."

"What happened over the weekend?" Cathcart pressed.

"I went to her house with Abby again." She looked at him happily. "I didn't want to break her rule again. She was in a Salvaggio rage, and Abby was fanning the flame!" Eden laughed at the memory. "Rafe let me give her a back massage to help her relax," she hesitated for a moment, debating on whether or not she should tell him what happened. Then she continued. "I didn't mean to, but I couldn't help myself, and I kissed her. I knew as soon as I did it I had screwed up, but then Rafe kissed me back."

"How did it make you feel?" asked Cathcart.

"It made me feel great!" Eden laughed aloud. "I didn't want to stop. But then suddenly, she stopped and stood up and said we needed to talk. I was hurt and didn't understand."

"What didn't you understand?" asked Cathcart

"She was telling me she didn't want me to do something I would regret," said Eden anxiously. "Why would I regret it? She said she didn't want to treat me like everyone else. She just wanted me to tell her the truth. She asked me if I wanted her to give me her heart, or if I was just doing this to use her and hurt her. I wasn't sure what she meant." She looked up anxiously. "I told her I didn't want to hurt her.

"Let's think about this calmly," suggested Cathcart. "It seems like she doesn't want you to regret having sex with her because she isn't sure if you're using her or if you really love her. Maybe she doesn't think you're really sure about her.

Maybe she's testing you like you tested her so she can be sure your feelings are real."

"But they are," Eden insisted. "I told her I love her."

Cathcart considered his words carefully. "Eden, you've been unsure of your feelings for a long time," he reminded her. "I think, if you really are sure about your feelings, you should let her lead when it comes to a physical relationship."

"I told her whenever she was ready, it would be right," Eden assured him. "She let me stay over and just hold her. But when I woke up in the night, she wasn't with me. She had gone into the guest room. I'm not sure why she didn't stay with me." She sighed. "I went in to lay down with her, but then in the morning, she was gone before I woke up."

"It's good you let her know you would wait," said Cathcart. "Now you just have to live up to your words. It's good if she wants you close, but if she needs space, you need to give it to her. Do you think you can?"

"Yes." Eden nodded. "I can. I'll do whatever she wants."

15

AT THE KIKI BISTRO, Rafe Salvaggio and Julia Hawthorn were at a table in the upper-level bar area where it was open for the event. From their vantage point, they overlooked the large crowd out for another big night of live music. Their friends were below, some out on the dance floor and others at another party table. Rafe was watching all the people as they came into the club and thinking about Eden.

It was frustrating how Eden still hadn't answered her questions or told her anything to make her believe she was telling the truth.

Time and patience.

Time only seemed to make it harder to be patient.

Eden kept asking for patience, but Rafe had never been very patient. All she could do was try to keep Eden close, watch where she tried to lead them, and hope it was real. She was still unsure about her, especially since she knew Eden was lying to her about the scheme with Jake.

Rafe had been worrying about her confrontation with Jake. There had been no sign of him, so she wasn't sure what exactly was happening between him and Eden. She had been waiting for signs to see if he would take some sort of action. Would he respond by immediately taking Eden away, or would he stay out of her way as she had told him? Eden was still here, and Jake hadn't been seen. So either her threats were effective, or Jake was telling the truth about how little influence he had over Eden.

There was also the hope maybe Eden was telling the truth—about not seeing Jake, at least. Rafe decided to go ahead with her plan to give Eden everything she wanted even if it meant losing everything in the end. While Eden was pretending to be in love, Rafe intended to do whatever it took to make Eden actually fall in love with her again. She could only hope, if Jake were telling the truth, Eden would change her mind or at least execute her plan in a less painful way.

Eden hadn't liked it, but they hadn't seen each other much over the last three weeks because of work and other things.

Mostly, it was just Rafe trying to keep an arms distance while she had time to process her conversation with Jake and not feel like she might explode again when she talked with Eden. But Rafe did her best to keep track of what Eden said about where she was going and who she was with.

To keep another line of controlled contact open and be a bit more assertive, Rafe had convinced some of the film students to call Eden and talk to her about speaking to their class. They were persistent, and Eden had no choice but to call her office to get information on being a guest speaker. Rafe had her assistant be very slow and vague about the procedure so Eden had to call back almost every day this week and come over to the house twice to pick up information.

But it hadn't been enough for Eden. In her relentless insistence to spend time together, she had shown up at the house almost every night last week after work. Her excuse was she was there so Rafe could spend a few hours with her and Bronte for family time. Rafe let her think she believed her. She figured if things looked easy, maybe Eden would not be as inclined to do the things Jake had reported she would do. The hardest part was when Bronte fell asleep, and they were alone.

Holding in her feelings while Eden was touching her, kissing her and whispering to her was the hardest thing Rafe had ever done—because it felt so right. Sometimes it was astonishing at just how relentless Eden could be, and it was maddening. Eden had always seemed to follow her heart and emotions when it came to being intimate and it was something Rafe loved about her. Sometimes it was hard to remember the things Eden was doing were just a means to a painful end.

Keeping a manageable distance and allowing time between Eden's visits helped.

But now it had gotten to the point where Rafe knew she had to give in to Eden or go mad with her desire for her. She wanted to give Eden what she was asking for, but she was still going to be protecting her heart, just in case. She couldn't afford to make mistakes.

Using the excuse she wanted to go to the concert, Rafe asked Letty to let Bronte stay with Lydia at her house tonight until she and Ephraim got home. She didn't want Letty to know what she was planning just in case things didn't work out.

Tonight she put all the other arrangements in place for her plan to make Eden's words a reality.

Now she just had to wait.

Julia glanced over and noticed how Rafe looked as if she were in another world. "Are you sure you want to be here? After the last amendment and everything, do you want to take the chance?" she asked wondering if Rafe was going to be pensive all night.

"I am worried about the amendment," Rafe said with a nod, "but Katheryn told me I shouldn't stop living my life. I know what I'm doing, Julia," she said. She smiled at the waitress who brought her a fresh drink.

"Does Eden know you're here?" asked Julia as she stirred the martini placed in front of her.

"I'm sure Eden knows exactly where I am," answered Rafe as she watched the door. "She's had an excuse to call me or see me almost every day this week."

"What about your promise to spend time with her?" Julia asked curiously. "What's she going to think if you take someone home tonight?"

"Don't worry about my promise," Rafe said wryly.

Julia smiled at Rafe knowing she was tired of everyone looking over Eden like babysitters. She looked over the crowd again for anyone she thought might be promising. "So, you see anyone good yet?"

"Not yet," said Rafe as she took a sip of her scotch on the rocks.

"I know I may regret this," Julia said gauging the feel of the night, "but do we want to make it interesting tonight? Another wager maybe?"

"No, Julia," answered Rafe as she smiled and shook her head, "no betting tonight." A woman approached them, and Rafe gave her a stare indicating the woman should go away.

"Oh, why not?" inquired Julia as she saw the woman turn away. "And how did you do that? The girl just did a U-turn. You could have let me have her." She pouted then took a mood-soothing sip of her martini.

"Because," she said and smiled wickedly, "I've come here with a plan. You'll be busy in a minute, and you can go get her later."

"A plan?" asked Julia and perked up a bit.

Rafe flashed a mysterious smile. "Yes."

16

ACROSS THE BAR, at a party table near the dance floor, Abby Van Falkov and Erica Sunley were checking out the crowd around the club hoping to see famous faces. As she looked through her camera, Erica spotted a familiar face in the upper bar area.

"Hey, there's Julia and Rafe," Erica said as she pointed, surprised to see them.

"Why didn't I know they would be here?" asked Abby irritably as she looked in the direction Erica had pointed. "I told Eden she better hurry and take her off the market. This isn't good," she said apprehensively. "I hope Eden shows up soon."

"Yeah, I'm surprised Rafe is going out like this. She promised to spend time with Eden," said Flynn not understanding why Rafe would come without Eden. From what Eden had told him, things were going well between them. Rafe didn't talk about Eden, just about the projects. She had even stopped talking about war.

"She told me she can't just stop living because of the injunction," said Jude. "And she didn't promise to not go places without Eden. Do you think they're still mad at each other after all this time?"

I don't know," said Abby. "I haven't talked to either of them lately." She looked up at Rafe again. "I can't believe they're claiming she is a deviant and immoral again. I mean, she can't help it if the girls like her and she's part wildling. Half the time she just walks in the room and does nothing, and women come up to her."

"I think you are missing the point, Abby," said Jude with a frown. "They're using whatever they can to stop the adoption for some reason."

"Well, all I have to say is Eden had better hurry up," Abby complained, "because the way those women are surrounding Rafe, she may just decide to accept one of their offers, and then what will Eden do? I just knew the crazed wild side of Rafe would haunt her someday."

"Abby, just stop with the wildling stuff," Jude scolded.

"Sor—*ry*," Abby said and rolled her eyes. She looked up and saw Eden. "Hey, Eden, you made it. Thank god!"

"Hi," said Eden, glad she found her friends. "I think Rafe is supposed to be here tonight. Her TA mentioned something about it. Have you seen her?"

Erica pointed up at Rafe. "She's up there hanging out with Julia."

"They're being surrounded, as usual," Abby said drolly. "Come on. Let's go out on the dance floor," she said before Eden could see the latest woman who was approaching Rafe.

"Yeah, the softball girls just got here," said Erica excitedly.

17

IN THE UPPER level of the bar, the women were already filled with enough liquor, and they had become brazen and brave. Rafe Salvaggio had just turned away another offer to Julia's chagrin.

"You could at least let me get a phone number," said Julia irked with Rafe. "So you're really not going to tell me your plan?"

"I don't need to tell you, Julia," Rafe explained. "You'll find out what it is soon enough."

"I hate waiting for things," said the silver haired woman disgruntled.

Rafe stood up and took the last sip of her drink. "Okay," she announced, "I've found her."

Julia looked around the bar with interest. "Who? Where?" she asked, desperate to go into action.

"See the beautiful golden blond woman over there?" asked Rafe as she nodded to a table below them. "The one wearing the green fitted mid-drift button-up blouse with cap sleeves, and the jeans with decoration along the pockets?"

"No, I don't see her," said Julia searching the area. "The only blonde I see over there is Eden." She looked at Rafe in confusion. "You mean Eden?"

"Oh, is that her name?" asked Rafe as she smiled coyly.

"Rafe, you're going to do it, aren't you?" Julia asked shrewdly. "You're going to seduce her!"

"No, I'm just going to give her what she wants," Rafe clarified with a shrug and then looked back over at Eden. "The plan is now in action. Pay close attention and keep other people out of my way."

"Oh, my god!" Julia laughed hysterically. "It's about time! Okay, let's go get her."

18

THE BAND WAS playing an upbeat song, and the dance floor on the lower level of the bar was so crowded it seemed like everyone there was dancing. Eden Kingsley was dancing with her friends, allowing her body to sway in motion with the music. Dancing was something, before moving to California, she never imagined herself doing. Not only because of her shyness and anxiety, but also because of being taught dancing was another entry on a long list of sins.

Meeting Rafe, and making so many other friends she was comfortable around who had encouraged her, was what finally got her to get out on a dance floor for the first time. Whenever she danced with Rafe, it seemed like she could just focus on her, and she was fine. But when it was just her and the girls, she had to push through what she thought of as a little stage fright until she could focus on the music or a rhythm.

It took two drinks, Abby's antics, and a whole song, but Eden had finally tuned in with the music. She was trying not to think about what Rafe was doing across the bar with Julia when a girl stepped in to dance with her. Eden looked at the girl and almost lost the focus she had as her shyness threatened, but she was able to push it away. She decided to stop worrying, just have fun, get lost in the music, and to just dance with her friends again.

Rafe and Julia took their time making their way down to the dance floor. By the time they had made it through the crowds of women, the band had stopped playing and announced they were taking a break. Rafe gave the DJ a nod, and she queued up a song with a slow, powerful beat exuding, along with the singer's soulful voice, a penetrating sexual vibration. Rafe saw the girl who had been dancing with Eden was moving in on her again. When the girl looked up, Rafe gave her a hard, threatening stare. The girl hesitated. Rafe signaled Julia to take care of it. Julia moved in and took the attention of the girl away from Eden. Eden took losing her dance partner with grace and watched with amusement as Julia swept her away. Rafe stood still behind Eden, then reached out and brushed her hand softly and slowly down Eden's back.

Eden turned around quickly at the unexpected contact. She was surprised but happy to see she was face to face with Rafe. Rafe didn't move but just looked into her eyes. Eden looked back into Rafe's eyes and saw an unfamiliar fiery look in them. She caught her breath as uncertainty rushed through her. A spotlight shined down on them, and Eden suddenly felt self-conscious about what was happening.

Rafe tilted her head down and breathed onto Eden's lips, then kissed her deeply before moving from her mouth to her ear. *"Ciao bella, posso avere questo ballo?"*[4] she asked in her smooth, sexy, Italian then took Eden into her embrace and began to move to the rhythm of the music, keeping them under the spotlight.

Eden swallowed hard at the sensation and the scent of Rafe as it seemed to overwhelm her. "Hi," she managed hesitantly.

As they danced, Rafe moved her hands lightly down Eden's back then up her body. "I haven't seen you in here for a while."

"No," Eden said as jealousy made her start to wonder how often Rafe had been coming here to dance with women. She decided it had to have been in the past, so she didn't care as she felt the warmth of Rafe's body against her. She laid her head against Rafe's shoulder. There was no need to search for anything else to focus on anymore. Her body relaxed as they moved to the music.

Rafe pulled back from her slightly and stroked her silky golden hair as Eden looked up at her. "You know who I am?" she smiled seductively.

Eden looked at Rafe confused but entranced by the smoldering desire she saw in her gray-blue eyes. "Of course, I know you, Rafe," she said with a smile, wondering why Rafe was asking her such a question.

"Good," Rafe whispered as she moved Eden slowly around the dance floor. "But you have to remember what I told you. I've changed a lot," Rafe said, and Eden could feel her breath on her lips. Rafe stopped dancing as she held Eden under the spotlight and placed her face close to her ear. "Do you know who you want?" she breathed. Rafe pulled back and looked intently into her eyes.

---

[4] Hello beautiful, can I have this dance?

Eden looked back with wide eyes not sure she heard right so didn't answer. Then her heart skipped a beat and her face flushed red as she realized Rafe was asking if she wanted Jake or her.

Rafe saw her sudden understanding cross her face. "I think I know," Rafe said close to her ear. "I want you with me tonight, okay?" Rafe pulled away slightly and watched Eden nod her head in relief. She leaned forward and kissed Eden on the lips lightly, once, twice, and then waited for Eden to bring herself into the third kiss, and when she did, Rafe kissed her deeply, relishing the taste of her.

Rafe began to move again to the powerful beat of the music pressing her body against Eden as they moved with a hypnotic sway. She took Eden's hand and placed it against her cheek then moved it down slowly until Eden's fingers were near her lips. Looking into Eden's eyes, she kissed the tips of her fingers then folded her hand around Eden's and held it to her chest. Rafe moved her face close again, and Eden fell into her kiss. Lithely, Rafe moved her kisses to Eden's cheek and neck and then spoke directly and softly into her ear. "My car is just outside. Do you want to come home with me?"

Eden heard the words she had been hoping for, and her body trembled as she nodded, unable to believe what she had been waiting for was actually happening. "Yes," she breathed as she looked up at Rafe.

"*Dimmi*,"[5] she whispered. "Tell me you want to," Rafe said with a seductive smile.

---

[5] Tell me,

"I do," she said as she looked at Rafe's smile, and her heart beat hard in her chest. "I want you to take me home with you."

Putting her hand on the small of Eden's' back, Rafe pulled her close and put her lips close to her ear. "Then what? Tell me what you want."

"Make love to me," Eden said shakily because the sensation of Rafe's voice in her ear was making her weak.

"What?" Rafe chuckled softly in her ear. "Make love? Are you sure that's what you want tonight? I don't need to take you home to make love to you. I can do it right here and now," she said and kissed her neck as she unclasped her bra through her shirt with one slight movement.

Eden could feel Rafe's presence surrounding her senses, and she felt the sudden freeness as her bra loosened. Rafe's body felt good pressed against her as they moved across the dance floor. Eden looked down and saw Rafe had covertly undone a button on her shirt and watched as she ran her fingers lightly over the small amount of cleavage revealed. Eden looked up into Rafe's eyes feeling the rush of thrill as it shot through her core from her touch.

She knew what Rafe wanted her to say. Still, after all these years, it was something she was shy about saying, even in private. She could feel herself flush red because she wanted to say it. Her body wanted her to say it. She closed her eyes and leaned her head against Rafe's shoulder then turned her head so her words would reach Rafe's ear. "I want," she swallowed, "I want you to fuck me." She couldn't help smiling at the feeling of unfettered exhilaration rushing through her having said those words to Rafe again. She was the only person who would hear those words from her lips, the only person she had ever felt free enough to express herself in such a way.

Rafe pulled Eden's face up gently by her chin and smiled. "I think we should go now. Are you ready? I love you. Tell me you love me," she asked as she kissed her then broke away and looked deeply into her eyes, awaiting her answer.

"I'm ready," Eden said breathlessly. "I love you."

19

FROM HER TABLE, Abby Van Falkov watched the dance floor from the darkness and couldn't believe what she was seeing. The spotlight followed Rafe and Eden as they danced slowly and close amid the crowded dance floor. The voyeurs in the crowd couldn't help but watch with interest what small parts of the seduction they could see unfold. The scene looked all too familiar to Abby, and it didn't bode well.

"What's Rafe doing?" Abby asked with a whine of concern.

"She's going to seduce Eden," Julia told her, amused and happy at how Rafe was finally making a move.

"What?" Abby shrieked. "No! She can't do this to Eden!"

"Do what? Be a crazed wildling?" asked Jude as she wiggled her eyebrows then laughed.

"Exactly," said Abby very worried. "Guys, this isn't a good thing. We have to stop it!"

"Why?" Jude grinned. "They're hooking up. I'd think it was a good thing." She took a drink of her beer. "Maybe Rafe wants to try out the new bed she had delivered."

"No, no, not like this," Abby fretted anxiously. "Look at Rafe." she groaned. "She's making those moves and giving her those looks she does when she's on the hunt. Eden isn't meat for her!"

"Everyone is meat for Rafe." Stacey laughed. "Didn't you read the injunction amendment?"

"Not Eden!" insisted Abby angrily. She looked over at the dance floor and watched Rafe as she moved with Eden. She could tell by the way Eden looked at her Rafe was doing the 'thing' she used to do to all the girls. The 'thing' Rafe did to get three girls into her bed before she found Greer. All her sexy talk and sexy moves that made girls think she was making a promise, but really, she was just playing her wildling game. Rafe was supposed to be taking getting back with Eden seriously, not treating her like a one-night stand she could throw away. "If she does this, and hurts Eden, she'll really lose everything."

"I don't think she's going to hurt Eden," Flynn said anxiously as he watched them on the dance floor.

"She told me she's going to give Eden what she wants," Julia said mysteriously than sipped her drink.

"What do you mean?" asked Abby perplexed. She watched as Rafe led Eden off the dance floor. "I've got to talk to Eden," she announced and walked away.

"Abby, don't," Jude called after her, but Abby ignored her.

20

AS THEY MADE their way through the crowded bistro, Eden Kingsley clung tightly to Rafe's hand. Rafe's gaze cleared a path for them, but their progress to the door was interrupted when Abby caught up with them and took Eden by her arm.

"Hey, Eden, where are you going?" asked Abby anxiously. "I mean, you just got here. I thought we were going to hang out."

"Oh," Eden flushed red. She felt like she did when she and Rafe had just started dating, and they would sneak away from everyone to make love. "Rafe and I were just leaving. Maybe we can hang out later."

Rafe turned as Eden slowed and saw Abby holding onto her. She stepped back to them and took Abby firmly by the arm then spoke softly into her ear. "Hi, Abby. We were just leaving," she said firmly. "Why don't you go back and keep Julia and the others company," she said and began to escort her away from Eden.

"What the hell are you doing, Rafe?" Abby yelled angrily over the noise.

"I think it's pretty clear I'm taking your advice," she said with a smirk. "You're the one who's been campaigning for this for months."

Abby looked at her miffed and stomped her foot. "Not like this, Rafe! You can't do this to Eden! Use your wild soul-stealing powers on her!" People began watching the scene unfold between the three with interest.

Rafe looked at her with a slight smile. "I'll use what you call my *wildling powers* on anyone I choose," she said calmly. "Stay out of it. You worry too much."

"No!" Abby fumed and broke away from Rafe and returned to Eden. "Eden, you're not going home with Rafe, are you? I mean," Abby started flustered, "she, you shouldn't. Not this way." Abby was definitely agitated.

"Tell her it's okay, Eden," said Rafe calmly as she caught up and stood beside Abby.

"Abby, it's okay," said Eden as she looked up at Rafe with shining eyes in anticipation of what they were about to do.

"Tell her you want to go with me," Rafe said softly as she looked intensely into Eden's eyes.

"I want this," she said to Abby but looked at Rafe. "I love you," she said as she gazed into Rafe's eyes and blushed.

Abby looked from Eden to Rafe in dismay. "Rafe, you can't!"

Rafe stepped in front of Abby to block her from Eden's view. "Abby, you need to walk away now. It's really none of your business. You worry too much." She turned and faced Eden, still blocking her view of Abby, as a few people began whispering behind their hands. She spoke softly into Eden's ear. "I love you too. Don't change your mind. Not if this is what you want."

"I... I won't," she said and kissed Rafe again. As the kiss ended, Eden quickly grabbed Rafe's hand and then spun on her heel and led her away.

Abby watched Eden pull Rafe along as the crowd applauded and whistled. "How could she?" Abby said and stomped her foot again. She returned to the table distressed. "You guys, I'm telling you this is wrong."

"What's so wrong?" asked Jude laughing as she finished clapping with the crowd. "It's Eden and Rafe. Everyone loves to watch Rafe in action, and they've never seen her make moves on Eden. It was great!"

"No, it wasn't Eden and Rafe!" she informed them. "It was Eden and a Rafe she knows nothing about!"

"Not the 'wildling' Rafe?" Jude said dramatically.

"It's not a joke, Jude," Abby said angry and worried. "You saw it. Eden was totally entranced. Rafe's seduced her just so she can get her way. Now she's going to take her home, fuck her, and treat her like she's nothing—just like all the others she's done the same thing with." She was fuming as a tear ran down her cheek. "Eden won't know what hit her, and then it won't be possible for things between them to be the same again."

"The same as what, exactly?" asked Julia not seeing what the drama was all about. "Until tonight, there was nothing between them," she argued. "Rafe just got tired of waiting."

"They could at least tolerate each other," Abby snapped. "After this, I don't know," she stammered, "and what about Bronte?"

"Abby, I think you're worrying too much," said Jude calmly. She knew Abby was talking about herself and how Rafe had treated her more than how Rafe was treating Eden at the moment. She was fairly sure Rafe wouldn't do the same thing to Eden. "Rafe knows what she's doing."

"Yes, she does." Julia grinned at Abby. "She said she had a plan."

"She has a plan? A Rafe Salvaggio plan?" screeched Abby. "Oh, my god," she said in a panic. She remembered Rafe's plans involving danger, disappearing, and sex. Not necessarily in the same order or separately. "This is worse than I thought."

21

EDEN KINGSLEY PULLED Rafe Salvaggio out of the bar and looked back at her with questioning eyes. Rafe smiled, understanding Eden wanted to know the direction of her car. Rafe pulled Eden back toward her and led her down the sidewalk. When they got to the car, she opened the passenger door for Eden and watched as she slid quickly into the seat.

After closing the passenger door, Rafe walked around the car, watchful for Jake. She was worried he would show up and interfere with her plan. Because of his threat, she really didn't trust he would stay away, and she was sure he wouldn't if he really was in love with Eden as he claimed. She took a calming breath and got in the car with Eden. She looked over at her and could see her impatience.

"Are you ready?" Rafe asked softly.

"Yes, I'm ready," said Eden as she looked into Rafe's beautiful eyes.

"Okay," said Rafe as she put on her seatbelt and started the car. She pulled out of the parking lot, and as Rafe drove down the street, she put her hand between Eden's legs.

C. L. CATTANO

Eden felt Rafe's warm hand move between her legs, and she ached for her to move it up further. Her heart was beating hard, and she felt lightheaded thinking about Rafe and being with her again. Every time they were together, she had tried to show Rafe how she felt, only to have Rafe stop things. Feeling Rafe's hand move up her leg made her feel achingly rhapsodic. She only felt this kind of ache for Rafe. Having this ache again, and being this close to her after all this time, was excruciating.

They pulled into the driveway, and Rafe got out of the car. She saw Eden had practically jumped out of the car wanting to get inside. Rafe walked around to her and took her by the arm. She pulled her toward her and kissed her deeply as she pushed her against the warm car. She ran her hands over Eden then pulled back.

"Are you sure you want this?" Rafe asked giving her the chance to stop.

Eden looked up at Rafe as she felt the warmth of the car against her. "I want this," she said breathlessly feeling the torment of desire run through her body. Eden reached out for Rafe and pulled her back to her, kissing her lips. She felt Rafe pull back as she took her hand and led them into the house.

Just inside the front door of the dark house, Rafe pulled Eden close, pinning both of Eden's hands against the door while she kissed her deeply. She suddenly pulled away from Eden and looked into her eyes. "Is this really what you want?" Rafe asked again softly, giving her another chance to stop. She didn't want there to be any doubt Eden was consenting in case Eden made another amendment or some other charge against

98

her later. She hoped the phone recording in her pocket would help if it came up.

"Yes," breathed Eden and arched herself toward Rafe.

"You know I love you," Rafe whispered between their kisses. "I want to do this because I love you."

"Yes," Eden answered back. "I love you too." She kissed her again. "I love you."

Rafe took Eden by the hands, turned her around, and pushed her backward through the house with her kisses. As they made their way to the back of the house, Eden tried to go toward Rafe's bedroom.

"No," Rafe whispered through her kisses. She maneuvered Eden into the guest room and closed the door behind them with her foot. Rafe stopped them in the middle of the room, pulling Eden to her by the front of her shirt, and kissed her. She moved her kisses to her cheek and neck, then put her lips to Eden's ear, and whispered. "Do you still want me?"

"Yes." Eden breathed as she clung to Rafe and ran her hands over her, feeling the firm shape of her body. It had become familiar to her again over the last month and she ached to know more.

"Tell me," Rafe whispered. "Say my name."

"I want you, Rafe," Eden whispered back breathlessly as she moved her head against Rafe's, her hands caressing her hair, shoulders, and breasts.

Her hands still gripping Eden's shirt, Rafe smiled when she heard the words. "Show me," she said quietly, and with a sudden swift movement, Rafe pulled Eden's shirt open, causing the buttons to be lost in the night.

Eden took a breath of shock and surprise before looking up into Rafe's hungry eyes as she pulled her to her lips passionately, the condition of her shirt immediately forgotten.

Rafe stripped Eden's ruined shirt off while kissing her deeply and made short work of her bra already barely hanging on her. She pulled Eden close to her by the waist of her jeans, unbuttoning them as Rafe kissed her neck, her shoulders, and chest, only interrupted when Eden pulled her back to her mouth. Rafe pulled away from Eden's kisses and stopped to look at the woman she loved. She saw Eden's lips waiting and the desire in her eyes. It was too late to stop now. Rafe knew she was past the point of no return. Rafe leaned in and kissed her again, taking her kisses down along Eden's body until she came to her open jeans and lace underwear.

Eden stepped out of her shoes as Rafe knelt in front of her, kissing her body and pulling her jeans down over Eden's hips and then to the floor. Eden kicked her jeans away, pulling Rafe up and kissing her deeply again while slowly unbuttoning her shirt.

Rafe helped with the buttons and stripped her own shirt off as Eden unfastened her slacks. They slid to the floor easily because of the weight of the phone in the pocket, and Rafe stepped out of them revealing her naked figure.

Taking in Rafe's body with her eyes, the desire to consume it took over Eden's senses. She was lost in the warmth, texture, taste, and scent of Rafe. Excitedly, she moved against Rafe, kissing her and frenziedly caressing her and feeling her soft skin, breasts, and her stomach. She took Rafe's hand and tried to lead her to the bed, but Rafe pulled her back.

Holding Eden out at arm's length, Rafe looked into her eyes. "No," she said softly. "I want to look at you."

Keeping her hands in contact with Eden's body, Rafe made a slow circle around Eden taking in the sight of her body without a word. Rafe ran her hands lightly over Eden's body, the curve of her hips, the smoothness of her back, the swell of her breasts and the faint scar on her stomach, all so familiar to her.

This was the woman she loved, the woman she wanted to make love to forever. Tonight may just be forever. She wanted a memory she could keep in the private recesses of her mind in case she left her again. No, she couldn't allow herself to think this way. She wanted Eden to fall in love with her and never leave again.

Eden was watching Rafe, unsure of what she was doing or thinking. Rafe had never asked to look at her like this with such hunger and intensity. Self-consciousness and uncertainty ran through Eden, but she pushed it back, allowing Rafe to take the lead as her warm caresses flowed over Eden's body and melted her.

Rafe took Eden's face in her hands, pulling her closer and kissing her passionately, as she wrapped herself around her pressing her warm body against Eden. The love chemicals in Rafe's brain crashed together making it hard for her to think but heightening the amatory sensations as they ran through her body, making her tremble at the touch of Eden's skin, lips, and tongue against her own.

Eden felt Rafe's body quaking against her, and she looked at her as Rafe ran her hands over Eden's face and hair. "You're trembling," Eden whispered.

"I know," Rafe said in a shaky whisper. "It's okay," she said between her kisses. "I love you." She put her head against Eden's and said, "Only you do this to me."

"I love you too," Eden said as she caressed Rafe's face and looked into her shining eyes. "I love you so much." She could feel Rafe's trembling body calm as her body heat rose under her hands. She noticed the changes in Rafe's body. She had become leaner than she was before, her muscles etched now, with a strength to match. But her scent was the same, her skin still so soft and her lips so sweet. Rafe was who she wanted, who she loved. Eden wanted to prove it, to show Rafe, to let her feel the fact of her love.

Eden tried again to take Rafe to the bed, and this time, Rafe offered no resistance. Encouraged and excited she could take the lead, Eden kissed Rafe all the way onto the bed and climbed over her, kissing and touching her body with every part of hers as Rafe's warm hands caressed her. Eden looked down into Rafe's face and saw the passion she was feeling in her eyes.

"I can't believe we're here." Eden ran her hands down Rafe's warm body. "Your body is so beautiful," Eden whispered as she caressed Rafe's breasts then fell toward her lips again. Rafe lifted her head up to meet her. Eden took her mouth to hers and kissed her deeply, pushing Rafe back down into the pillow.

Eden moved her kisses down Rafe, savoring the taste and the texture of her skin against her tongue as she filled her mouth with Rafe's breast. She felt Rafe's breath quicken, and desire ran through Eden as she explored and revisited the body of the love she thought she had lost.

Rafe ran her hands over Eden's hair and threw her head back as Eden kissed and teased her body with her tongue, and an intense desire overcame her with Eden's every touch. Her mouth filled once again with the sweet taste of Eden's tongue as she kissed her. Her mind and body knew this touch, craved this kiss, and had been deprived of this woman for too long. The love she felt for Eden, the love she couldn't let go of, echoed through her heart and body.

A soft moan escaped Eden as Rafe's warm hands pulled her hips down, and she could feel Rafe move her leg up between her legs. She knew Rafe was going to try to overturn her. Eden pulled away from their kiss, pushing Rafe's arms up and leaning back on her knees, pinning Rafe down. Eden smiled at her and licked her lips.

"I've been thinking and dreaming about having you in this position a lot," she said huskily.

"Oh, really?" Rafe chuckled and watched her nod. "Well, you've got me here. What are you going to do about it?" she asked as her eyes sparkled. Rafe saw the flush of desire in Eden's face and could feel how wet she was as she pressed her leg against Eden.

"Do you want to hear about it or do you want me to show you," asked Eden lustfully. Her body tingled with need as she hovered over Rafe.

Rafe smiled up at Eden, breaking free of her grip, and running her hands over her. "Well, are you sure you remember what to do? Maybe I should give you a little reminder," she teased then pulled Eden down and kissed her.

Eden broke away breathless and pushed back up, looking down into Rafe's face. "Oh, I remember what to do," she breathed out. Eden's mouth watered at the thoughts running through her mind, and she needed to swallow. "I can't wait to show you exactly what I remember," she confessed and watched as Rafe gave her a sexy smile then arch her eyebrow in a challenge.

Eden accepted the challenge with a kiss. She broke away with a grin then looked down Rafe's body, seeing Rafe was open for her. Eden set a slow pace as she took herself down Rafe's body to where she had been invited. She explored Rafe's body as she did the first time they made love, only this time, she knew the terrain by heart.

Eden knew kissing Rafe in the spot between her neck and collarbone drove her crazy. She knew dragging her hair over her body would make her nipples harden. Eden knew Rafe liked it when she teased her nipples with her tongue by the moans coming from Rafe's lips. She knew pressing herself against Rafe and making sure she could feel how wet she was made Rafe squirm under her.

She wanted all of it to happen and everything else she could remember. She wanted the kisses to those familiar places along her body to say 'remember this' to her. She wanted to make Rafe see she didn't need Lauren or Greer or any of those other women. She wanted Rafe to need only her, to want only her. Eden wanted Rafe to have no doubt she was sorry for ever leaving her. Eden wanted her to see they still had a strong connection even though they were apart for so long. Most of all, she wanted Rafe to believe she loved her.

Through the sensual fog created by her mind, Eden could feel Rafe touching her. Eden looked up as Rafe sat up and put her hand over the hand Eden had covering her breast. Rafe reached out for her with the other and pulled her into a kiss. Breaking away, Eden looked down at where her hand was resting against Rafe's firm abs and at how close she was to her goal. She looked back up at Rafe and could see the desire in her eyes. It caused a surge of heat and light-headedness to run through her. Eden knew, somewhere in her mind, Rafe wanted to kiss her and touch her back, and she wanted it too, but at this moment, she had no willpower left. Only the primal need for what she had denied herself, the need for Rafe.

There was no fast. There was no slow. There was an instinctive passion as Eden gently but firmly pushed against Rafe's abs, forcing her back against the bed. Eden swore she heard Rafe laugh as she moved back down her body, covering it with kisses, licks, and gentle bites.

Eden had arrived, salivating as she looked at the open, waiting lips between Rafe's legs. She swallowed and then gently delved her tongue inside Rafe with a short, tantalizing stroke. Rafe arched at the sensation, and Eden felt her offer more of herself. Eden was lost in the warmth, texture, taste, and scent of Rafe. She moved excitedly against Rafe, sucking and licking her, frenzied, and pushing her tongue inside her.

Taking Eden's hand again, Rafe held it tight. Then she sat up and pushed Eden's head gently back with her other hand.

Eden looked up and saw Rafe struggling on the cusp. "I'll go slower," she breathed. "I'll make it last." Pushing her head against Rafe's hand, she put her tongue and lips back onto her swollen nerves. Eden paced herself as Rafe's hands ran through her hair. She felt Rafe arch herself up, demanding more of the perfect torment she knew was threatening to overcome her.

As Rafe's scent and taste filled her mind, she probed into her gently, drinking, teasing, and tasting. She could not get enough. Her mind and soul felt starved for this feeling, this closeness, and the connection that needed no voice. Touching her again, breathing her scent, tasting her again, was bringing Eden back to life and filling the emptiness she had felt for so long.

Eden felt Rafe touch her again, gently directing and holding her head in place. She heard Rafe's fast breathing and knew she was almost there. Eden swept her tongue over Rafe's clit and pressed into it giving it all her focus. She heard Rafe encouraging her and felt herself become wetter. Suddenly, Rafe curled forward with a cry of pleasure then leaned back again as Eden kept her tongue moving against her until Rafe sighed heavily and took deeper breaths.

Feeling Rafe's body relax, Eden smiled as she went down to lick up the sweetness flowing from Rafe. Then crawling up Rafe on her hands and knees, she kissed her. Sitting up, Eden reached back down between Rafe's legs, dipped her fingers into her, and then brought her wet hand up, touching Rafe's mouth, tracing her lips and kissing her again, reveling in her taste.

"See," Eden breathed onto Rafe's lips, "I remembered everything." She kissed her again. Eden couldn't help grinning as she lay on top of Rafe between her legs, grinding against her and kissing her.

Rafe looked up at Eden who grinned down at her, proud of herself. She loved the feeling of Eden moving on top of her and watched as her golden hair fell forward over her flushed face. She reached out and pushed the hair back then trailed her fingers lightly down her beautiful face. Memories filled her mind of how they used to be before it all came crashing down. She was glad Eden was proud of herself for being able to take a trip down memory lane, but Rafe had plans to go a different direction tonight.

Thoughts and worries intruded and darkened her mood, so she closed her eyes to try to hide it. There had been no angry pounding on her front door by Jake, and she doubted there would be if it hadn't happened by now. She thought about her conversation with Jake and wondered if she had made the right decision or if he was right, and she was only going to hurt herself more in the end.

Was she doing this for the wrong reasons? Was this really just a reminder fuck and the reason why Eden became angry when confronted–because it was the truth? Was this why Eden kept saying she needed time and patience because the truth was already right in front of her? Rafe took a deep breath fighting the building pain in her chest. Rafe felt Eden still on top of her and kissing her face and neck gently. Panic filled her as she felt she couldn't breathe. She had to make her stop. She had to get her off.

Rafe put her hand on the back of Eden's neck, adjusted her body, and overturned them quickly onto their sides. Then she buried her face in Eden's neck, breathing in her scent, trying to calm her panic and force the pain in her chest to go away.

This is right, she told herself. She was doing this because she loved her, and she wanted her back. She wanted Eden to love her again. She wanted her family back, and she would do anything for this chance.

Eden ran her hands over Rafe's body and felt her breath on her neck. Rafe was very still, and Eden wasn't sure why. She wondered if she had done something wrong. Eden started thinking maybe it was because she had promised to make things last and then she lost control. Maybe the sex wasn't good for Rafe, and she regretted getting together again. Maybe Greer or the other women made Rafe feel something she hadn't. Anxiety swept through her.

"Hey," Eden said shakily, "are you okay?"

"I'm fine," said Rafe softly as she recovered and pushed away all those dark thoughts. She fought to get back to the place where she was sure her plan to give Eden what she wanted would work. Rafe moved her lips closer to Eden's ear. "Tell me what you want," she said softly and began to massage the muscles in Eden's neck with the hand under her, moving her other hand over her lower back and hips.

Bringing her hand up, Eden lifted Rafe's face so she could see her eyes. "I want you," she said and pulled her into a kiss. "I love you," she said as Rafe poured more kisses over her and warmed her body with her hands.

"*Dimmi*,"[6] Rafe breathed through her kisses. "Tell me. Tell me what you want from me." She ran her warm hands over her, kneading and caressing her as she kissed her face and neck again.

The touch of Rafe's lips on her neck, the sound of Rafe's voice in her ear, and the feel of Rafe's hands caressing and loosening her muscles made her body heat rise, and a fine sheen of sweat began to cover Eden's body. The heat between her legs was rising too, and she wanted more of Rafe. She tried to wrap her legs around her again, but Rafe put her hand on her hip.

"I want your body against me," Eden said softly as she struggled to move her hips. What Rafe was doing to her lower back felt sublime. "I want to show you how wet I am for you."

A rush of desire ran through Rafe, and she couldn't help her smile. She kissed her neck and licked the salty sweat from above Eden's lips. "That's what you want?" Rafe asked softly as she ran her hand up Eden's spine slowly and firmly then back down again to her lower back. "You want to show me things?" She pulled Eden's leg up over her side and ran her hand up and down Eden's thigh and hip, pressing and massaging. "Okay," she said and pushed Eden leg off gently. She pulled away from Eden and quickly made her way to the end of the bed where she stepped onto the floor.

She looked down on Eden, who was on her back with her legs slightly opened. Rafe could see Eden was aroused because peeking out from the slightly parted lips between her legs was her engorged pink labia. She looked from between Eden's legs

---

[6] Tell me

up to her flushed face to her amazing brown eyes, and then Rafe arched her brows, waiting.

It took Eden a moment to catch up with what had just happened. Eden went from having Rafe's hands warming and arousing her to laying on her back looking up into her eyes. "Rafe," she said muddled. "What?"

Rafe grabbed Eden's ankles and dragged her down, bringing her hips near the edge of the bed. She then propped Eden's feet on the edge so her knees were in the air. "You said you wanted to show me something," said Rafe with a rakish smile. "I'm ready."

Eden pushed the damp hair from her face, propped herself on her elbows and laughed. "Come here, and I'll show you something," she said invitingly.

Rafe leaned forward between Eden's legs and put her hand on Eden's stomach right above her pelvic bone. "If it's what you want," said Rafe with a smile.

Eden lunged out, grabbed Rafe, and pulled her down onto herself, kissing her. She felt Rafe's hand press into her stomach. It didn't feel bad, but Eden wanted her hand down further. She writhed against Rafe's firm hold, and at a frustratingly slow pace, Rafe's hand moved down. She could feel the heel of Rafe's hand on the top of her pelvic bone, and she could feel herself throbbing, needing more, and wanting her hand lower.

"Please, Rafe," she breathed as she pushed her hips against her.

"I like what you're showing me," Rafe whispered with a smile. "Tell me what you want me to do now. What do you want?"

Feeling Rafe's hand move down slightly, Eden closed her eyes and bit her lip as she realized what Rafe wanted. She took a breath, opened her eyes, looking into those blazing gray-blues, and shivered when she saw a feral glint in them, surprising her. She couldn't help smiling back at Rafe as she kissed her.

"I want you to fuck me," she said breathlessly when they broke away, all inhibitions about words forgotten as she felt Rafe begin taking over her senses and taking control of her body.

Removing the hand between them, Rafe thrust her abs between Eden's legs. She felt the warm wetness she knew would be there while Eden wrapped her legs and arms around her. As Rafe kissed Eden, she could taste her salty essence. Rafe drew Eden up and stood with her in her arms. She felt Eden's wet warmth as she slid down her until she was standing.

Kissing Eden hungrily, Rafe ran her hands over her as she pushed Eden backward until she had her backed up against the bedroom door. Rafe pulled herself away and looked into Eden's eyes, smiling with an impish grin and fire in her eyes. She held up her hand and with two fingers, placed a firm love tap over the center of Eden's chest between her breasts claiming the quickly beating heart inside Eden for her own and keeping her fingers in place until she felt her heartbeat calm.

The tap echoed through Eden like ripples in a pond. "What are you doing to me?" Eden asked, unsure of what was happening, but she couldn't break away from Rafe's piercing eyes.

Rafe didn't answer. She just looked at her with the burning intensity of an artist at work and envisioning the creation about to come into existence. She began to move her two fingers slowly down Eden, pressing firmly into her wet, slippery skin so the trail left would be felt long after her hand moved on. From Eden's heart, Rafe's fingers continued their descent down Eden's body, ending inside her where Rafe could feel the smooth, wet sensation, setting Eden on edge.

Eden arched at Rafe's touch while she held onto Rafe's shoulder with one hand and the door handle with the other. "Oh, yes," she gasped. "I missed your touch," she moaned.

Rafe moved her fingers around and through Eden then brought her wet hand up, following the trail she had made back over her body to her stomach, to her heart, to her neck, over her chin, and to her lips, gently touching them, and lacing them with her sex and desire.

Putting her hand to her own lips, Rafe tasted the woman she loved for the first time. She licked Eden's lips needing more of her. Rafe sucked Eden's lower lip, and then took her kiss deep as the sensation sparked through her mind, making her feel like falling. She pressed Eden against the door and used her tongue and hot kisses to follow the sex trail she had made while caressing every part of Eden's body with her warm hands. She went down the sex trail, slowly touching her body and licking up every drop of Eden, over and under her chin, down her neck, through the valley of her breasts, and over her stomach until she was on one knee, kneeling in front of her.

Rafe put her arm through Eden's legs parting them. She then lifted one, resting it on her shoulder as she moved in to taste directly from her.

Eden couldn't move from her position as she held the door handle with one hand and had the other clinging to the doorframe. She was reeling from Rafe's love tap, the hot kisses, and the reaction of her body to how Rafe was touching her and not understanding exactly what was happening but knowing every nerve in her body was reacting to it. She didn't care as long as Rafe didn't stop what she was doing. Her heart was pounding inside her again, and Rafe's tongue was making her lose her mind.

"My god, Rafe! Please," she panted desperately, "I don't know if I can take it," she said as she leaned her head back on the door. "Oh, I need you to fuck me," she pleaded shakily as a tingling sensation washed over her body hitting every nerve.

With her shoulder, Rafe pushed Eden's leg higher lifting her slightly, then leaned her shoulder against Eden's thigh and held her open and against the door. She put her face against Eden's middle and slipped her fingers along the edge of her, slowly creating a desperate need inside her.

As Eden called her name and encouraged her, Rafe smiled to herself and slid inside Eden, rediscovering the texture and warmth now wet, swollen, and aroused. Rafe made her explorations and carefully made sure she was in the best position before finding her rhythm.

Eden matched it holding herself up with both hands on the doorframe and the ball of her foot. Her leg was giving out, and she had no choice but to let herself down onto Rafe's hand for further penetration.

As Rafe felt Eden's weight push down, she slid out then pushed back up inside her deeper while her tongue and lips wrapped around her sensitive nerves.

Eden cried out and reached down to touch Rafe's hair, clenching her fist, not wanting Rafe to stop but unsure of just how much more she could take. Suddenly, she felt a new sensation forming inside her, running through her body, pounding through her heart, and forcing her lungs to release their air over her vocal chords in an uncontrollable siren call of pleasure she couldn't control or stop. She didn't know what Rafe had done, and her mind couldn't comprehend what had happened yet because little waves of ecstasy kept rolling over her.

Rafe slowed her rhythm to keep her on edge for a little longer and moved her fingers deeper inside Eden. She was patiently beckoning and coaxing as Eden's body became immobilized by the need for liberation, and Eden's cries encouraged her.

Eden could feel Rafe pressing against the inside of her leg next to where her tongue was circling her clit. Eden could feel Rafe's fingers deep inside her stroking gently against her sensitive swell—it felt so good. Rafe moved her fingers, and Eden felt a familiar filling sensation inside, joined by the sensation of Rafe's tongue, as those magic fingers slid in and out and over and through her. Eden could only hold on to Rafe, her fingers tangled in her dark hair curled from the light sweat covering her. Eden's entire body was on overload with excruciating pleasure, and her body was screaming for the release Rafe was keeping from her.

Rafe suddenly moved her fingers, striking the unfamiliar place inside her again, and simultaneously targeted her clit directly with her tongue and lips. Eden felt the release coming and something else strange but familiar—yet her mind couldn't focus enough to remember. A shock of rapture ran through her imprisoned body and mind, taking her words away and cutting off her cries for Rafe, leaving only uncontrollable primal sounds to be unleashed. She suddenly realized what the familiar feeling was and she started to panic. Then all thought stripped from her mind, and she felt herself pour out onto Rafe. Eden could feel the vibrations in her throat as she cried out at Rafe's touch, coaxing more from her than Eden knew she had. It just seemed to keep cascading out as her body continued to spasm.

Rafe's heart beat fast at the sound of Eden's cries of pleasure as she flooded over her. Eden poured out uncontrollably over Rafe's hand and down her arm and onto her chest, over her breasts and body. Rafe had called out and knew from the flow down her own legs she had come hard as she felt Eden's orgasm contract tightly and release around her fingers.

Rafe felt Eden quake with the unexpected, powerful sensation, a result of what she had done to her. She could feel Eden throbbing inside and see she was unable to control her own body as her legs weakened and her body convulsed. Rafe took all of Eden's weight on her shoulder, pressing her against the door as she pulled herself out of Eden slowly and gently, feeling every spasm Eden had from the shockwaves caused by her movements.

She lowered Eden's leg from her shoulder. As soon as Eden's foot touched the floor, she began to slowly slide down the door from weakness. As Rafe stood, she took Eden's hand and untangled it from her hair. She held Eden up as she kissed her way back up her body. She rubbed her glistening wet body against Eden, finding her lips with her own and grinding her knee against her still throbbing center while kissing her deeply.

Eden let Rafe help put her arms around her neck. She looked up at Rafe looking down on her. Rafe's face seemed to glisten as she looked at her with shining wild gray-blue eyes and an open-mouthed grin. Eden couldn't look away from Rafe's eyes as she felt her body slowly move against her. Eden found some strength from somewhere, though she wasn't sure where, and ran her hands through Rafe's black curls and pulled her face down to kiss her. Pulling her closer, Eden moved her kisses to her neck. Eden laid her head against Rafe's shoulder as her desire-clouded mind succumbed and was overwhelmed. Then she lost her strength and began to shake with weakness.

Rafe pulled Eden's shaking body against hers and lifted Eden up, carrying her back to the bed where she laid her down gently and kissed her. She tried pulling away, but Eden wouldn't let go.

"You're so beautiful," said Rafe softly and kissed her again.

Eden wanted to keep holding onto Rafe, but her arms were too weak, and she was still shaking. Slowly, her arms loosened and slid down Rafe's shoulders and then her arms. She looked up at Rafe.

"I can't move," Eden said shakily. She tried to say more, but nothing came out.

"It's okay," said Rafe softly and pulled a blanket over them. "I'll keep you warm."

Taking her time, Rafe filled Eden's mind with sweet whispers, and slowly warmed her body with kisses and caresses, soothing her muscles and reawakening her desire.

Eden felt the brush of Rafe's hair and face against her cheek, and she lifted up her chin and felt her kissing her neck, causing a small spark of desire. Eden felt Rafe's mouth on hers again, and with her kiss, she felt Rafe breathe into her. The breath caused the spark of desire to inflame and run through her, filling her with the strength she needed to gain back enough control of herself to function again, and to feed the intense hunger she had for Rafe, who she had been deprived of for so long.

They couldn't stop touching each other, kissing and tasting every part of each other's bodies. They quickened and slowed their passionate attentions to keep each other in a state of euphoric excitement. Their combined scent filled the air around them. Rafe sat up, threw off the blanket, and then pulled Eden to her, lacing their bodies together so they could reach each other's wet centers and sensitive nerves.

Eden could feel Rafe's body heat infiltrating her making her vulnerable and more sensitive. Eden already felt so weak from what had happened before and, as Rafe's presence filled her, Eden felt something open up inside her. Tears fell to her cheeks as Eden realized what she was feeling. It was the memory of the fact her heart had made a promise, one she could never break no matter what. A promise she had made the first time she told Rafe she loved her and they had made love. The promise she would never stop loving Rafe no matter if they were together or apart.

Eden wiped her tears away quickly before Rafe could see them. She let go of herself as Rafe stirred her senses to their breaking point. Her breathing quickened, her already sensitive body electrified as Rafe moved against her.

Eden's quickening breath alerted Rafe she was on the edge of her climax again. Rafe slowed her pace and held her, pulling her tighter as she kissed her face and neck. "Stay with me," Rafe whispered.

Eden pushed herself against Rafe moving through her warmth and trying to focus, but she didn't know if she could do this after being apart for so long. She felt like she would lose her mind in ecstasy.

Suddenly, a flood of pleasure burst open and washed over her. She cried out as Rafe held her close, and her body trembled as she felt the flow of her release.

"Oh, god," she breathed her head spinning. "I," she started but cried out in shocked pleasure as Rafe pressed against her clit again, then sliding inside her, leaving her thumb on her clit and sending sparks through her brain.

Eden finally caught her breath again and looked at Rafe, who was grinning at her. "That wasn't funny," Eden said, and Rafe pushed into her again. "Ah, Rafe," she said softly then felt Rafe pull back out gently. "You're killing me. I don't know if I can take anymore. Let me touch you."

Eden tried to put her hand back between Rafe's legs, but Rafe kept her hand in place between Eden's legs. Rafe turned them so Eden was on her back. She climbed up to her knees and leaned over Eden so she could reach her breasts with her mouth. Rafe cupped Eden's breast in her free hand then leaned into her and took it into her mouth. She ran her tongue around her nipple lightly then let it slide slowly out of her mouth and kissed it. "You have perfect breasts," Rafe whispered and started on the other breast.

"Fuck," groaned Eden softly and felt Rafe's hand move slightly between her legs as her thumb retrieved some of the released wetness. Eden swore she could hear Rafe laugh softly at the fact Eden had cussed, but at the moment, she couldn't do anything about it.

Massaging and sucking Eden's breasts and stomach, Rafe carefully spread her attention between them and mixed her intensity of pressure and suction. Eden arched up against her when she wanted more, and soon, her body was flowing and wet again, and her pelvis was moving against Rafe's hand seeking more there too. Rafe took her kisses to Eden's neck and lips then whispered in her ear, "Are you ready now? Tell me what you want," she breathed.

Eden opened her eyes and looked up at Rafe, barely able to stop herself from crying from the overload of sensation her senses were carrying. "I just want you to make love to me, Rafe," she said softly blinking away her tears. "Please," she started, and Rafe kissed her.

"If it's really what you want, I'll make love to you," said Rafe tenderly as she looked into Eden's liquid brown eyes. She could see the golden specks in them—and somehow, there were other colors in her eyes. Rafe adjusted her body and pulled Eden to her, cradling her in her arms across her lap. She settled Eden's hips down onto the bed between her legs and Eden wrapped her arms around her neck.

Rafe pulled Eden close, kissed her, and ran her other hand slowly down her body, gently spreading her legs, making her way back to where Eden was waiting for her. "Tell me you love me, Ede," whispered Rafe.

Hearing Rafe call her Ede again while they made love caused a burst of warmth to flow out of her heart and through her body. It was the only nickname she ever missed because it came from such a happy and loving time.

"I love you," said Eden as she felt Rafe's hand move over her, feeling her body flow for her because of the memory Rafe had awakened.

Rafe kissed Eden, and a moan came from her throat as she slid her fingers through Eden's hair and over her nerves lightly. "I love you too," said Rafe and slid herself inside Eden who gasped and held her tighter.

Rafe held herself still for a moment then slowly began to rock with Eden while pushing and pulling herself in a slow and deep rhythm .

"*Bellissima Ede*," she whispered as she pushed deep into her and waited for Eden to breathe in, then rocked her back and pulled out slowly. It was controlled so Rafe could watch Eden's pleasure build with each push as she kissed her or offered her a whisper. "*Ede, mio cuore*," Rafe said as she slid inside Eden again and felt a rush run through her at how wet

Eden was becoming. Holding Eden close again and breathing in her scent as she moved inside her made Rafe feel like her world was right again. She wanted Eden to feel this was where she belonged. Rafe pushed into her again, easily sliding deeper. "*Mi ami, Ede,*" she breathed and kissed her.

Eden clung to Rafe and moaned into her kiss. "Oh, god, Rafe," she breathed, "I love you." Taking measured breaths mixed with moans of pleasure, she could feel Rafe deep inside her and then gently pull out bringing more wetness with her. She could feel herself responding to everything Rafe was doing with her hands, her lips, and her words. She had missed the way Rafe used everything from her body to her voice to make love to her. No other lover had come close to giving her this feeling or had been able to make her respond this way.

"*Per sempre Ede,*" breathed Rafe as she pushed deeper into Eden making her moan and grip Rafe's hair in her hand tightly as she rubbed her head against her. She felt Eden tighten slightly around her fingers, so she held her hand in place and kissed her until she relaxed.

Rafe lowered Eden so her back arched across her legs and ran her free hand over Eden's breasts and stomach while pulling out of her slowly. Rafe bent her knee and shifted her leg putting it under Eden's hips and bringing them up slightly. Eden was so wet now Rafe could feel it running down her own leg. She put her hand back between Eden's legs, fondling and stroking until her hand was wet again. She put her thumb on her clit and heard Eden's sharp breath as her body surged at the sensation, so Rafe held still for a moment before removing her wet hand from Eden's core and using it to coat Eden's stomach.

"Ede, are you ready," asked Rafe softly. She looked down at Eden who nodded. "Me too." She smiled then leaned over her and traced her lips with her wet hand before tracing her own.

Eden reached out and wrapped her arms around Rafe's neck. When Rafe sat up, Eden was once again held in her arms being kissed, tasting herself, and being rocked lovingly. She felt Rafe move her hand back over her body and between her legs then slide inside again. This time, though, Rafe was going faster, and she had Eden at an angle where she had more leverage. There was also more passion, causing arousal and, with it, more lubrication.

"Oh, yes, Rafe," Eden moaned encouraging her. "Don't stop! Oh, god! Yes," she cried out. "I love you!"

Rafe could feel Eden start contracting and releasing and could hear her breathing change as she reached closer to her climax. "Do you want my mouth on you or do you want to touch me?" Rafe asked heavily.

Eden looked into Rafe's beautiful face framed by her wild dark curls and couldn't resist. "I want to touch you," she whispered. She felt Rafe pull her closer and angle her slightly. Eden knew then the rest was up to her.

She released her arm from Rafe's neck and reached straight down past her breasts until she felt Rafe's abs then lowered her hand until she found those waiting parted lips and entered. Eden immediately found her hard clit and had the satisfaction of hearing Rafe gasp at the sensation. She could feel Rafe was close. Eden wished she could have held on so they could have come together and wanted to make it up to her now. She moved against her harder, and Rafe's breathing quickened.

Eden felt Rafe's strokes push in and out of her faster and felt her thumb strike her clit harder each time. Eden worked to match her and not lose her again. She felt Rafe push hard and deep into her then pull out, rubbing her clit so fast and hard Eden lost awareness of the scream she let out and the fact she was biting Rafe's collarbone. She only became aware again when she felt Rafe pull her head back to kiss her. Just as their lips were close, their faces touched, and a sudden dizzying wave of intense shockwaves ran through Eden as her release came and her body shuddered. As Eden's body shuddered, she felt Rafe flow over her hand and Rafe's breath against her face, as she let out a hoarse cry of pleasure. Somehow, she had stayed with Rafe.

Rafe laughed as shock waves shot through her as her body shook. She kissed Eden deeply as they shook. Gently she stroked Eden's body, burying her face into her neck and hair, breathing in her scent, and holding her tightly. When Rafe found her strength, she lifted Eden from her lap and settled her next to her before bending over to lick her stomach where she had covered it with her sex. She then licked between Eden's legs, and Eden held Rafe's head and moaned when Rafe's tongue caused shocks to charge through her. When Rafe was finished, she pulled the blanket back over them, and they embraced each other, holding onto the shared sensations they had experienced until their breathing slowed and warmth began to take over their bodies and minds.

Eden looked into Rafe's beautiful, smiling face as she held her with eyes full of sated passion and desire. She lifted her face to kiss Rafe again and looked into her eyes with wonder as she saw something new in her again.

"Thank you," said Eden tenderly.

"For what?"

"For making love to me."

"No problem," said Rafe and smiled. "Just tell me what you want, and I'll do my best to give it to you."

Eden chuckled and pushed Rafe's dark curls from her face. "So," she said softly, "what was the other thing you did to me?"

Rafe looked at her with a slight frown for a moment then smiled again. "I gave you what you wanted," she said seductively.

"Was that what I wanted?" Eden laughed softly.

Rafe looked at her innocently. "You said you wanted me to fuck you. You didn't give me specifics." It had become too warm, so she pushed the covers off, exposing their naked bodies.

"I'm so jealous of your abs," said Eden as she ran her hand gently over Rafe's body, marveling again at the definition beginning to show in her abs.

"I've been working on them for a while," Rafe said as she closed her eyes enjoying Eden's touch. "No tickling."

"Don't worry." She chuckled. It was amusing to Eden, for someone so dominating in her work and most aspects of her life, how Rafe was so ticklish. She moved her hand up to Rafe's breast loving the feel of the nipple in the palm of her hand. She sat up, moved her body over Rafe, and took her nipple into her mouth sucking gently at first, then a bit harder until Rafe grabbed her and gasped. Eden kissed the nipple gently then sat up and ran her hands over Rafe's arms. "I can't believe you carried me back to bed," she whispered and kissed her breast again.

"I've been lifting weights." Rafe chuckled and flexed her bicep. She thought she could have carried Eden anyway with the adrenaline rush she always got when they made love. She felt Eden take her breast in her mouth again. "Oh, yeah," she moaned, "that's making me lose my mind."

Eden released Rafe's breast from her mouth and smiled. "I think I lost my mind and all control of my body because of what you did to me," said Eden as she thought about what Rafe had done and how her body had felt. Eden remembered the panic when she thought she was going to pee. She looked at Rafe again. "I don't think I ever came like that before in my life. I just remember you glistening."

"I thought you liked different now," said Rafe looking at her with a grin and winked.

Eden looked down at her, unsure what to make of her comment, and shook her head. "It was definitely different," she said with a frown trying to remember when she said she liked something different.

"It felt like you were enjoying it," said Rafe remembering Eden's cries of pleasure and how her body had reacted and how her own had body responded, as well. She pulled Eden over so she was all the way on top of her. She tried to push her legs apart but Eden resisted.

"Oh, I liked it," Eden assured Rafe with a smile as she leaned forward then kissed her and ran her hands through her dark curls again, moving her hips in a slow grind against her. She felt Rafe grab her hips and pull her tighter against her hard abs.

"I know something else you might like," Rafe whispered lustily into Eden's ear.

"Yeah?" Eden managed to ask before she found herself in motion and falling back.

Rafe had somehow managed to push her backward so Eden was lying on her back spread wide open, with her legs to either side of Rafe. Rafe sat up on her knees and looked at her with a grin.

"What just happened?" laughed Eden.

Rafe tossed her a pillow. "Here, just in case you want to watch," she said and grabbed Eden's hips then pulled her closer.

Eden looked down and saw Rafe was touching herself and looking at her. "Fuck," she moaned as she felt herself begin to throb and become wet again. Eden heard Rafe chuckle then felt Rafe's wetness on her as Rafe pushed against her. She felt herself tighten inside at the feeling. Eden couldn't believe Rafe was making her so ready again. She watched her and couldn't deny the want of her.

"Rafe," she called and reached for her. Rafe took her hand and pulled her up so they were facing each other. Eden looked into Rafe's desire glazed eyes. "What do you want, Rafe?" she asked and kissed her.

"Per sempre," she said, so softly it sounded like a sigh. She kissed Eden back softly and felt her take hold of her hand.

"You're the only one my body begs for," Eden said hearing her sigh. She took Rafe's hand and put it between her legs so she could feel how wet she was for her. "Do you want my body to beg for you?" She looked into Rafe's eyes and saw her hunger.

"No," said Rafe when she found her voice. She pushed Eden back and climbed over her. "You never have to beg." She kissed her and then lost herself to the passion she could feel pouring out and into the one it was meant to fill. Rafe took control of Eden's body, and among Eden's cries and moans of pleasure and calls of encouragement, Rafe gave willingly everything Eden's body begged for and more.

22

A FEW HOURS later, Rafe Salvaggio felt Eden relax in sleep as she sighed against her. Slowly she untangled herself and kissed Eden lightly before gently pulling herself away and getting out of bed. She looked down at Eden's naked body again, and it was hard to look away. Her golden hair spilled across the pillow, and a few strands were across her face. Her body at riveted attention and a dark rose color not long ago was now relaxed and a soft blushing pink. The soft blond hair between her legs she kept trimmed short, because she thought to shave it all off wasn't sexy on her, was now almost transparent because it was dry.

Picking the blanket up off the floor, she gently covered Eden so she would stay warm. She couldn't stay the night with her. Rafe didn't think she could take it if Eden called out Jake's name while she dreamed.

Eden sighed and smiled as her whole body tingled. She reached out and opened her eyes in confusion when she couldn't find Rafe. She saw her stretching naked in front of her and smiled again. As Rafe picked up her clothes, Eden's questioning eyes followed her. She was unsure about why Rafe was gathering her things as if she was leaving. Eden suddenly wondered if she had done something wrong.

Rafe sauntered back to the bed when she saw Eden was awake and leaned over her, brushing her golden hair back. She smiled and kissed her again, and whispered into her ear, "I hope I can always give you whatever you want. I love you." Rafe slipped her still recording phone under the bed then walked naked out of the guest bedroom as Eden watched, unable to react before she was gone.

Entering her own room, Rafe headed for the bathroom where she took a long hot shower. When she was finished, she put on her pajamas then lit her meditation candles. She sat down on the floor, put her hands on her knees, and stared at the reflection of herself in the dark window in front of her.

Her mind started going through the night, remembering everything Eden had said and done. It was hard to believe all of it was a lie. But she may know the truth tomorrow. If Eden called Jake tonight or even called out for him in her dreams, she would have it recorded on her phone.

She began to worry she may have crossed the line when she agreed to make love to Eden. Then, to make things worse, she had to say those words to Eden while she did it. She knew why she said them. She wanted to remind Eden of what they used to have.

Now, if it turned out Eden didn't love her and Jake was right, she had just ruined a good memory for herself. Rafe shook her head and sighed. It couldn't be helped. She would give her whatever she wanted, even all those memories—but not her heart.

Not yet. Not until she knew the truth.

"Don't jump. Don't fall in love again yet," Rafe demanded in a harsh whisper to herself. "She could be gone tomorrow."

23

WITH A SATISFYING stretch, Eden Kingsley woke, her body still feeling the erotic sensation of being with Rafe the night before. She laid in bed after Rafe had gone, wondering why she had left, but determined to take Cathcart's advice to give Rafe space and take her lead when it came to being together. She slid out of bed and saw at some point in the night, Rafe had been in the room. Rafe had cleaned up the floor in front of the doorway, and she left her a pair of her pajamas. Eden slid naked into the soft pants and pulled on the top, buttoning it as she went into the bathroom to brush her teeth with the guest supplies Rafe always kept.

Stepping quietly out of the bedroom, Eden went over to Rafe's room and tried to open the door, finding it locked. She shook her head a bit confused but decided not to knock. She went back to the bedroom, stripped the sheets from the bed and threw them in the laundry, then went into the kitchen and began making breakfast.

Eden was surprised Rafe actually had food in the house and was almost finished cooking when Rafe walked in, dressed and ready for the day.

"I couldn't resist the smell any longer." Her mouth curved into a smile. "Can I have some?"

"Sure. I'm making breakfast for both of us." Eden smiled back at her. It made her happy to be cooking a nice breakfast for Rafe again as she used to do on weekends

"Great," Rafe said as she walked up behind Eden. She kissed the back of Eden's neck, reached around, and touched her between her legs. "*Ho bisogno di caffè,*"[7] she said as she pulled away quickly and went to make herself an espresso.

Caught a bit off guard, Eden fought down the sensations Rafe just caused in her. "I," she cleared her throat, "I called Letty and Ephraim. Ephraim was home and said he'd meet us at The Kiki Bistro this afternoon with Bronte."

"Okay," said Rafe as she set up the espresso machine and turned it on.

"Can I borrow a shirt? The one I had on last night..." She stopped blushing as she thought about last night.

Rafe looked over, drew her lower lip between her teeth, and then touched the collar of the pajama top Eden was

---

[7] I need coffee,

wearing. "This one looks good on you." She winked. "Just don't steal my pajamas," she joked. She pulled it down off Eden's shoulder to kiss her there and on her neck. She saw a small bruise on the edge of Eden's shoulder. "What's this?" she asked with a raised eyebrow.

"I can't wear this out," Eden started to explain, but laughed, happy Rafe was reminding her about their old joke. Eden used to wear Rafe's pajamas sometimes, and Rafe would act worried Eden wouldn't give them back. Rafe getting them back became a very sexual or very comical game depending on the mood. Eden felt her shoulder as she looked at the bruise Rafe had pointed out. "It's just a bruise," she said as she waved her off.

"From last night?" asked Rafe with a slight smile.

"Yes," Eden said hesitantly.

Rafe looked intently into Eden's eyes. "Are you sorry?" she asked very softly.

"No," Eden whispered.

"Good," Rafe said as she kissed the bruise then smiled at her. "I wouldn't want you to file a restraining order against me or anything." She went back to the espresso machine and poured herself a small cup.

Eden looked at Rafe with bewilderment. "You're very funny, you know?" she said as she stepped over and kissed her. "I love you."

"I'll get you a shirt," Rafe said as she put her cup and saucer between them and took a sip of her espresso, "after breakfast."

24

AFTER A BIG breakfast, Eden Kingsley watched Rafe walk out onto the patio with a cappuccino, her phone, and her tablet to read. After she had finished cleaning up in the kitchen, Eden took the shirt Rafe had given her to wear and went back to the guest room to take a shower and get dressed for the day.

Looking in the mirror over the dresser, Eden inspected the small bruise on her shoulder. She smiled at the fact she had no idea when or how it happened. She turned to pick up her clothes and put them on the bed. As she held her shirt up, she shook her head. The buttons all popped off, and the fabric ripped in a few places, so there was no saving it. She tossed the ruined shirt on the bed then walked into the bathroom and took off Rafe's pajamas.

In the shower, Eden felt some pain on the inside of her leg and sat down on the edge of the tub to find out what it was. There was a thumb sized bruise in the crease where her leg met her torso. She laughed at how she could almost draw a straight line from it to her clit. She looked at her inner thigh as the warm water rained down on her and saw another fairly large bruise Rafe's shoulder had formed there.

She gingerly touched the tender skin. "Jeez," she hissed in pain. "Oh, my god, that hurts."

She looked up, letting the water wash over her face, and got lost in the memory of the night before, still feeling the sensations inside her. She put her hand to her heart, feeling it quicken, and ran her hand down over her breasts to her stomach and touched herself lightly as her mind replayed what her body and senses had experienced. She couldn't help but smile.

"No." She laughed softly to herself. "It's oh, my Rafe," she said as she laughed at her own joke.

Last night was the most intense and incredible sexual experience she had ever had with Rafe, or anyone else. Rafe had always been able to make sex last a long time. She had never forgotten how sometimes Rafe could cause her to have several orgasms and was somehow able to drag them out and drive her crazy. Other times, they would run into the bedroom to have sex, and then later in the night, they would make love again slowly. But last night, it was as if Rafe pushed her body to the limit and took her sweet time doing it.

Eden had no idea she was even capable of having so many orgasms in one night, let alone one flooding the floor. She was still recovering from it, and she was amazed it had really happened. She was also still sorting through and figuring out which emotions she should feel because there were so many she wanted to break into, from Aflutter to Zen. She could feel herself get a little wet from the memory.

Eden stepped out of the shower and dried her hair then wrapped herself in a towel. She looked in the mirror and ran a comb through her wet hair before she put some of Rafe's lotion on her legs and arms. Then she decided she would go do her hair in Rafe's room so she could use the good blow dryer.

As Eden stepped out of the bathroom, Rafe immediately swept Eden up into her arms.

"I thought you'd never come out," Rafe told her through her kisses. "Tell me I can have you again," she said as she pulled the towel away and picked her up.

Eden lost herself to Rafe once again.

25

THE LUNCH CROWD at The Kiki Bistro had found its way in for a meal and was finally clearing out. Julia Hawthorn was sitting at a round table at the front of the bistro with Abby, Jude, and Flynn. They were talking about their night and finishing their lunch. Stacey came in and got a pre-made sandwich and a drink from the self-serve drink station Letty had out on Saturdays, and then she walked up to the table.

"Hey, everyone," Stacey said as she sat down and looked around. "Eden's car is outside, but I don't see her anywhere."

"You don't know?" asked Julia with a knowing grin. "She went home with Rafe last night."

"She did?" Stacey laughed. "That's great!"

"No, it's bad," said Abby with an annoyed frown at Julia for bringing the subject up again.

"Why?" asked Stacey. "I thought you wanted to get Eden back from hetero land!" The redhead laughed.

"Stacey, please stop saying those things," said Flynn, anxious and offended because he felt it belittled everything Eden had gone through.

Stacey ignored Flynn and turned back to Abby. "Why is it a bad thing?" she asked as she ate her sandwich.

Jude put down her glass and rolled her eyes. "Abby thinks Eden went home with Rafe's dark wildling side," she informed her wryly.

"She did!" said Abby agitated. "You didn't hear our conversation. She *made* Eden tell me she wanted to go with her."

"I think you're over reacting," Jude told her and took a bite of her food.

"Really? You'll see!" Abby exclaimed as she pointed at Jude with her fork.

"I can see right now," said Jude as she pointed toward the window. "They're coming in. Look, they're fine."

"Yeah," Stacey agreed. "They're holding hands and everything. What happened to your wildling?" She laughed mockingly.

Rafe and Eden walked down the sidewalk toward the entrance of the bistro holding hands. Eden was smiling and talking to Rafe, feeling the best she had in a very long time. Rafe was looking around for Jake and preparing for the possibility he would challenge her publicly after the events at The Kiki Bistro last night.

Rafe opened the door for them, and they walked to the counter and placed a food order for lunch. When they finished, they saw everyone over at a table near the window, and Eden smiled as she approached the table, bringing Rafe along by her hand.

Jude saw them coming first. "Hey, did you guys have a good time last night?" she asked, knowing the subject would antagonize Abby, but she knew everyone thought pushing her buttons was funny.

"Did we?" asked Rafe as she looked inquisitively at Eden.

"Yes, yes, we did," said Eden with desire in her eyes and a smile. "We really did," she said and kissed Rafe then ran her hand down her back.

Abby put down her fork, and it clanked against the plate. "I think I'm going to be sick," she said under her breath.

Jude heard Abby and smiled. "Sit down and join us," Jude offered and moved her chair over for Rafe and Eden.

Stacey watched as they pulled up chairs to the table. "So, Eden," she said as Eden sat, "did you get to meet Rafe's wildling side last night?" She looked up and caught a hostile look from Rafe. Stacey swallowed in fear and looked down quickly.

"Wildling?" asked Eden bewildered. "I'm not sure what you're talking about," she said oblivious to the look Rafe had given Stacey.

"It's nothing. Stacey's just trying to be funny," Jude said as she saw Rafe looked as if she wanted to reach out and strangle Stacey. "Right, Stacey?"

"Right," Stacey agreed quickly, very alarmed with the look Rafe gave her. "I just meant to ask if you had a good time last night."

"She already answered Jude's question," said Rafe in a low voice as she glared harshly at Stacey.

"Oh, yeah." Stacey laughed nervously. "She did, didn't she?" Stacey looked down and concentrated hard on her sandwich.

"Well, you look radiant, Eden," said Julia hoping to change the subject and lighten the mood.

"Thank you." She blushed at the compliment as the waiter brought their food and drinks. "This looks good." She moved her chair closer to Rafe's and reached out to touch her to reassure herself everything from last night was real and had actually happened.

Letty saw Rafe eating her lunch from across the room and went to their table. "Hey, you guys. Did you just get here?" she asked cheerfully.

"Yes," said Eden. "Do you know if Ephraim is on his way?" She picked up her iced tea and drank a little over half the glass. "God, I'm so thirsty," she said as she sat her glass down.

"He is," Letty confirmed. "He just called." She looked at Rafe and saw she was looking around for something. "Are you okay, Cugina?" she asked then looked from Rafe to Eden, who were sitting very close together. "Am I missing something?"

As Letty had Rafe distracted, Stacey leaned over toward Eden. "A little dehydrated, are you?" She snickered.

"Shut up, Stacey!" Flynn hissed and kicked her under the table causing her to yelp.

Rafe smiled at Letty and rubbed Eden's hand resting on her leg. "I'm just fine."

Eden ignored Stacey and Flynn as she looked from Letty to Rafe. She locked eyes with Rafe and couldn't help it as a big smile appeared on her face. "She's very fine. Very, very fine," she said as she touched Rafe's face and hair then leaned in and kissed her again.

"Wow," said Letty with surprise. "I guess after a kiss like that, she is definitely doing fine. Well, I have to get back to the counter." She leaned over Abby. "It's about time," she whispered and walked away glad it looked like Rafe was happy again.

"I really do think I'm going to be sick," groaned Abby softly.

Rafe sat restlessly for as long as she could. All morning, she had been debating on whether or not to listen to the recording on her phone and worrying about whether or not Jake was going to show up. She dropped her fork and wiped her mouth. "Excuse me, I'll be back," she said and left the table to look around for him.

Abby moved into Rafe's vacated chair. "Eden, are you really okay?" she whispered concerned.

"Why wouldn't I be?" Eden smiled still feeling Rafe's warmth. "The only thing not doing well is the shirt I was wearing last night." She laughed and pulled the soft flowing bamboo shirt she was wearing away from herself to show it to Abby. "This is Rafe's shirt." She picked up her tea and drained the glass. "I need to get another drink. I'll be right back," she said as she stood up and headed toward the drink station.

Abby jumped up and followed her, upset by what she saw at the edge of the shirt. "What's on your shoulder?" she demanded.

"What?" Eden asked as she refilled her glass.

"Right there," Abby said as she moved Eden's shirt and revealed the bruise under it, "on your shoulder. When did you get that?"

Eden looked at her shoulder and smiled at the mark left by Rafe the night before. She had almost forgotten about it. "Oh, it's nothing. It's just a little bruise," she said waving Abby away.

"Did Rafe hurt you?" she hissed barely above a whispered screech. She couldn't believe Rafe would physically hurt Eden.

"What's wrong with you?" she asked as she saw Abby was getting upset over nothing.

Abby grabbed Eden's arm distraught. "What happened last night? Did Rafe hurt you?"

Eden pulled her arm away. "Rafe didn't do anything to hurt me, Abby," she said looking at her like she had lost her mind.

"What? She didn't? Are you sure? Is she making you say that?" Abby shot out her questions, wanting to find out just what Rafe had done to her.

"Abby, stop," Eden said worried about her friend. "What's wrong with you?"

"Just answer the questions," she demanded frantically.

Rafe had been looking around for any signs of Jake without being too obvious. She had also been watching to see if Eden was expecting him to show up, so she saw Abby follow Eden. She had walked up beside Eden as Abby was questioning her. "What if she doesn't want to answer your questions?" she asked and looked at Eden. "Do you, Eden?"

Eden put her hand on Rafe's arm and smiled at her. "It's okay, babe."

"No, it's not okay," Abby said defiantly and looked hotly at Rafe. "You can't do this! You can't hurt Eden."

"I don't want to hurt her." She smiled with amusement. "I love her." She leaned in and kissed Eden and whispered to her. "I love you. Tell me you love me."

"I do, I love you," Eden breathed, reeling from the taste of Rafe.

Rafe put her arm around Abby and turned her away from Eden. She put her face close to her ear. "Abby, this wildling knows girls don't break easy," she whispered very seductively. She looked at Abby's shocked face and smiled impishly as she walked away.

Shaken, Abby looked from Rafe to Eden, who hadn't heard Rafe's whisper. "What did she do to you, Eden? What's going on with you two?" she demanded.

Eden watched Rafe as she walked away, openly staring at her body. She loved the way Rafe moved in the world like it was hers for the taking, and as far as she was concerned, Rafe could take her anytime. Smiling at the thought, she turned back to Abby. "Abby, your concern is appreciated. I got the bruise last night, and yes, Rafe caused it, but it's okay. She didn't hurt me. I didn't even know it was there until this morning. I assure you, I was feeling other things," she said and couldn't help her grin. "You should see the one on my inner thigh. It really hurts, but it was so worth it! I think I may have one on my bum too from this morning!" She laughed and grabbed her tea glass from the counter. "Come on. Let's go sit down."

Abby followed Eden closely. "Oh, my god. You have got to be kidding me," she said as they walked. "She did this to you after her big production last night with the spotlight and the crowd?"

"No," Eden looked over her shoulder. "It's, oh, my Rafe!" She laughed then stopped walking and leaned in close to Abby. "Abby, she did things to me," she confessed shuddering with a thrill at the memory, "I didn't know could be done! I can still feel her." She trilled as the feeling of love butterflies thrummed through her.

"This isn't right!" Abby hissed. "What things?"

"Abby." Eden grinned and bit her lip. "I'm not going to kiss and tell but," she hesitated and looked around then leaned in close, excitedly, "well, I think I can now officially say I know what it means to have someone F your brains out!" She laughed giddily as a rush ran through her at the thought of what Rafe had done, and her face flushed red.

"Oh, my god!" Abby groaned. "This can't be happening." She shook her head in disbelief. "You actually think this is a good thing?"

Eden looked at Abby then looked over at Rafe. "If you knew how many times she gave me a world altering orgasm last night, you'd think it was a good thing too," she said and nodded her head yes before giving Abby a pat on her back. "She's right. You do worry way too much." Eden smiled then made her way back to the table and to Rafe.

Rafe watched Eden make her way back to the table, followed closely by Abby, who had an angry scowl on her face. She leaned over and whispered to Jude, "I love tormenting Abby when she's freaking out over nothing. She's all upset because Eden has a tiny bruise." Rafe pulled her shirt back to show Jude the bite marks Eden had left on her collarbone. Jude looked at it and arched her eyebrows as Rafe winked.

"Keep this under your hat, though," she said softly as she covered the bite mark. "I don't want her messing with Eden about it or have Stacy worrying I'll become a zombie." She chuckled.

Jude nodded and put her hand over her mouth to stifle her laugh and hide her smile from Abby and the others.

Eden ran her hand over Rafe as she sat next to her. "What are you guys talking about?"

Jude watched Abby stare menacingly at Rafe as she sat at the table. She jumped in before Abby could start anything. "Nothing," Jude said quickly. "Hey, there's Ephraim," she said and waved at him.

Ephraim made his way to them carrying Bronte. "Hello, here we are," he said and handed Bronte to Rafe.

Rafe ignored Abby's stare and took Bronte. "*C'è la mia neonata. Ti sono mancato?*"[8] she said and kissed her on the cheek. "Look. There's your mommy. Say hi." She turned to Eden. "Do you want to hold her?"

Eden smiled at them as Bronte put her hands on Rafe's face. "No, it's okay, babe. You keep her with you."

"Did you hear that? Your mommy says I can hold onto you for a while," Rafe cooed to Bronte. "I'm going to take her to see Letty, and then we can go get ready for her art lesson," she said to Eden.

"Okay," she said and gave Bronte a kiss.

"Let's go see Zia Letty," said Rafe to the baby as they left the table.

---

[8] There is my little girl. Did you miss me?

As soon as Rafe left, Abby started in again because she knew she would get nowhere with Rafe around. "Okay, what the hell is going on, Eden? Why are you guys acting so weird all of a sudden?"

"What are you talking about, Abby?" asked Eden as she ate the last of her lunch. "I told you everything's going good. Rafe and I are—" she couldn't help smiling, "we're fine. Last night was, well, it was so incredible!" She laughed happily.

"Abby, they aren't acting weird," Julia intervened knowing Rafe didn't like Abby rambling on about her wildling obsession, especially to Eden.

"Are you kidding me? They're acting totally weird," shrieked Abby in frustration.

"Abby, really, everything's fine. Please, stop worrying," Eden tried to reassure her. "There's nothing weird going on, and things are going to be great." She looked up and saw Rafe come out of the back office where she had gone to see Letty. "There's Rafe. I'll see you guys later," she said and went over to meet Rafe and Bronte.

"I've got to go too," said Flynn. "Bye."

"See ya, Flynn," said Abby. She watched them all leave then looked around the table at her remaining friends... and Stacey. "You can't tell me you don't see it. Did you see the way Eden was looking at Rafe? It's like she was entranced or something!" Abby whined. "It's like one minute they're at each other's throats, then Rafe puts her wildling moves on her last night, and now Eden says they're great and everything is incredible!" She shook her head and couldn't believe they didn't see it too.

"Come on, Abby," said Julia. "You're the one who's been helping Eden convince Rafe to spend time with her. Well, she's spending time with her. Quality time," Julia said with a wink.

Abby looked at her with a scowl. "They were supposed to be working things out and talking," she said hotly. "It seems like things are moving really fast with them all of the sudden."

"Well," said Jude, "maybe there are some things better said without words." She gave Abby a knowing look.

"What about the fact Rafe was looking around here like Ninjas were about to jump out at any second?" Abby demanded and wondered if maybe Rafe was really looking for a way to escape and take off like she used to do when those girls would come looking for her, believing they were in a relationship with her. "Then she was looking at Eden with that look of hers!" Abby looked at everyone, and she knew they thought she was crazy, but she didn't care. "Eden may not be able to see it, but something's definitely going on with Rafe," Abby claimed as she sat back and crossed her arms in anger.

"You mean with the *wildling* inside her?" asked Stacey as she laughed. "Abby, it's probably nothing."

"Nothing?" Abby shouted. "Rafe pretty much confessed she was hurting Eden. She told me she knows girls don't break easily! Did you know Eden is all bruised up?" She just didn't understand why Rafe was treating Eden like all those girls she used to fuck and then throw away.

"Abby, Rafe's just messing with your head," Jude explained with a laugh knowing Rafe had sex bites from Eden. "But she does have a point—girls are pretty tough."

"It's not a joke, Jude," said Abby, wishing they would take her seriously.

"Of course, it's not," said Julia, "but Eden assured us everything was fine. She wouldn't lie or let Rafe actually hurt her."

"She would if she didn't know what was really happening," insisted Abby.

"You need to be careful, Abby," said Julia firmly. "Rafe already has enough problems without you accusing her of abusing Eden."

"I'm not!" Abby swore. "I'm just saying she's treating Eden like she treated women before, and it's not good. Did you see the bruise on her shoulder? And she said she had one on her inner thigh too. Eden actually told me she had her brains fucked out last night."

"Eden actually said she had her brains 'fucked' out?" asked Julia in shock. "She rarely uses those kind of words."

"No, well, she said she knows what it means to have someone 'F' your brains out now. She didn't actually say *fuck*," admitted Abby. "But still."

Jude looked over in surprise at Stacey and covered her mouth trying to hold back laughter. "Oh, my god. She did it!" She laughed hysterically.

"I didn't think she would! She was so against it!" Stacey howled and joined in the laughter.

"Well, every girl has the right to change her mind," added Julia with a grin knowing the subject would agitate Abby.

"What are you guys talking about?" Abby asked angrily, not understanding why they were laughing.

"Abby," started Jude grinning and trying not to laugh, "Rafe and Eden," she paused and tried to control herself, "let's just say they may have tried something new last night."

"Yeah," Stacey joined in excitedly. "Rafe was wearing jewels last night!" She laughed so hard, tears started coming out of her eyes.

"What are you guys talking about?" Abby demanded again in frustration.

Julia put her hand on Abby's shoulder to calm her down. "I think they're saying Rafe strapped it on last night for Eden," she said calmly.

"She did!" Jude laughed and tried to breathe. "I think she really did!"

"Oh, no." Abby shook her head in denial. "It can't be true. Rafe would never do such a thing. I know she wouldn't," insisted Abby.

"Whatever! How do you know?" asked Stacey as she laughed and wiped watering her eyes.

Abby just looked at them hard until they calmed their laughter. "When we dated, I tried to get her to use one. She laughed at me and said if I wanted to be with her, she had to be enough. She then proceeded to—to prove to me how she was enough. The things she could do," Abby said earnestly and shook her head at the memory.

"So that's why you're always so jumpy about her and the things she does." Jude chuckled. "You're still kind of hot for her after all these years."

"I'm not hot for her!" said Abby defensively. "I mean I can't forget what happened," she confessed weakly. "I don't think I'll ever forget what happened," she mumbled. "But she's my friend now, and I'm telling you this could be serious."

"Why don't you tell us exactly what you're talking about, Abby?" Julia asked hoping she would not regret it.

"Yeah," said Jude, "tell us how her strapping it on for Eden can be so bad."

"You guys know Rafe," Abby said as her mood swung to empathy for Rafe. "I mean, she's this super sensitive soul with an over flowing amount of passion in her." She looked at their amusement and was determined to make them understand. "When she explained to me why she wouldn't use one, it was like she had made her reasons a part of her soul! She said it was like someone adding paint to a Picasso. It's crazy, I know," she said as they all looked at her funny.

"Well," said Jude wondering if Abby had lost her mind, "she may have changed her mind about it last night."

"This is serious." Abby pouted, now worried Rafe was the one in trouble. "She compared it to creating a painting and told me it puts distance between the canvas and the artist and she said the distance is the difference between something very good and a masterpiece."

"What does that even mean?" asked Jude looking at Abby with amusement.

"I don't know. I know I'm not explaining it well," Abby said frustrated, "but it's kind of like it's against her nature."

"Abby, Rafe knows what she's doing," Julia tried to reassure her. "I think she was just giving you a seduction line." Julia knew Rafe had just given her a line. She also knew Rafe wasn't a stranger to 'strapping it on' as Jude put it or many other sexual feats. Having known her since high school, and knowing many of the girls Rafe had dated, she was privy to many details spilled by those girls when they gushed about Rafe. So if Rafe did do it for Eden, it wasn't as if she were outside her comfort zone.

"Well, while she was telling me about it, we did have really great sex," Abby said thinking maybe Julia was right and maybe Rafe was still just the wildling who she needed to watch. "I mean, really great."

"Abby, don't worry," Julia patted her hand, "Rafe has a plan. She knows what she's doing."

"But what exactly is her Salvaggio plan? Guys, we have to keep an eye on her," Abby insisted because she knew something was up.

"Abby, you keep an eye on her," Jude suggested. "I'm sure she knows what she's doing."

"I agree with Jude," said Julia. "Rafe and Eden know what they're doing. You should just let it go."

Abby looked at all of them with a frown, disgruntled they weren't taking her seriously. They didn't know Rafe and her wildling ways the way she did, so they would never understand. She knew something was wrong. She didn't know yet if it was Eden or Rafe who was in trouble, but she was going to get to the bottom of it.

26

AFTER A BUSY and productive day at work, Eden Kingsley was in Dr. William Cathcart's office for her regular Monday appointment. She was feeling very good and confident today, still thinking about her weekend with Rafe. After they had taken Bronte to her art lesson, they went back to Rafe's house and had a relaxing evening. It was very hard for Eden to leave and go back to her apartment. She had hoped to stay the night again, but Rafe didn't invite her. She also didn't see her Sunday because Rafe said she had work to catch up on. She didn't press the issue because she didn't want to do anything to make the mood of the weekend change. She was determined to let Rafe lead like Cathcart had advised.

"Come in, Eden," Cathcart said as he motioned her into his office. "How are you doing today?"

"I'm good," Eden said. She walked into the office, smiling as she sat on the couch. "I'm really good."

"What would you like to talk about today?" asked Cathcart as he sat across from her.

Eden looked at her hands and hesitated. "I was with Rafe this weekend." She looked up and smiled. "She was," she started hesitantly, "I don't know how to describe it. Surreal, I guess."

"Surreal?" Cathcart repeated.

Eden nodded thinking about how to say what she was feeling. "It was like I was with Rafe, but a very different Rafe. It's kind of hard to explain."

"What happened?" asked Cathcart.

"She made the whole thing into what Abby called a big production. I'm not sure why she thought she had to do it like that."

"Like what?" Cathcart asked.

"It was like," Eden stopped, looking for the words, "like she wanted everyone to know what she was doing. We were under the spotlight on the dance floor, and Abby said everyone in The Kiki Bistro was watching Rafe make her 'moves' on me."

"Well, you told me women come up to her constantly now to hit on her," Cathcart reminded her. "Maybe it was her way of telling them she isn't available anymore." He paused to let her think about the possibility. "How did you feel about the whole thing?"

"I felt like," she stopped and smiled, "it was like when we first met. She looked at me, and I couldn't look away, and I didn't want to look anywhere but at her." She thought about Friday night. "I really don't remember anything except for Rafe. She told me she wanted me, and I could hardly wait." She laughed at the tingle the memory caused. "If she wanted to, I probably would have made love to her right there on the dance floor under the spotlight."

"So, you talked to her about your fears?" asked Cathcart trying to ascertain why this sudden change came about.

"No, not really." Eden looked down. "Not yet." She looked back up at him thoughtfully. "But I think you're right. I think she wanted everyone to know we're together and she wants me. I'm going to start telling her things," she hesitated, "but I think I still need to go slow."

Cathcart took a moment to consider what Eden was telling him. "You should talk to her about how you're still hurting over her infidelity first, Eden," he said pragmatically, "especially since you've had sex. She needs to know why you've been having such a difficult time, and what your expectations are of her if you're going to be in a relationship again."

Eden frowned as she thought about everything she was keeping from Rafe, and then closed her eyes for a moment. Then she thought about what Rafe did after they had sex.

She looked up at Cathcart. "She said she had changed, and I felt like there was something new in her but," she hesitated and fidgeted anxiously, "something was missing too. It felt like some part of her was missing," she said and shook her head to clear it. "Maybe I'm imagining things." She sat back in her chair and sighed. "She... she didn't stay with me all night. While we were making love, she held onto me like she thought I might disappear. I wanted to fall asleep in her arms. I'm not sure why, but she just got up and left," she revealed trying to figure it out. "She told me she hoped she could always give me what I wanted, but she left and went to her room. Why do you think she left?"

"I don't know," said Cathcart.

"Do you think it's part of her testing me?" asked Eden worried she was right.

"Eden, you're going to have to ask her if you want to know," said Cathcart. "How did it make you feel when she left?"

"It made me feel..." Eden hesitated, sad and worried. "It made me feel confused because I didn't understand why she had to go." She looked up at him and took a breath. "She didn't ask me to stay the night again, either. I keep thinking about the night we spent together. I wonder if I disappointed her," she said softly

"Why?" he asked calmly.

"Well, I know she did a lot more for me than I did for her," she said and blushed. "I felt great, but there were a couple of times when I thought maybe Rafe wasn't," she hesitated, "wasn't satisfied with what I did for her. She didn't say anything," Eden said quickly and left it there.

"I'm sure she knows sometimes it takes time to get back in sync after being apart," Cathcart assured her. "I'm more concerned with you feeling like something was missing. Last time we talked about sex, you said you weren't satisfied with Jake, yet you were willing to stay with him. Are you having a similar experience with Rafe?"

Eden looked up at Cathcart and frowned. "No," she said sharply. "It's not the same." She took a breath to calm herself. "I'm very satisfied sexually with her. I'm happier than I've ever been. I feel better than I have in a long time, and I've only spent one night with her." She shook her head, trying to make the jumble of thoughts in her head make sense. "By something missing I mean it feels like she's holding something back or something. I don't know. I can't really put my finger on it." She put her face in her hands and rubbed her temples because not knowing worried her. "Maybe it's because she didn't stay the whole night," she said softly.

Cathcart made a note then looked at Eden for a moment. "I can see you're concerned, and what I hear you saying is it's upsetting because something seems to be missing," he said calmly, "but I don't want you to hyper focus on this and miss out on the positive things happening and the things going right. I've noticed a pattern of you doing this when you start to feel anxious or have feelings of guilt or stress about something. You hyper focus on an issue or some small thing and then make a decision or a choice without looking at the bigger picture, and sometimes it ends up having a negative impact on your life."

Eden looked up at him in confusion and tried to think of something she may have hyper-focused on, but she just couldn't see anything. "Like what?" she asked at a loss.

"Most recently," Cathcart revealed, "you've been hyper focused on Rafe and everything she's been doing instead of focusing on yourself." He watched as Eden frowned not liking what she had heard. "But," he added, "there were larger, underlying reasons for your focus we were able to bring out into the open. Now, you've been able to have a positive experience with Rafe, and I think we should focus on the positive in this session."

Eden sat back on the couch and crossed her arms thinking about Cathcart's words. She knew he was right. She had been super-focused on Rafe. She felt like she was still focused on her. The difference now was she had more good things to say about her than complaints. Eden leaned her head back and sighed. "I want to focus on the good things," she said softly.

Cathcart smiled slightly, knowing it had to be a relief to her to be able to talk about Rafe and her feelings for her again without looking for something to be angry about. "What was your perfect moment?" he asked, allowing her to interpret the question in any way she felt comfortable.

"Perfect moment?" Eden repeated and thought about the question. "I think it was when she called me Ede again."

"Ayday?" Cathcart repeated.

"Close," Eden laughed. "Less of the 'y' sound." She waited as Cathcart said it a few more times. "It's just a silly nickname she started calling me," she said. "No one else uses it. My friend Abby calls me Edy sometimes. I don't really like it, but I think she mostly started it to try to correct Rafe and just still uses it sometimes. Abby doesn't know why Rafe calls me Ede, though. When Julia gets drunk, she is always making fun of how Rafe says my name." Eden laughed and shook her head. "But I like how she says it."

"How does she say it?" asked Cathcart with a smile.

"Oh, she can say it like you and I do," Eden assured him, "but I told you she's half Italian, right? She was raised in Italy, and Italian is her first language. Sometimes, when she is excited, drunk, or distracted, she will slip into her accent or even into Italian. Sometimes, she hears a word, and when she repeats it, she says it how her mind interprets it. Like my name. She knows the word Eden and how to say it in Italian, so when she repeats it, she says it how she would in Italian rather than English. So, to her, my name is pronounced 'Adan' rather than Eden."

"I see," said Cathcart as he nodded. "So how did she end up calling you Ede?"

Eden looked down at her hands and bit her lip. For a long time, Rafe only called her Ede in private. Then it was like a secret code between them, and she knew when Rafe called her Ede when someone was around she was saying she wanted to be making love to her. Over the years, it turned into a term of endearment and nickname when Rafe began using it more in public, but the origin was still something only the two of them knew. She had never told anyone the story, and she didn't think Rafe had told anyone either. It started out as something very silly and ended up as something loving and romantic.

It had been a long time since Eden thought about the incident surrounding her nickname. It started not long after Eden had moved into Rafe's house and they had taken a trip to Italy. They were out with a group of people Rafe knew at a private party in Milan. Everyone was having fun laughing and getting drunk. Rafe had a really painful case of the hiccups Eden and a few of Rafe's friends were trying to help cure without much success. As people arrived, Rafe would try to introduce Eden, and she would only be able to get out the first part of her name—Ede—before she got cut off by a painful hiccup.

A couple of Rafe's friends spoke English, and Eden was able to tell them her name and talk with them for a while and answer all their many questions. Somehow, the gossip spread through the party and people were coming up to confirm the news Rafe was off the market. It was apparent they were all very surprised Rafe had brought Eden to Italy and even more so when they found out Eden was living with her. Before the night was over, everyone was calling her Ede, and Rafe tried to apologize, but Eden knew it wasn't something she could help.

Everyone seemed to enjoy teasing Rafe about Eden, so they made a game of it. They would go up to Eden, making sure Rafe could hear, and say things like *bellissima Ede, mi ami Ede, per sempre Ede, Ede mio cuore* and other things Eden didn't understand but, according to Rafe, were very dirty. Rafe would pretend to be mad at them and run them off while yelling things at them in Italian. They would all laugh and pretend to apologize, and then would bring more wine and kiss Rafe to make up with her. Eden thought they were all very dramatic and loud and a lot of fun once she got over her initial shyness.

Later, Rafe took Eden back to the apartment they were staying in, and she said all of those things as she made love to her, speaking in both English and Italian. *I love you, Ede. You're beautiful, Ede. You're my heart, Ede. Love me, Ede. Forever, Ede.* Afterward, they lay in bed and laughed about Rafe's hiccups and the fact Eden had a new name. Rafe told her she wanted to be remembered as the one who said those words to her and for them to mean something. At the time, it was the most romantic thing Rafe had done for her. Eden never picked up a lot of Italian, but those words she never forgot because Rafe said them to her many times.

Shaking loose the memory, she looked up at Cathcart and couldn't help blushing again. "I don't think I should tell you about it," she said softly. "It's not some big secret. It's just ours, you know?"

"I understand," said Cathcart. "We're not here for you to tell me all your private moments."

"Okay, good," Eden said softly as she nodded. She took a breath and sighed heavily as she remembered Rafe saying those words to her Friday night and when she said *per sempre Ede*. She wanted to say, *yes, forever*, in her ear, but all she could do was nod her head against her. She hoped Rafe felt her yes. "Anyway," Eden said softly, "when she was holding me in her arms, and I heard her call me Ede again, it was definitely my perfect moment."

"When you think about such a perfect moment, doesn't it make more sense she wasn't keeping score on who did the most for whom?" Cathcart asked quietly. "Isn't it more likely she was just trying to be a good lover?"

"She is," said Eden as she thought about Rafe and all the moments she had given her when they were together. "She's a very, very good lover."

Cathcart looked at his notes and tapped his pen on the notepad a few times. His normal procedure when a patient came into the office was to make a basic emotional assessment upon arrival and again, before they left to track their progress. Most anxiety patients like Eden had assessments seeming very erratic at first. They would go from very low to very high for a while, then settling into moderated lows for a period of time, then gradually build into a normal mid-range where they were handling the highs and lows well on a daily basis without having severe anxiety problems.

What he saw in Eden now, however, was troubling because she wasn't out of her erratic period yet and barely out of a low. She had a month of more lows than highs. Today was an obvious high day, but the session was ending as a moderate. He was worried she was going to put a lot of her emotional well-being into the sexual relationship with Rafe. If something happened to end the relationship again, it could set Eden back, especially if she wasn't prepared.

"What do you think will happen when you talk to Rafe about your fears and expectations?" he asked calmly.

Eden looked at her hands and sighed. "I don't know."

"How will you feel if she decides she needs time away to decide if she wants to be in a relationship exclusively with you?" he asked gently.

Eden snapped her head up in surprise. "What?"

"I know you slept with her," he said evenly, "but it doesn't mean she's in an exclusive relationship with you. She could see other people if she chose too, and so could you."

"No," Eden said softly as she shook her head. "I don't want anyone else." She thought about how Rafe danced with her under the spotlight and how upset Abby was about everything. "But why would she do what she did on the dance floor then?" she asked softly. "She was telling everyone she was with me again."

"Possibly," said Cathcart. "I hope it's true."

"Why are you trying to make me doubt her," she asked in confusion.

"I don't want you to doubt her, Eden," said Cathcart. "I want you to make sure you're looking at things realistically." He watched as Eden sat back on the couch and crossed her arms defensively thinking about his words. "There are a lot of emotional things happening right now for you, and for Rafe. You've taken a big step in your relationship by sleeping together. It's a big deal emotionally." Cathcart watched as she fidgeted with her shirt. "Eden, you seem to want to go back into a relationship with Rafe very quickly, and I understand your eagerness. You feel better and happy again because you've stopped being angry and you're working through your fears. But based on things happening over the last month, and even this weekend, Rafe doesn't seem to be going at the same pace. We've discussed this before."

"I know," sighed Eden, "don't push her. Let her lead when it comes to a physical relationship. I did," she insisted.

"You need to give her emotional space too," said Cathcart. "She needs time and space to be able to process her emotions."

"Maybe it's why she didn't invite me to stay over again," Eden said as she tried to reconcile what she had heard with what Rafe had done.

"Possibly," said Cathcart. "Some people need physical distance from people or situations to help themselves manage their emotions. Everyone is different. Some people need to talk, some journal, some run or do something else physical, and others read or play video games. The most important thing is if what they are doing is actually helping them. The next thing is for them to be allowed to do what they need to do by the people around them. This means, if the physical distance is what helps her, you have to accept it and allow her the time and space to deal with her emotions. Do you think you can? Do you think can allow her some space?"

"Yes," Eden said weakly. She sighed knowing it would be hard. "She never had to have distance from me before."

"You were both very hurt over things surrounding your break up," Cathcart reminded her. "And you two haven't had some of the hard conversations you still need to have."

"I know," groaned Eden and put her face in her hands.

"I've been talking to you for weeks about the conversations you need to have with Rafe," said Cathcart calmly. "I know the reason you haven't talked to her yet is because you're afraid." Eden lowered her eyes confirming his words. "Now you've had sex with her and were upset she didn't invite you to stay another night. You obviously have expectations she doesn't know about. It isn't fair to Rafe, or to yourself emotionally, if you have expectations and then one day, she fails because you didn't say anything."

Eden rubbed the back of her neck nervously. "But she says she loves me," she said softly. She knew he was right, and she needed to talk with Rafe. There was so much even Cathcart didn't know about, though. But she and Rafe were just now in this really good place, and she was afraid of losing what she had gained. "I don't want to drop this on her right after we took such a big step forward," she said shakily. "I just feel like I need a little more time."

27

REVEREND EZEKIEL CAZZAK was a devout man of his God. He had a holy mission to fulfill given to him directly from his Holy Father in a vision. In this vision, he saw an army of dark angels carrying pure and innocent children away from the light of God and down into the sinister blistering blackness of hell. They carried the innocents down a dark and well-worn path then threw them into a billowing black flame where their souls were stripped from their bodies. The oozing masses of pure and pliable bone and cell were refashioned into soulless minions of hell. The extracted souls were then entrapped and used to create weapons meant to be used against the host of heaven and the God who Reverend Cazzak claimed as his own.

The vision wavered and transformed, and the reverend saw himself standing under the bright light of God and crowned with a circlet of light. Behind him was a faceless mass kneeling in supplication to God. The only remarkable thing about them he noticed was every one of them had a red flame upon their forehead. He watched as a legion broke away from the mass, marched forward, and drew swords from their sheaths as they went into formation. The reverend realized he was watching himself on a battlefield. He turned to see who he was fighting and saw what looked like the entire world facing him. He was terrified and overwhelmed at the thought of facing a hoarded mass so infinite.

He watched himself order the charge of the legion wondering how he could so calmly send so many to their certain death. As he watched the legion cut into the enemy, he noticed something strange. The legions were cutting through the enemy, and though their swords made killing blows with every swing, only a few bodies fell. From most of the fallen bodies, demons appeared, and the legions fought to destroy them. A few of the bodies released souls hidden inside them, souls stolen from their intended host and purpose. When those souls appeared, a special squadron deployed and rescued it from the battlefield then relayed it back behind the front line to safety.

The reverend tried to follow the special squadron and the souls rescued, but he was unable to move forward. Instead, he found himself pushed further back into the wave of humanity in which the enemy lay hidden. Driven so far back behind enemy lines, he could no longer see the righteous battle on the front lines. He didn't understand why he would be pushed away from seeing the battle he was leading.

When he woke, he tried to forget about the dream and go back to his ministry. Though he worked hard, it seemed nothing went right. Every sort of scandal and sin seemed to tear his flock apart. Families were lost to each other and the church. It seemed the whole world had erupted into chaos. Along with these failures, the vision haunted him until he knew he had to seek help before the people around him began to believe he was going mad.

The reverend revealed his vision to an ancient holy man who was able to interpret the visions God sent to earth in the form of dreams. The holy man revealed the reverend would be a great leader who would someday lead a great heavenly host against the enemies of God. But before it could happen, a mission had to be completed. The holy man interpreted the vision's meaning of God's plan for the reverend. God required the reverend, through his ministry and church, build an army of specialized secret soldiers, and lead them for His glory to complete the mission demanded of them in the vision. The reverend was to head God's mission on Earth to save the innocent children from the dark forces who would use them so evilly. The dark forces, the reverend was told, used the unrighteous to create children in a way that mocked God's plan for them.

Based on the trials the reverend had gone through with his ministry, the essence of God's plan was clear. The righteous family has a master who rules and answers only to God himself and the leaders of his church. The master takes a wife, who is there to care for him and bear his children, raising them in the manner God intended as outlined in the Good Book and in the doctrine of the church.

When a child isn't raised in righteousness, it's God's will that Reverend Cazzak and his followers intercede and save those innocents, in the name of God, by any means necessary. Throughout the years, because of his personal God-like love, the reverend included saving the mothers whenever possible. Not only did he feel it was more humane for the children, but it helped with the legal issues they sometimes had to address. But the holy man was clear the reverend must concentrate on the innocent children above all others and focus on those innocents who are most at risk. Those innocents created by the most unrighteous in the eyes of God are the souls that must be saved. The most unrighteous, who must be watched and their actions curtailed, are many and include, but not limited to, those who have children outside of proper marriages. This includes homosexuals, single women, unmarried couples and anyone who creates a child by any artificial means and not raised in the proper God sanctioned manner. God had led them to many innocents throughout the years in every manner of unrighteous situations where they were able to save innocent souls. The reverend was very proud of the thousands of missions accomplished by his soldiers.

Their headquarters in California focused on the unnatural creation of innocent children by homosexuals, and they had made great strides, saving many children. They had good networks and systems in place throughout the State and worked in a lotto pattern to avoid attention by focusing too much in one area. Recently, though, it seemed the men assigned a mission in the name of God in L.A. were facing formidable adversity in completing their current mission.

This was the reason Reverend Cazzak had come to Los Angeles, California and was once again in the deserted strip mall home to the local offices of the Stewards to the Protection of the Innocence and Morals of Youths. It was after hours, so only a few key staff members were there with a small night shift. The Steward comptroller had been happy to lend his run down yet well-organized office to the reverend once again. The Mission Soldiers, Jake Thompson and Daniel Fuller, were called again into Reverend Cazzak's presence to discuss the problem with the Kingsley charge.

Reverend Cazzak sat behind the secondhand desk looking over the large file for the Kingsley Mission and was not happy. He looked up at Jake who was sitting across from him patiently in one of the two matching heavy wood framed office chairs with threadbare and faded gold and brown toned upholstery.

"Jake," Reverend Cazzak began then cleared his throat, "things have gotten out of control with your mission." He paused and looked at Jake so he could see his disappointment.

"It's been a month since you've reported anything on your mission. You've failed to extract your charge, Bronte Kingsley. You've failed to keep the mother and her consort apart, and everything you have given to the lawyers for amendments to stop the adoption has been fought by the lawyer and thrown out. This last issue with the internet pornography is still hanging in there, but some strong arguments have been submitted against it. Now I understand they're trying to rekindle their relationship and the Salvaggio woman has actually challenged you," he said incredulously. "How did you let things get in this state?"

"I don't know how things got this way," said Jake nervously running his hand through his short hair. "This has never happened before."

Cazzak closed the file, sat back in his chair, and looked at Jake with a frown. "I don't care how you do it, but you need to fix this."

"I know it sounds bad, but I know for a fact they're still on rocky ground, and I'm sure I can fix this so the injunction will have a chance," Jake assured him. "I know Eden is still keeping things from Rafe." He laughed to show some confidence. "If Rafe knew about some of the things happening, she never would have thought she had to challenge me. I can use it as an asset to break them apart again."

"Stopping them from continuing with their relationship is a start," Cazzak said as he tapped the file, "but what you need to be doing is making sure the innocent girl's adoption does not go through. We need to stop it, Jake. It is an abomination to our Christian traditions," Cazzak began his preaching. "A child should be raised in a household with a mother and a father. It's the order in which God's plan is meant to work as outlined in the Good Book. Only by following the plan to the letter can we find salvation. Every household must have a master to guide them, and only a man can fill said position. It is faithless people like those two, who are creating children unnaturally and stealing innocent souls from the righteous, who deserve them. By doing this, they are causing all the strife in the world and bringing damnation to us all. Why did you let the Kingsley woman out of your sight?" he demanded.

"She wanted to break up." Jake shifted nervously. "I tried. I've been trying to get her back, but she's adamant she doesn't want me. I know she was attracted to me and things were going fine. I'm still really not sure what happened there."

"I suggest you find out what happened and quickly," Cazzak threatened.

"I know," said Jake afraid of what might happen if he let the man down. He had heard stories of failures in handling certain situations where soldiers were sacrificed, and some situations were worse than others. But Jake knew he was one of the best, so he thought it should count for something. "I need to figure out why nothing I say to Eden has had any effect, and why she started talking to Rafe again. She can't really want to be with Rafe again. The woman is so screwed up in the head she doesn't really know what she wants from one day to the next. It was a struggle, but she really was beginning to come back into God's light." He sighed and shook his head.

"Jake, I'm giving you the chance to redeem yourself," offered Cazzak, seeing himself in Jakes concern for the woman's soul. "If you don't fix this before we have to go to court, and the injunction gets thrown out, and the adoption is granted before we can rescue the child, you're finished," he warned firmly. "If you prove to be an asset, we will help you, but if you become a liability—" He needed no further words. "You understand we can't afford liabilities. Our work is too important."

"Don't worry, I'll fix this. I won't be a liability," Jake promised.

"Good." Cazzak nodded. "Remember, if it's not fixed, you're finished. God be with you then because we will not."

28

WALKING INTO THE house, Rafe Salvaggio left the girls having a good time in the pool and enjoying the warmth of the sun. She headed to the dining room where she began to pick up the plates from the table and stack them up. Eden had invited all the girls over to swim and invited almost everyone else they knew to come over for a dinner party later tonight. At the moment, Eden and Flynn were out grocery shopping, and Rafe was wondering what was taking them so long. Eden wanted to celebrate and ask for the support of their friends since they were trying to work things out. Rafe was unsure about why she had agreed to have the dinner party so soon.

After she made a big deal out of taking Eden home to make sure word got back to Jake she was serious, she thought he would show up at some point. But so far, there had been no attempts by Jake to take Eden away as far as Rafe knew. Several times, she had attempted to listen to the recording on her phone, but she found a lot of it was indecipherable. There were times when she thought about deleting it but changed her mind because she might need to give it to Katheryn as evidence if Eden filed something against her. Then she would remember why she was doing this with Eden, and she was firm again in her mind she would do everything in her power to convince Eden to love her again. She would not tolerate Jake's interference, even if she heard his name in the recording.

Things had seemed to be going well for the last two weeks, or they were uneventful at the very least. Once again, Rafe had been trying to keep informed about what Eden was doing, where she went, and who she had seen over the last couple of weeks. It was still a difficult task because of her work schedule, but Rafe figured, if Eden was meeting Jake, she probably would only do it when she was certain it remained a secret.

It was very hard to trust Eden knowing so many things Jake told her were true and worrying the rest was just as true. Eden still insisted she needed time and patience, but for Rafe, those commodities were running low. She wasn't even sure anymore Eden really had anything true to tell her. She thought maybe Eden was just biding her time until the court date to put her plan into action, just as Jake had said.

The consolation for Rafe was at least Eden hadn't filed the restraining order yet like Jake said she would before the court date. So it looked like it was possible her plan could work.

Rafe had let Eden spend several evenings with her when she asked and let her stay the night again last weekend, as well.

She hoped showing and telling Eden she loved her would break down her desire to take herself and Bronte away—or make her want to tell her the truth about what she was hiding and about her plan.

Making love to Eden made Rafe feel alive again. She never wanted to stop. She had to force herself out of the room when Eden stayed over before she fell and lost her heart. Sometimes, the pain she felt in her chest when she thought about Jake's words and Eden's lies drove her out of the room to find relief. It was easier when Eden had to leave and go back to her apartment, but not a lot. She would give Eden everything she wanted, but not her heart. Not again, not yet. It was still something Eden had to earn. Rafe didn't want to feel such dark pain again, and she knew it could all end in a heartbeat because it had happened before. She would stay in control of her heart, and it would not happen again.

Thinking about the situation was giving Rafe a throbbing headache, and her mood was going from bad to worse. Waiting for the world to fall out from under her was very stressful. She hoped she could make it through what she considered 'Eden's Play' tonight. She was not sure why Eden wanted to involve all their friends in her plan. Maybe she thought, on top of everything else, she could make her look like a fool in front of them.

Jude walked in from the patio and found Rafe putting dishes away in the dining room cupboard. "Hey, aren't you coming back out?"

Rafe slid the dishes into the cabinet and then pulled out a different set. "I just need to get out the dishes first," she said irritably.

"I'll help," offered Jude. "Where do you need them to go?"

Rafe took the plates to the table. "Let's set them up in here because I think this is where the food is going to be set out unless Eden and Julia have other plans. Eden insists I can't help her, but if I don't, she'll never get everything done in time," she said and knew her irritation showed. "Julia is supposed to be helping her, but she's laid out by the pool."

"So, you let Eden arrange this all at your house?" asked Jude curiously. "Are you guys really, you know, 'together' together now?"

"No, well," Rafe frowned, "yes, kind of, but don't say anything."

"Why not?" Jude asked as she set out plates.

"Eden wants to tell everyone at the get-together tonight," Rafe explained. "Will you be coming back for it?"

"Definitely, but I might be late," said Jude and winked insinuating she had a hot date. "I've always had hope for you guys."

"We're just going to try to spend more time together," said Rafe as her headache intensified. "We're going to take it slow."

"You guys love each other," Jude said like she knew it was a fact. "I know there's a lot of bad history, Rafe, but you guys had a lot of good too. If you guys can remember the good and try to get there again," she said encouragingly, "maybe you could move forward faster."

"Thanks," Rafe smiled, knowing her intentions were good but she just didn't know what was really going on. "I just need her to be sure she's staying with me for the right reasons. I don't want to rush in, and then in a few months, find out it was a mistake."

"It'll work out," said Jude trying to keep things positive. "I know you two love each other."

"Yeah," said Rafe musingly, "but what kind of love is it?"

Jude set the last plate out and smiled at Rafe wanting to reassure her. "Abby has been really worried about you," she revealed. "She thinks there's something weird going on."

"Abby really is a funny girl," said Rafe dryly. "Why does she think that?"

"Because when you and Abby hooked up, you wouldn't strap it on for her." Jude grinned.

Rafe shook her head wondering what the hell their hook up at least seven or eight years ago had to do with anything going on now. She looked at Jude who was grinning and realized it was just Abby being her crazy self and she chuckled. "If I thought I loved her, I might have considered it," Rafe winked and laughed, "but I just gave her a little technique instead. Plus, I loved the story I told her. And sometimes, it can be just as fun not giving into girls as it is giving in."

Jude laughed and nodded her agreement. "She thinks you're going to use your wildling ways on Eden."

"Well, I'll be sure to torment Abby about the things she's telling everyone," said Rafe with a wry smile as her head throbbed.

"You're okay, aren't you, Rafe?" asked Jude with concern. "I know how hard this whole thing has been for you."

Rafe smiled through her pain. "I'm fine," she said with a nod. "Thanks, Jude."

The front door opened, and Flynn walked in carrying several grocery bags. "Hey," he said happily. "Where do you want this? Eden's outside."

"Put it in here," Rafe said and led him to the kitchen where she made room on the counter. "Does she have any more?"

"Just a couple," said Flynn as he headed toward the front door. "Don't worry, I'll get them."

"Thanks. We'll be out by the pool," she called after him. "Come out when you're done."

"Okay, thanks." Flynn waved back at her.

Rafe walked back out to the pool and sat on the lounger next to Julia. She leaned back and closed her eyes against the pain in her head and the pressure she was beginning to feel in her chest.

Julia lifted her sunglasses to look at Rafe with a slight frown. "Are you okay?" she asked as she dropped her glasses back down. She was sure it was driving Rafe crazy because she wasn't in charge of the dinner party.

"I'm fine," said Rafe, her eyes still closed as her head throbbed. "I just need to relax for a bit before I see Eden."

"It looks like your plan worked," said Julia. "You got the girl,"

"The plan is still in action," said Rafe rubbing her temples.

"The plan," she stammered. "What are you—" She halted her comment as Eden came outside. "Eden's here."

"I know," said Rafe as she put her arm across her forehead, her fist on her chest, and tried to swallow back the pain she was feeling.

Eden walked out to the pool where she saw Rafe lying back with her eyes closed and arm over her eyes and smiled. She straddled her then moved her arms aside and kissed her forehead. "Hey, you. Are you okay, babe?"

Rafe smiled at the sound of Eden's voice and the feel of her weight over her. "I'm fine," she said softly then opened her eyes and looked intensely into Eden's eyes. "Tell me what you want," she whispered.

Gripped in Rafe's burning gray-blue gaze, Eden swallowed. "I want this," she whispered and kissed her.

Julia shook her head at whatever Rafe was up to and stood up. "I think I'll go start preparing the food for tonight," she said. Eden looked up at her and smiled as Julia headed for the kitchen.

Rafe pulled Eden back down for another passionate kiss then pushed her back abruptly. "We should stop," she said and gently pushed Eden up and off her as the pressure in her chest seemed suffocating and her head throbbed with pain. She stood and forced a laugh. "We're driving everyone away."

"Yeah," Eden tentatively agreed, confused as to why she would push her away. "Yeah, I guess."

Rafe turned and saw Flynn come out of the house. "Hey, Flynn, will you help Eden light the grill for Julia?" she asked. "Thanks," she said then walked away to get some aspirin before she got an answer.

"Rafe, are you okay?" Eden asked as she followed Rafe inside.

"I'll be fine," she mumbled. "I just have a headache. I think I'll go lay down for a while." She walked to her bedroom with a grimace of pain on her face.

Julia looked up and saw Rafe head down the hall toward her room then Eden walk into the kitchen. "Is she going to be okay?" she asked Eden. "Is our unorganized dinner party driving her mad?" She laughed. "You know, she's been complaining all day about how disorganized and unplanned this thing is? Look," she pointed at the dishes on the table. "It's is the second set of dishes she's pulled out. When I told her we were having salmon, she threw up her hands, stormed inside, and changed the plates. She's worse than last time when she was driving Abby insane. You said she promised you could handle everything."

Eden looked at Julia with worry in her eyes. "She promised, but she just can't help wanting things to be perfect. I think she's been very worried about where I'm going and what I'm doing when she's not around," she said as she started helping Julia. "She's trying to be subtle, but I think she's worried I'm going to leave again. I'm not going to," Eden said and looked hopefully at Julia. "I want to stay with her. I hope doing things together like this will help us break down some walls, and we can work on trusting each other again."

"Why don't you go in and keep her company and keep her from taking over," suggested Julia as she pulled out her puff pastry dough. "I'll knock out these *vol-au-vents* and pop them in the oven then start the rest. Maybe you can reassure her you want to stay with her at the same time."

"I..." Eden hesitated. "I can't."

"Why not?" asked Julia as she unfolded the dough and began cutting circles for filling.

"It's just we," Eden paused, "we agreed, her room is off limits to me right now."

"What? Why on earth did you guys agree to something like that?" Julia asked in surprise.

Eden started chopping vegetables for the salads. "I talked to her about it one day because she seems to go to her room a lot and locks the door. She just doesn't seem to want me to go in there yet."

"Eden, this is strange even for Rafe," said Julia as she shook her head in bafflement. "Don't let Abby know. Who knows what she'll make out of it."

"No, I don't think it's strange." Eden stopped cutting and looked at Julia. "I think there are other reasons she needs it too," she said. "She still has a lot of rules to protect herself. She didn't really say much, but I told her I understood she needed a place where she can go and be alone. Some place just hers so she can think or deal with all the emotional things happening right now. I think it's fair since she is letting me be here practically whenever I want."

Julia was not really sure how to respond to what Eden was telling her. She had no idea what Rafe was up to with her so-called plan or if this was even part of the scheme. "Well," she said as she put her pastry in the oven, "I suppose it's positive you're at least thinking about each other's well-being."

"We are," said Eden with a smile as she went back to work on the salads. "Things are going fast, and there are a lot of emotional things happening. I still have a lot of things I still need to talk to her about too." Eden put the vegetables she had chopped into the salad bowl. "Rafe needs a place to help her cope, and Dr. Cathcart said I should give her space when she needs it. I go to Dr. Cathcart," she explained, "and Rafe goes to her room."

29

ALMOST EVERYONE HAD arrived for Eden Kingsley's dinner party at Rafe's house, and everything was beginning to take shape. Rafe had finally come out of her room after having taken something for her headache and getting some rest. Still on the edge of a painful headache, she was trying to push through and be a good host for their company.

Guests were scattered throughout the house and out onto the patio eating Julia's *vol-au-vent* pastries filled with a sweet and savory filling. Letty, Bronte, Ephraim, Stacey, and Flynn were out by the pool lounging or swimming. Julia and Eden had set out all the food they had prepared in the dining room buffet style, to Rafe's chagrin, so they could take plates out to the patio to eat but keep the food inside.

Rafe was in the living room with Eden and Abby when the doorbell rang. She opened the door for their guests. "Annie, I'm glad you came," said Rafe and gave the art teacher a hug.

"Thanks for inviting me," Annie said as they entered the living room pulling a sandy haired young man around to introduce him. "This is my boyfriend, Rob."

"Welcome, Rob," Rafe said and shook his hand. "This is Abby, and this is my good friend Eden," she said as they all shook hands. "Guys, this is Rob and Annie."

"It's nice to meet you, Rob," said Abby as she gave Rafe a puzzled look. "Annie is a great art teacher."

"She is," said Rafe ignoring Abby's look. "We're lucky to have her." As Annie and Rob came inside and Abby led them away, a beautiful brunette woman made her way up the stairs, and Rafe greeted her. "Hello, you must be Selina. I'm Rafe."

"Nice to meet you, Rafe," said Selina with a slight Latin accent and smiled. "Julia has told me all about you."

Rafe laughed carefully through her headache trying not to make it worse. "I'm sure." She motioned to Eden. "This is Eden. Everyone is out on the patio," she said with a forced smile. "Follow me."

30

RAFE SALVAGGIO LED Eden and the others out to the patio where everyone had started to gather around the table. Letty had put Bronte in her booster seat, and the guests began claiming their seats for dinner. As everyone settled in, Rafe started the introductions.

"Everyone," Rafe called out and signaled for quiet. "Most of you know Annie, Bronte's art teacher. This is her boyfriend,

Rob." She motioned to Selina. "This is Julia's date, Selina. Annie, Rob, Selina, let me introduce you to Stacey, Flynn, Ephraim, and my cousin Letty," she pointed to each, "and Selina knows Julia, and Annie already knows the beautiful Bronte. Our other guests Jude and her friend should be here soon." She noted Annie and Rob didn't have drinks. "Eden, can you get them some wine?"

"Sure, I'll be right back," said Eden happily and left to get them wine.

Abby leaned into Julia "What is going on with Rafe?" she whispered. "She just introduced Eden as her good friend."

"Not again, Abby," Julia complained. "You always think something is wrong with her. Give it a rest," she said as Selina sat next to her. She welcomed her with a quick kiss. "I'm going to help Eden make sure all the food and wine are ready for everyone."

"Okay," Selina smiled, and Abby began her interrogation before Julia was inside the house.

Jude came in through the back gate and walked up to the patio with a beautiful, voluptuous brunette on her arm. The beautiful woman was wearing deadly looking stilettos and a very revealing low cut evening dress, clinging to her in all the right places, revealing her sensuous curves. Her hair was full, and not a strand was out of place. Her makeup was flawless from the eye shadow giving her bedroom eyes to her perfect pouty bow lips painted crimson red.

"Hi, we're here," Jude announced. "Sorry we couldn't get here earlier but," she grinned, "you know."

Abby gave Jude and her beautiful date the once over look. "Yeah, we know," she said with a snarky sneer.

Jude ignored her and looked at Rafe. "Rafe, this is Ms. Scrumptious Luv," she said with a grin. "Scrumptious this is Rafe Salvaggio."

"It's a pleasure," said Ms. Luv and offered her hand to Rafe.

"Oh, brother," mumbled Abby under her breath. It looked like she was going to have to put up with a Cabaret girl phase with Jude now.

"The pleasure is mine, Ms. Luv," Rafe said with an easy smile as she took her hand and brought it to her lips then kissed the back of it gently as she looked into her eyes. "I don't know how I'll ever be able to repay Jude for bringing a guest as delicious as you to my table as company for us all to enjoy for the evening. I hope we don't disappoint you, Ms. Luv."

Scrumptious laughed and turned slightly pink in embarrassment. "You really are a temptress, aren't you?" she asked as Rafe released her hand. "You can call me Scrumptious," she said and ran her fingers down Rafe's face and over her lips.

"Welcome, Scrumptious," said Rafe then she gave Jude a wink. "Jude, you know almost everyone so I think you should do all the introductions personally with her. Scrumptious is too special to do them any other way. She should be treated like a fine wine, she needs to be savored."

"Absolutely." Jude grinned proudly and led Scrumptious away as the beautiful woman clung to her and they laughed at Rafe's words.

Abby glared at Rafe and huffed in frustration. "Really? She needs to be savored? She's a glorified stripper." She waited for Rafe to respond, but she just looked at her with those freaking wildling eyes and sipped her wine. Abby's temper began to flare because it was as if Rafe and Jude were both sabotaging their lives on purpose. "I swear both you and Jude—"

"Okay, everyone, everything is ready," Julia interrupted as she came back out and with a couple of carafes of wine and sat them on the table. "Let's go inside for our plates and get something to eat."

Eden looked around to make sure everyone had filled their plates and had a drink as they all returned to the table. "Okay, does everyone have food and a glass of wine?" she asked and waited for their acknowledgments. She looked around the table again at all the faces of their friends. "Rafe and I would like to thank you all for coming," she said and beamed at Rafe for a moment. "We wanted you all here because Rafe and I just wanted to let you all know we're going to be seeing more of each other. We hope we can work through things and make each other happy again, and we would really appreciate your support. So, thank you for coming to our dinner party," she said and raised her glass in a salute and the others followed.

"That's great, you guys!" said Jude as she touched her glass to her date's glass then took a sip of wine.

"Yeah, it's great," said Annie with a smile and gave Rob's hand a pat of affection.

Selina leaned over to Abby. "I love this music. Who is it?"

"It's Jen Foster," she told her. "I brought it. Do you think it's up too loud?"

"No," Selina assured her. "I love her voice. I'll have to get her download or a CD."

Rafe watched a moment as everyone began eating and talking and then leaned over to Eden. "I'm sorry about earlier," she whispered. "I wasn't really fine. I just wasn't feeling good. But I feel a little better now," she said and kissed her cheek.

"So what made you guys decide to throw a party?" asked Annie from down the table.

"Simple," said Rafe as she looked at Eden. "Eden said she wanted it."

Everyone noticed the intense look she gave Eden, and it was all Abby could do not to throw her fork at Rafe.

Rafe smiled and leaned in to whisper in Eden's ear again. "I'm glad this is what you want," she said in her low sensual voice.

Eden smiled at the whisper and the feel of Rafe's breath on her ear. She regained composure and looked at Rafe. "We both wanted it," she said softly. "We have a daughter together, and things are going good between us, and we wanted to share it with our friends. It just feels right," she said as she put her hand on Rafe's leg to feel the comfort of her closeness.

"I can see why you're together," said Selina who couldn't help noticing them whispering to each other. "There's a lot of, I don't know, electricity or something between you two."

"There's definitely something between us," Rafe said with a small smile as she touched Eden's hand as it rested on her leg.

Eden took a drink and looked away knowing Rafe was implying they still had things they needed to work on. "So, how do you like the salmon?" Eden asked everyone, hoping to change the subject. "Julia did a great job."

"Thank you," said Julia reveling in the attention. "But the plates make the meal." She chuckled and gave Rafe a smirk as Rafe shook her head.

Letty lifted her glass. "I'm just glad you two finally got your acts together," she said and took a drink as calls of 'here, here' sounded around the table.

"We still have a lot of ground to cover, Letty, but we're starting out really well. Right, babe?" Eden smiled at Rafe and watched her take a sip of wine with her bite of salmon. She didn't know why Rafe always agreed to let Julia cook salmon when she clearly did not like it. She always ate it without complaint, though.

Rafe smiled weakly and could feel her headache resurfacing. "I think so," she said and took another sip of wine to clear her palette. She looked intensely at Abby who was staring back in her annoying way. "If things don't work out, you'll take me back won't you, Abby?" she asked remembering the stories Jude said she was telling everyone. "I know I can give you what you want," she winked at her, "if you'll let me try." Across the table, Jude snickered because she knew what Rafe was doing.

Abby looked at Rafe in shock. "I..." she stammered, "I... Rafe, you better hope things work out, or you'll be out in the cold!" she yelled down the table.

"Me? Out in the cold?" Rafe said coyly. "Abby, it would never happen." She smiled slightly. "When someone loves me, they love me forever," she wrinkled her brow to fight her pain, "even if they don't know it." She looked at Eden very seriously. "Right? You never stopped loving me, did you?"

"Conceited much?" Julia asked wryly as she picked up her wine glass and gave Selina a knowing look.

Eden looked at Rafe, unsettled by what she was doing. "No, I never stopped."

"See, Abby," Rafe forced a grin at her. She looked back at Eden. "It's okay if she's still in love with me, isn't it, Eden?"

Eden hesitated then understood Rafe was teasing Abby. "Only if it's from afar," she said and sipped her wine.

"I'm not in love with you!" Abby said defensively.

Rafe smiled at her impishly and spoke seductively to her, "No, just with the things I can do to you."

"I know I'm already in love with just the possibilities of you, Rafe!" Scrumptious laughed from the far end of the table then sipped her wine.

Jude saw the looks both Eden and Abby gave Scrumptious and knew she better step in to help. "Rafe, you're worse than I am!" Jude laughed out loud. "You're going to start a fight if you don't stop teasing them."

Rafe laughed lightly through the pain in her head. "Abby, it's what you get when you start telling stories to people," she said with a frown.

"I didn't tell," Abby stopped and looked at Jude. "You told her what I said? How could you?"

"What did you tell?" asked Eden puzzled about what they were talking about and why the woman with Jude would be in love with the possibilities of Rafe.

"Oh, she was sharing stories of our past." Rafe looked hard at Abby. "Our *private* past," she emphasized, "with Jude and who knows who else."

"Is this something I should know about?" asked Eden anxiously shaking her head in bafflement, wondering if the scrumptious woman was talking about the stories.

"No!" screamed both Jude and Abby at the same time.

Rafe leaned over and gave Eden a quick kiss. "Don't worry. It was a long time ago."

Rob, along with the rest of the table, had silently enjoyed the exchange. "So, you two," he said pointing from Abby to Rafe, "you know, were together? And you're still friends?"

Abby dropped her fork with a clank clearly exasperated with how the conversation had been turned on her. "We weren't for a while, but Rafe has this way about her," she said as she frowned. "Even if you're hurt and pissed, you still want to be around her for some reason," she said sarcastically.

"I had to leave you, Abby," Rafe said with simulated sympathy. "I was pursuing true love," she said and rubbed Eden's back.

"I know," Abby smirked, "you told me, but you better not screw your true love up again because picking up the pieces after you—is a pain in the ass. No offense, Eden."

"None taken," said Eden anxiously. "Can we please change the subject?"

"Sure," said Rafe with a shrug. Rafe glanced up seeing something move behind Abby. Her expression hardened and her temper ignited. "Maybe you should have tried to seduce

Eden instead of Julia," she said evenly as she saw the movement again.

Julia choked on her bite of food and coughed. She wondered how Rafe found out about the drunken and embarrassing moment when she and Abby stayed in Rafe's entertainment room during the storm.

Selina looked at Julia then Abby with a smile and shook her head but chose to stay silent.

Rafe continued to look past Abby angrily. "You two seem to have a lot of the same needs. Then maybe she wouldn't have had to leave me for a man."

Abby, thinking Rafe was looking directly at her with her fierce look, became upset. "What's your fucking problem, Rafe?"

"Guys, please," said Eden, worried things were getting out of hand. "Stop."

"Yes, Rafe," said Letty concerned with Rafe's sudden anger, "stop it!"

Rafe looked around the table then past Abby again. "My fucking problem is some people seem to be doing a lot of interfering in my life lately, and I don't appreciate it. I won't tolerate anyone interfering," she said in a low and angry voice as she saw the movement again.

"Oh, I get it," screeched Abby angrily. "This is because of the night I didn't want you to take Eden home."

"Abby," Eden broke in, looking from Abby to Rafe nervously. "Rafe. Please!"

"Excuse me," said Rafe. Then she got up and walked determinedly into the house.

"I'll fucking excuse you straight to hell!" Abby yelled irately at her as everyone stared after Rafe in silence.

31

RAFE SALVAGGIO WALKED through the house and went straight out the front door then made her way around to the side of the house.

"Hey! What the hell are you doing?" Rafe yelled menacingly, the sound of the music covering her voice from the guests on the patio. As the figure turned, Rafe felt the justification lock in for her anger and knew, if released, there would be no reprieve, no mercy, and no regrets. There would only be obliteration for Jake because right now, Rafe wanted nothing less than to murder him. "Get off my fucking property, now!"

"How did you know I was here?" he asked as he stood his ground.

"I saw someone trying to look over the fence," she said evenly as she sized him up, "and all the people I'm expecting are here, so I knew it had to be an uninvited guest."

Jake laughed nervously because he was not expecting to confront Rafe, and he could see she was angry. He nodded toward the gate. "I've come to get Eden," he declared, deciding to make the best of the situation.

Rafe gave him a condescending smile. "You won't ever be taking Eden from my house again."

"You really do think you can keep me away from her, don't you?" he asked shaking his head sadly. "You do realize you aren't actually doing anything to convince her to stay with you, right? She's just letting you think you are so she can get what she wants."

"You're right," said Rafe as she kept a forced smile on her face, "she's getting what she wants. I told you it's what I'm giving her."

"You're so fucking stubborn!" Jake snapped angrily clenching his fists. "She doesn't love you! She's using you, and you just stand there like an idiot and let her!"

"Just get the hell out, Jake. Leave, or I'm calling the police," Rafe growled, "then she'll know you're here and know you've told me everything about her plan. Then we'll see who she loves," she said scathingly. Jake stepped toward her, and Rafe put her foot back and raised her fists "Back the fuck off," she warned menacingly.

"What are you going to do?" asked Jake with a laugh. "Fight me? Beat me up?" He laughed again. "You're ridiculous." He looked at her and her cocky attitude and all the trouble it had caused him with the reverend and decided she needed her ego taken down a bit. "Maybe I should beat the shit out of you right now. Maybe I can knock some sense into your head!"

Rafe saw his intent long before Jake stepped into his sloppy attempt to backhand her. His hand never made it close to her face because she knocked his arm aside and punched him hard in the mouth sending him reeling to his knees in surprise. She immediately immobilized him by pushing his arm up behind his back and kicked him hard in the ribs then pushed him into the ground. As she backed away, she bent and picked up a large rock from beside the fence and wielded it threateningly.

"Get the fuck out of here," said Rafe breathing hard mostly from anger.

Jake sat up slowly and touched his lip wincing in pain then looked at the blood on his fingers. He took a breath and wiped the blood on his shirt. "Fuck," he said softly as he held his ribs. He looked up at Rafe and saw the rock in her hand. "What do you think you're going to do with that?" he asked mockingly.

"Knock you the fuck out!" Rafe growled. "I told you to disappear. So, I suggest this time you actually do it."

Jake used the fence and pulled himself up. He chided himself for getting sloppy and letting a woman get in a solid punch. He thought about going after her but stopped and took a breath. He had to be careful and not do anything to make the situation harder for the Stewards. Getting involved with the police for assault would not be good. It was probably a good thing Rafe got in her punch. Rafe seemed to be full of surprises, as always. Luckily, he had a few of his own.

"We shouldn't be fighting," Jake said softly. "I'm sorry. I shouldn't have taken a swing at you. I've just been so worried. Not knowing what's happening is driving me crazy, I guess." He ran his hands over his face flinching when he touched his lip then tried to straighten his clothes. He took what he hoped looked like a brave breath and looked up at Rafe. "I knew you had her here," said Jake grudgingly. "What are you doing, holding her hostage or something? I heard about what you did to Eden at The Kiki Bistro." He looked at her suspiciously. "Did you fuck her already?"

"I'm not holding her hostage," Rafe said, barely containing the anger inside her. "She wants to be here. This is her idea." She looked at him with murder in her eyes. "I know she's not fucking you," she sneered unwilling to give him any information about herself or Eden.

"Rafe, you have to stop this," Jake pleaded feigning concern for Eden. "You're the one allowing her to hurt herself now." He sighed heavily. "She won't stop this on her own, and it's gone too far. I need you to stop this, Rafe. Don't let your addiction for her make you selfish or foolish. If you aren't stopping it for yourself, at least stop it for her. She's doing this to hurt you, but someday, it may end up hurting her too. Especially if Bronte ever finds out what she's done to you." He watched Rafe's eyes narrow and knew he had her attention. "Think about it," he said gaining confidence. "Someday Bronte will want to know who her real father is, and she'll find your friend in Italy. What will he have to say to her about Eden and what she's done to you again?" He gave her a moment to think about the question. "If you send Eden and the baby back to me, I can make sure Bronte knows you and your friend. Then Eden won't ever have someone saying bad things about her or hurt her relationship with Bronte." Jake paused for a moment as Rafe frowned. "Don't let it happen. Tell her you don't love her— tell her it was all just your addiction and a mistake. Send her back to me. I'll convince her to change her mind about the adoption and doing this to you, I swear."

Rafe looked a Jake defiantly. She didn't need any man, especially Jake, to fight her battles. "But I do love her. I told you," Rafe reminded him as she re-gripped the rock. "This is more than an addiction, and I think deep down Eden knows it. I'm giving her what she wants no matter what. She's not going back to you," she said evenly as she tossed the rock from one hand to the other.

"Rafe, eventually she will, and then what? What will you do then?" he asked with concern. "You're setting yourself up for failure and pain."

"Why do you care?" Rafe laughed bitterly. "What does it matter to you?"

Jake looked at her and shook his head in sympathy. "I've been through a separation and a divorce," he said candidly. "I know you sometimes dream things will go back to the way they were. Sometimes you feel the same way years after the breakup," he paused, "but things can't go back, Rafe. Not with Eden, anyway. She really is in love with me. She even left me a note the other day, so I'd know she was okay." He pulled a note out of his pocket and tried to hand it to her.

Rafe snatched the note and looked at it. She saw it was clearly Eden's handwriting. Dated Tuesday, just four days ago, and Eden was telling Jake not to worry. She said she couldn't wait to get back to him and she loved him. Eden had even drawn a little picture of two hearts hooked together at the bottom of the note. Rafe frowned as she remembered Eden drawing the same thing on notes when she wanted to leave a hint she was in the mood to make love. She crushed the note and threw it at Jake working hard to hold back her rage.

"Nice to know," she said shortly.

"Rafe, don't you understand," Jake said as he shook his head sadly, as he picked up the note and smoothed it out. "It means she isn't in love with you."

"No," she said sternly, "it *does* mean she's in love with me. I told you, I think she's fooling *you*," said Rafe stubbornly.

"Rafe, she's doing this because she doesn't love you," Jake argued, "and the fact you hurt her when you fucked around on her! You're acting fucking insane!"

"And you're just fucked!" she growled furiously. Letting her anger out, she hurled the rock at him hitting him hard in the chest then quickly picked up another.

"You fucking bitch!" Jake cried out as he bent over in pain holding his chest. "I'm trying to help you!" he gasped angrily.

"I don't need your fucking help!" Rafe fumed. "I need you to stay the fuck away!" she said brandishing the second rock.

"I'm going, because I don't want to lose her," he said reigning in his anger, "but you should listen to me!" He turned and walked away slowly and deliberately. The situation was escalating, and he didn't know how much longer he could hold off fucking her up. He couldn't endanger the mission.

Rafe watched him walk away and stayed where she was until she heard a car engine start and the car pull away. "I'm not fucking listening to you," she mumbled to herself. She forced her fist open to drop the rock then turned and walked back to the front of the house. Her body heated with fury as her head throbbed, and it felt as if something was pressing painfully into her chest.

As Rafe walked up the stairs of the front porch, Eden opened the door and stepped out. "Rafe, what are you doing?" she asked, clearly upset Rafe had been gone so long. "What's wrong?"

Rafe sat on the top stair and leaned her head into her hands trying to calm herself and cope with the searing pain in her head made worse now by the note Jake had shown her.

"Nothing, I'm sorry," she said wishing Eden would go back inside in case Jake came back.

"Why did you say those things to Abby?" asked Eden as she sat down beside Rafe, thinking she was still mad at Abby. "You know she cares for you. She's a really good friend."

"I know," said Rafe as she rubbed her aching head. "My head hurts, I'm not in a good mood," she said quietly trying to hold in the panic as an invisible hand pressed against her chest. "I'll tell her I'm sorry."

Eden reached over, took Rafe's warm face in her hands, and kissed her forehead and face. "You're so warm," she said concerned. "Do you need to take some more aspirin and lay down again?"

"No. I don't know," Rafe said, not knowing what she wanted to do about her headache and everything else. She leaned into Eden then kissed her. She pulled her close then lay back with her on the porch and held her tightly. "I don't want you to hurt anymore, Ede," she whispered to try to control her shaking voice.

"I know," said Eden and gently put her head against Rafe. "I don't want you to hurt, either."

"I love you," said Rafe softly. "I need you to kiss me. I need you to tell me how you feel again. I need you to tell me you don't want anyone else but me. You don't want to be with anyone else."

Looking down into Rafe's eyes, Eden could see she was in pain. "Okay, I'll tell you," she said and kissed her sweetly. "I love you," she whispered, "I want you," she kissed her forehead, "I need you," she kissed her closed eyelid, "I don't ever want to be without you," she kissed her other eyelid, "I don't want anyone but you." She kissed her deeply, running her hands fluidly over her body then over her face and through her hair as Rafe clung urgently to her. "I love you."

Rafe felt like she was being crushed with every word and every kiss, but she wanted them all. She didn't know how Eden could say those words to Jake and hint she wanted to have sex with him in her note then turn around and say them again to her and sleep with her. Nothing made sense anymore. She felt Eden's kiss on her face again, and she looked up at her not sure what to say or even if she should say anything.

"Thank you," she said softly, "thank you for what you're giving me right now." She pulled Eden to her and kissed her deeply, taking comfort even if Eden meant it to be something else.

The front door opened, and Abby looked out and saw Rafe and Eden laying on the porch kissing. "Oh, gross," she said cynically.

Eden smiled as she looked up. "Hi, Abby."

"Hi, sorry," she said and started to go back inside.

With her eyes still closed, Rafe loosened her hold on Eden. "Hey, Abby," she called out to stop her.

"Yeah." Abby stopped and turned back.

"I'm sorry I'm in such a fucked up mood tonight," apologized Rafe.

Eden rubbed Rafe's temples. "She isn't feeling good. A headache," she explained.

"I'm sorry for the things I said to you," said Rafe. "I didn't mean any of it. I'm not mad at you." She hesitated. "I..." She didn't know what else to say. She couldn't tell her who really made her angry.

"It's okay," said Abby accepting Rafe's apology. "I'm not really trying to interfere, you know. I just don't want you guys to hurt each other anymore."

"We know," said Eden. "Don't we, babe?"

"Yes," Rafe sighed, "we know. Thank you, Abby. You're a good friend, the truest friend."

"Come on," Eden said as she pulled Rafe up. "Let's go in and get you some aspirin," she said. "We still have guests, you know.

32

AFTER TAKING MORE aspirin, Rafe Salvaggio spent some time alone to calm her mind and was finally feeling better. She had decided to push her visit with Jake out of her mind for the night and concentrate on being a good hostess and helping Eden. Everyone had finished dinner and was enjoying some good conversation with wine while scattered throughout the house or outside enjoying the pleasant night.

Annie and Rob were impressed by the art Rafe had throughout the house. Annie was awestruck when Rafe took them to see the private collection in the room she had converted to a gallery. They finally returned to the dining room and stood in front of the painting of the Blue Woman.

"Wow. This one is really intense," Rob observed and looked at Rafe. "It looks a little like you."

"It is me." Rafe chuckled looking up at the piece.

Annie looked at the signature. "This is by Professor Noble," she said surprised. "You guys dated for a while, didn't you?"

"Yes, for a while." Rafe smiled thinking about Greer.

"She's having a show in New York next summer with Beth. Is this going to be in it?" asked Annie.

"No, not this one," Rafe said shaking her head, "though the photograph in the gallery at the Conservatory might be in her show. She says it's the only art she's done on a human canvas. Well, where it's documented, anyway." She smiled and winked. "I'll bet she's done it before, but it was never recorded," she said with a laugh. "Since she's seen my photograph, she's started calling me her canvas."

Eden saw Rafe was back from the gallery room, so she went over and stood next to her. "What are you guys talking about?"

"This painting," said Rafe as she pointed to the Blue Woman.

Rob looked at Eden curiously. "You must really like art, Eden. I don't think I'd want a painting like this of Annie, one an ex-lover did, hanging where I'd have to look at it all the time," he said honestly. "It would be like a daily slap in the face."

Eden put her hand to her face remembering Greer's visit to her office. "Sometimes, a slap in the face can be a good thing," she said softly. She looked up at him and smiled. "I don't live here." She paused fighting the jealousy still gripping her. "This is Rafe's house and her art. It's not up to me what she hangs on her walls."

"Oh, okay," said Rob and arched his eyebrows. Then he and Annie moved to look at another piece.

"I'll take it down if you want," Rafe whispered to Eden.

"No," Eden said and kissed Rafe for being sweet and offering to take it down. "I can see you in it now. She did capture you on canvas, but I have the real thing. Plus, it's a good reminder for me."

"I hope I have the real thing too," Rafe said puzzled, unsure how it was a 'good reminder' for her of anything. "Rob, bring Annie and come into the living room. I'll show you a painting I did I think you'll like."

33

AFTER CHECKING ON Bronte, who had passed out from exhaustion earlier in the night, Eden Kingsley pulled the guest bedroom door halfway closed and went to find Rafe. All the guests had gone home, and the house was finally quiet again. Not counting the drama at the beginning of the dinner party

Eden thought things went very well. The biggest change was Rafe had started to feel better. It was so good to see her smile again and hear her laugh. It seemed like everyone's mood changed once Rafe was feeling better, even Abby's had changed. Before the end of the night, Abby was actually talking about doing an interview with Ms. Scrumptious Luv and had called Erica to put it on their calendar.

Eden smiled as she walked outside and saw Rafe relaxing on the double lounger by the pool. She went over and stretched out next to her quietly. She reached out and took her hand lacing their fingers together. Everything felt perfect.

The image of two hearts joined together kept appearing in Rafe's mind. She turned her head and looked at Eden. She knew one of those hearts was meant for Jake on Tuesday when the note was written. But she had made love to Eden just a few days before, and they spent family time together on Wednesday. They also spent some intimate time together after Bronte was asleep, though they ended up not having sex. Rafe wondered if the reason they didn't have sex that night was because Eden wanted Jake. No, she was sure it was mutual. It was late, and they both had work and early morning meetings.

The image of two hearts joined appeared in Rafe's mind again. She gently unlaced her hand from Eden's and got up from the lounger. She picked up her wine glass and swallowed the last of it then put the glass back on the table. She stepped in front of the lounger and faced the pool lit subtly from within. She suddenly thought to feeling warm salt water around her would help stop the despair threatening to let itself loose. She pulled her shirt over her head and tossed it aside.

As Rafe striped in front of her, Eden watched with a silent smile as she stretched and shifted her body as it reacted to the vision of Rafe's softly sculpted body being unwrapped. Her breath quickened as she watched Rafe reach behind her back and unhook her bra, then slide it off and discarded it with the rest of her clothes. Eden always loved the shape of Rafe's shoulders and the curve running from there, along her waist, and over her hip, then down her long legs. She crossed her legs as Rafe slid her underwear over her slender hips then down her legs and kicked them aside. Her eyes locked on Rafe's round ass, and she had to bite her lip to stop the sound escaping her. Eden knew she was bright red from watching Rafe, and the anticipation for her to turn around so she could look at her was excruciating. She couldn't wait to feel Rafe's hands on her again.

Rafe felt the night air on her skin and could feel Eden's eyes on her, as well. She could hear Eden breathing. She leaned her head forward then stretched her neck from side to side and rolled her shoulders as she tried to calm her frustrations about the note and the image of the two hearts. Knowing all this time, Eden was thinking about Jake and wanted him and was missing him shouldn't have been surprising. She was sure it wasn't surprising because Jake was the one she was trying to convince Eden not to want and not to miss, after all. It was seeing it, seeing the note. The evidence—the two hearts combined—was what hurt. The truth always hurt.

Rafe dove into the pool, feeling the warm water surround her as it washed away a salty tear having dared to fall from her eye. Lately, there always seemed to be at least one traitor tear she couldn't stop before she could slam her wall of control up on her emotions. Tears were for great beauty, children, mourning, and people who lost control. She promised herself she would never lose control again. She swam laps to burn through her anger at herself and the fact she had allowed her heart to get too close. She knew Eden had already made her choice and maybe she was a fool to think she could change her mind. Jake called her insane for doing this. But she felt like it would be insane if she didn't do it. The hard part was figuring out how far over the line she could go before turning back would no longer be an option.

Rafe grabbed the edge of the pool and pulled herself out of the water, breathing heavily from exertion. She pushed her hair from her face, wiped the water from her eyes, and then looked up at Eden. She was gone. Rafe looked around the patio then turned toward the pool stairs and was surprised and a bit wary of what she saw. She had seen the image somewhere before. A blonde woman walking naked into the water as waves lapped on her. It used to be a vision that made her smile, but she couldn't find it in her right now. Rafe slipped back into the warm pool then stayed motionless as Eden made her way toward her. She thought tonight, rather than going to Eden as she usually did, it would be appropriate if Eden made a choice to be with her or go home to Jake. Then all of this could stop.

Eden glided through the warm water and made her way to Rafe. She had been watching her swim laps naked with her strong, sure strokes. She was surprised when she dived into the pool because she expected her to turn around and make love to her. The more laps Rafe swam, the more Eden realized the night must have been very stressful for her, and she was working it off. She felt guilty she may have pushed too hard too soon, but she thought the night had gone well, they got through it, and now all their friends were supporting them. Right now, she just wanted to take Rafe's stress away.

Eden eased through the water until her body was against Rafe's, pushing her back against the pool wall. "Did your swim make you feel better?" she asked softly as she ran her hand over Rafe's shoulder and down her chest and her breast, watching as her nipple hardened.

"No," she said candidly. "I may not be very good company tonight. You might still have time to go out with the girls, or do something on your own you've been missing or needing to do," she said. Arms stretched out, she held tightly to the side of the pool with both hands, ignoring Eden's touches. "I'll watch Bronte, and you can get her whenever you're ready."

"I'm sorry you're not feeling well," said Eden as Rafe looked away from her. She reached up and put her hands around her neck pressing her body against hers. Eden loved how it felt to have her breasts pressed against Rafe. Moving her lips toward Rafe's ear, Eden licked her ear lobe then sucked it into her mouth and nibbled it gently. "If I leave," she breathed into Rafe's wet ear, "then I'll be missing and needing you." Eden kissed along her jaw, taking her head in her hands, turning it so she could kiss Rafe's lips.

As Eden released Rafe from her kiss, Rafe leaned her head back slightly and closed her eyes. Rafe gripped the side of the pool tighter as Eden kissed her neck and moved her leg up and down while pressing into her. Rafe leaned her head forward against Eden who began kissing her face again. "I just thought maybe you needed a break from me," she said thickly. "You can go relax and not have to deal with me," she said and swallowed before continuing, "be somewhere you can do something for yourself you might not be able to do if I'm around."

Eden pulled back and looked at Rafe, unsure what to think about what she was saying. "What?" She chuckled with uncertainty. "Rafe, I don't need a break from you," she said then kissed her softly. She pulled back and couldn't hide the desire building inside her for Rafe. "As a matter of fact," she said in a sultry voice, "all of the things I want to do for myself require you being around." Eden leaned in to claim Rafe's breast with her mouth and wrapped her nipple in her tongue, sucking until she heard her gasp. "Yes," she said, very happy with the results of what she had done. "I really like what that did for me." She leaned in, claiming Rafe's other breast, and smiled as she felt Rafe's arms wrap around her, finally.

As far as Rafe was concerned, Eden had made her choice. She pulled Eden up and kissed her deeply, determined she would never regret her choice. Rafe lowered herself slightly and pulled Eden's hips to her, so Eden had to wrap her legs around her. She reached her hand down between Eden's legs and heard her moan as they kissed.

"I want to see exactly what it did for you," said Rafe as she pushed her fingers through the layers protecting where the proof lay.

"It's there," Eden whispered in her ear, "I promise." She could feel Rafe getting closer, and she had to kiss her again.

It was almost imperceptible at first—almost. The slight texture change from water to water mixed with Eden's cum, but Rafe felt the difference. She slowly eased her fingers inside Eden, inching them in, then pulling them out and pushing back in quick enough so the cum didn't wash off, but slow enough as not to hurt Eden when the part of her fingers not lubricated yet went inside her. "I found it," she breathed into Eden's ear. "You were right. I wonder what else you could do for yourself and might require me." Rafe pushed deep into Eden making her moan and hold Rafe's neck tighter. "I liked how you sucked on my breasts. Maybe you could do the same thing to my clit. Maybe you could do that for yourself," she said softly in between kisses to Eden's ear and jaw.

"Oh, god, Rafe." Eden moaned, reacting to Rafe's words and kisses as she felt Rafe's strokes deepen inside her. Her breathing quickened as Rafe's strokes moved faster because Eden's body gave Rafe exactly what she needed. "I want to do it to you," she said and kissed Rafe again breathlessly, loving the sensation Rafe was causing.

Pushing in deep, Rafe held Eden close until they broke away from their kiss. "Okay," she said softly. Kissing Eden several more times, Rafe pulled out of her slowly.

Eden looked up at her with blatant disappointment on her face, and Rafe just smiled at her. Before Eden could say anything, Rafe lifted her up onto the edge of the pool and pulled herself out.

"Come on." Rafe reached down for Eden's hand, then pulled her up and led her to the double lounger. She lowered the back on the lounger to the point where it was at a nice angle, then, without a word, she sat down and lay back with her hands behind her head. "I can't wait to see what you do for yourself," she said with a rakish smile as she looked up at Eden.

Looking down on Rafe, who was displaying herself like a toy on a shelf as rivulets of water dripped down her body, Eden wasn't sure if she should laugh or be turned on—or both. One thing she was sure of—what Rafe started in the pool, Rafe was going to finish, one way or another.

34

THE EXTERIOR OF the industrial space was dated and grungy, but Masson Essex saw to the new interior build-out a few years ago. Inside, there was a large executive office, including a large restroom with a shower and a dressing room with clothes lockers. Next door, there was a separate meeting room for mission meetings and training. There was enough space left over in the building to park a van and for some industrial shelving to store tools, equipment, and other pieces and parts needed for surveillance.

Inside the large office, sitting on the desk, there was an older looking computer processor and a large newer looking computer monitor powered up. The light from the monitor emitted a soft glow over the room. Hidden with the wires cleverly concealed was a state of the art computer system with several processors and other high tech hardware connected to the monitor. There was concealed recording and video equipment hooked up throughout the building and tied into the computer system. The high definition sound system hummed along with the other machinery. Soft sounds were coming from the high-end speakers, but Mason Essex knew the volume was at just the right level to hear the sounds he wanted to hear. Sounds he had found lately he needed to hear. It had become an addiction he couldn't live without.

He leaned back in his oversized leather office chair he had bought because it was big enough he could fit a girl in it with him for sex. Right now, his ass was comfortably stuck to the leather seat, and his pants were around his ankles as the dark, brown-skinned girl on the floor between his knees slipped the condom on him. She finally got the timing down right and knew when she heard a certain part of the recording she needed to get ready to take him in her mouth. It was a good thing too, because even though he was beginning to like her, if she disappointed him again, he would send her back to her pimp and let him handle her. She had gotten much better over the couple of weeks she had been with him. Maybe she was sold cheap and was a bit strung out when he found her, but it didn't mean she couldn't learn. He took a breath, released it slowly, and refocused on the sounds coming from the speakers.

"Did you like that?" a soft voice echoed through the speaker. *"Yes,"* said a second voice even softer followed by heavy breathing and soft moans. *"You taste so good,"* whispered the first voice, *"I don't know if I told you, but I missed your taste."* The second voice, heavy and sultry, oozed from the speakers, *"I hope it did something for you."* "Oh, it

did," the first voice confirmed lilting upward breathily. *"Can you feel that?"*

"Now!" said Mason excitedly and then felt the girl take him into her warm mouth. "Oh, yeah!" This girl had promise. He could tell the sounds were working on her just as they were on him.

A soft moan came from the speakers. *"I can feel it,"* said the voice. *"It feels like you're doing a good job for yourself. What are you going to do next?" "This,"* whispered the first voice, and there were soft noises for a few moments. A soft chuckle came from the second voice. *"Is this for me now? I thought you were doing things for yourself."* The first voice answered with a little sass, *"I am doing things for myself, things requiring you, remember? And right now, I require you to finish what you started in the pool." "Oh, really,"* said the second voice after a bout of heavy breathing and the sounds of kissing. *"I was just checking things then. I can tell you're doing fine now, though."* There was a soft moan from the first voice and the second voice continued, *"Yeah, it feels like you're doing really well. Do you require anything else from me?"* asked the second voice sensuously. *"Please, Rafe,"* moaned the first voice, *"I need you inside me."*

"Yes, please, Rafe." Mason laughed as the girl kept the steady rhythm on his hard cock. He could feel himself twitch excitedly as the girls throat vibrated with a moan. He knew for a fact she was with him now, and it was going to be great this time.

"Is this all you need?" asked the second voice. *"I don't think it is. I think you require something else from me. Tell me*

what you really require." The first voice spoke with a sigh, *"Oh, Rafe,"* and breathed heavily. Then the room filled with the sounds of soft moans and kisses and more soft calls for Rafe. *"You need to say it, I know you want to say it,"* encouraged the second breathless voice.

"Say it!" called Mason desperately close to climax as the girl started moving faster along his length, using her hand and flicking her tongue over his head.

"What the hell are you doing?" barked an angry voice.

Mason, focused on getting off, barely registered the angry voice as he felt his chair kicked hard, sending him reeling and toppling him from the chair, taking the girl onto the floor with him as the voices continued from the speakers.

"I... I require you to," Eden said breathlessly, *"to fuck me, Rafe."* Her voice resonated through the speakers. *"Ah,"* she breathed out in a long breath barely able to breathe back in. *"Yes, Rafe, yes."* The room filled with the sounds of escalating passion. *"I love you, Rafe,"* Eden's voice echoed softly through the room.

"What the hell?" Mason groaned from the floor as he held himself with eyes watering. He untangled himself from the girl.

"Turn it off now!" Jake demanded in a fury.

Mason looked up at Jake furiously with watery eyes. "You could have killed me!" he screamed angrily as he struggled to make his way to the computer holding his throbbing and injured member. He turned off the sounds of Rafe and Eden having sex and glared at Jake. "Why the hell did you do that? She could have bitten my dick off!" he yelled pointing at the dark haired girl who cowered on the floor.

"Classy, Mason," said Daniel with a tolerant laugh. "Does the reverend know you get blow jobs in your office?"

Mason scowled at Daniel as he lifted his t-shirt, exposing his hard surfer abs as he fastened his baggy pants. "I'm a soldier too," he spat. "I can do what I want!" He shot a superior look at Jake. "At least I'm not failing a mission."

Jake clenched his fists wanting to punch him and then looked over at the hooker on the floor. "Get her out," he said evenly and nodded toward the girl in the corner.

Mason looked over at the girl and rolled his eyes. "Fine," he sighed. He pulled out his wallet and took out some cash. "Come here," he said to the girl firmly. The girl got up and walked over tentatively, and he shoved the cash in her hand. "Go down the street and get some food. Come back in an hour," he said and watched her nod. She started to leave, and he grabbed her arm hard. "Wait! Go to McDonald's and get a garden salad and water," he took the money back, counted out less money, and gave it back to her. "I don't want you going to Taco Bell. I can't stand the smell of that shit on your breath." He pushed her toward the door. "I don't want you buying drugs, so if you get a bump, it better not be with the cash I gave you," he warned. "Bring me the receipt for the food or Tony will get you back tonight." He smiled when he saw the fear in her eyes because he knew it meant she would comply. If it took fear to keep her clean for now, then so be it.

Daniel leaned against the desk and watched Mason deal with the girl for a moment before turning his attention to the equipment in the room. Mason was supposed to be a genius computer tech and sound engineer. They had recruited him to head all the surveillance in the area. Though he specialized in information procurement or hacking, and sound engineering, he was very good with all types of surveillance from phone tapping to aerial surveillance with remote control drones.

It was no secret Mason Essex was one of the reverend's favorite soldiers. Daniel thought one reason was probably because one time, for a mission, Mason was able to bug a law office. They knew everything the lawyers were planning and were able to crush them in court. It was probably also the reason Mason got away with things like having prostitutes in his office and saying the things he did.

Mason always complained the Stewards couldn't do anything high tech because they were too cheap to buy any modern technology. He said the Stewards were a low-tech operation because they had low-tech minds running the show. Most of the equipment did look pretty old, but it didn't seem to keep Mason from doing his job. Daniel wasn't sure how Mason would turn rescuing innocents from the unrighteous and immoral people whose hands they were undeservingly delivered from low tech to high tech. It seemed to Daniel as if they were pretty high tech with all the online things they did with social media and computers. Plus, they only had so many soldiers to send out to the more difficult missions like the one they were working now, and there was really nothing high tech about dealing with regular people.

Mason closed the door and made his way back to his chair. He sat it back up on its wheels and plopped down on it. "So, to what do I owe the displeasure," he asked acidly as he adjusted himself.

"I'm here for the tapes," said Jake shortly. He didn't hide the disgust he had for the shaggy looking guy. He wanted to write his behavior off to the fact he was young and grew up as part of an entitled generation, but this time, he had gone too far. Walking in and hearing the familiar voices of Eden and Rafe, then realizing what was happening on the tapes, and seeing the girl going at it on Mason made him snap. He didn't know why but he felt something like a fury of protectiveness, or maybe it was possessiveness. It was his mission, and he didn't like Mason getting off while listening to her, especially when she was having sex.

"Sure." Mason shrugged and pushed his chair back toward a file cabinet. He pulled open a drawer and removed a flat box. He opened it and pulled out a USB drive. He put the box back, closed the drawer with a slam, and tossed the drive to Jake. "There ya go," he said with a smirk. "It's not called a tape anymore by the way. It's a sound file." He looked at Jake and knew by the way he clenched the drive in his hand, Jake was still pissed, but Mason didn't care. "Do you want me to add the fucking to it?" he asked coarsely. "I don't usually find it stimulating but that Rafe chick can be a real mind fuck, and I really get off on it." He laughed crudely.

"You son of a—" Jake started and then went after Mason with the intent of beating the life out of him.

"Whoa!" Daniel shouted and pulled Jake off Mason. "Calm down, Jake!"

"Yeah, calm down, Jake!" said Mason trying to act unfazed by what it took for Daniel to hold Jake back. "What's the big deal?"

Daniel felt Jake relax and released him, but made sure he stayed between the two. "It's just been a stressful mission," he said looking from Jake to Mason. "It's taking too long, and the reverend has gotten involved personally."

"Were you able to bug Katheryn Hardam's offices and home?" asked Jake harshly.

Mason looked at Jake again and the anger he was displaying. Dealing with pricks like Jake was a pain in the ass. "No," he said with frustration. "I told you and the reverend, if you want me to bug her office, then you have to buy state of the art equipment. She has a sweep company and modern preventive devices. Whoever does her security is very good. You can't even pull her home up on satellite mapping systems."

"Well, what the hell can you do?" demanded Jake.

"Nothing," quipped Mason with another shrug as he rolled his eyes at Jake's dark look. "Listen, surveillance is about who has the best equipment. We don't have it. So it means you need to get information another way. Figuring out what other way is your department."

"Hack in," suggested Daniel.

"Can't," said Mason as he stretched. "They use a closed in-house network not hooked into the internet for internal work. For correspondence and external research, they have the best security and firewalls money can buy. I told you, she hired a really good security firm."

"Shit!" yelled Jake in frustration. "We have to win this case if we end up going to court."

"Then don't end up in court," suggested Mason with a sneer as Jake glared at him. He noticed Jake's lip was swollen, bruised, and split open. "Your face looks like shit." He snickered and looked at Daniel. "Did he tell you what happened the other night?"

"Shut the fuck up," growled Jake realizing what Mason may have heard because he had been at Rafe's house Friday night too.

"What?" Daniel asked as he looked from one to the other in confusion. "He tripped in the dark."

Mason let out a big mirthful laugh and wiped a tear from his eye. "Tripped?" he squeaked and managed to control himself. "No," he said and cleared his throat. "Rafe punched him in the mouth," he said and laughed again.

"She what?" asked Daniel in surprise and looked at Jake. "She punched you?"

"I have it all on file," Mason confirmed happily. "She knocked him on his ass!"

Jake glared at Mason as he wanted to throttle him. "It's all part of the mission," he said evenly. "She likes to think she's powerful, so I'm letting her think she is," he said in what he thought was a convincing lie.

"Right," mocked Mason knowing Jake had lied. He looked at Jake, and even though he was smart, he couldn't help himself from torturing people he thought were idiots. "You know what I think?" he asked with mock thoughtfulness. "I think you have a thing for Rafe." He smiled and watched Jake go red with anger. "It's just a thought," he said acting innocent and looking over at Daniel. "If he does, it could affect his mission."

"Mason, come on," said Daniel exasperated with how they were bickering. "Jake doesn't have a thing for Rafe. You're just mad because Jake thought what you were doing when we walked in was offensive."

"Right," said Jake with a nod, too angry to say more. *I don't have a thing for Rafe. I don't,* he told himself. She was just part of his mission, and Mason needed to respect it.

"I don't know. Sounds like tough love to me," Mason said with a smarmy tone. "A beautiful woman beats you up and has you telling your buddies you tripped in the dark like a scared housewife!" Mason burst into peals of laughter holding his side.

"She's not beating me up," said Jake with a clenched jaw and tried to get his hands on Mason again, but Daniel stopped him.

Mason looked at Daniel and arched his brow. "Daniel, what do you think the reverend will conclude?"

Shaking his head as he pushed Jake back, Daniel had no idea how to answer Mason's question. He looked at Jake and couldn't understand why he wasn't defending himself more. Instead, he was just getting angry and physical. It wasn't how they were trained to do things. He ran his hands through his hair and sighed. "It's true, isn't it?" he asked hoping Jake would deny it. "You're attracted to her in some way."

"Don't listen to him, Daniel," said Jake in a harsh, angry whisper. "He's grasping at anything, so we won't report him for misuse of mission surveillance tapes and having a hooker in the building."

"Come on, Jake!" Mason goaded. "Admit it. You wanna get sweaty with her!" He laughed again, queued up a file, and hit play.

Rafe's sultry voice came through the speakers, *"You need to say it, I know you want to say it."*

Mason turned his chair around and looked at Jake with a sneering smile. All the mission soldiers he dealt with were just like Jake and thought since their assignment was to go out and fuck some lesbian, they were special and everyone should kiss their asses. The only thing making it bearable to deal with them was finally being able to take their ego down a notch. He thought about what he knew of the mission Jake was on, which was a lot, and suddenly, it clicked for him—this was the perfect opportunity to vaporize Jake's ego. He just needed a little time and a little information, both of which he had plenty of at his fingertips.

"Anything else?" Mason asked impatiently. He was ready for them to leave so he could get back to the girl and then start on his new pet project.

"Yeah," said Daniel, "we need to use the portable listening equipment again."

"Fine," Mason sighed as he grabbed his clipboard and made his way out of the office to the warehouse.

The equipment was stored on the shelves in labeled tubs to keep off dust. Mason pulled out the two tubs they would need and opened them to check the contents. When they looked it over, he made them sign the checkout form on the clipboard then took their photo with the equipment. They finally got everything packed into Jake's SUV and went on their way.

Mason went back to his office to wait for the girl and lay out his plans for his pet project he had decided to call *The Jake Off*.

35

IT WAS A busy Friday morning in Rafe Salvaggio's office. She was trying to get all of her calls in and take care of anything urgent so she and her TA could take the afternoon off. Since she was able to leave the office early, it meant she could work in the photo lab for the rest of the day. Being in the dark room and playing with the light and chemicals reminded her of when she went to work on her conservation projects.

Though construction was quite different from photography, she was still always looking closely at details, scouting locations, creating plans and composing different elements, and recording minute details. In the darkroom, she was mixing chemicals to develop film and using photo enlargers to print photos. The enlargers—both color and black and white—took a lot of patience and attention to detail. Adjusting light, filters, time, the negatives, and other factors to make an interesting print by hand was a true art form.

The photography project she would be working on today though would not involve the dark room. This time she would be spending time in the digital lab because the assigned project in the class she was auditing was using digital media. She used a professional Nikon digital camera rated best in its class, and it came with several lenses and effect filters. The Conservatory used the academic edition of Adobe Suite, and the professor was on top of regularly updating the software and making certain the students had access to other online options for photo editing.

Rafe had been out very early in the mornings all this week taking photos of surfers. She was happily surprised at their openness and willingness to let her photograph them—even after she told them, despite her 'super cool' camera, she was not with a big sports magazine. In return for their kindness, she brought them breakfast treats from the Bistro and USB drives with copies of the photos she took.

She caught many great moments of them out on the water using her telephoto lens. Both the young men and women were impressive riding the waves on their colorful boards. Sometimes, it looked to Rafe like the waves were actually chasing them to shore. On a couple of days, a few of them were tearing across the water on boogie boards doing flips and other amazing jumps into the water. After they came in exhausted and lined their colorful boards up in the sand, the photos became more personal.

Usually, someone was there to build a fire so everyone could unashamedly strip out of wetsuits in front of it, and then slip into dry clothes. Rafe was careful not to take photos while they were changing—until they all, as the kids put it, 'went National Geographic,' and said everything was fair game. She was careful to take tasteful shots subject appropriate, and they all loved what she showed them on the display screen.

When they were dressed and dry, they would hang out by the fire to warm up and talk about their rides and the waves as

Rafe took their photos and captured the excitement on their faces. Every one of the kids out there seemed to have busy and successful lives in school or at work, and Rafe enjoyed talking with them.

Rafe smiled as she remembered one particular kid who just really seemed to need someone to talk with about everything from life in general to help with his future. He was into everything technology and felt all the restraining forces in his life were holding him back. He was a smart kid, and he had sent her information on some amazing new digital imaging software for her photography. She already forwarded the information to the photography department to see if it had academic applications. In return, she had sent him information on opportunities available to help him expand his experiences and help him feel less restricted. She was glad he had taken the initiative to look into the information she had given him. He was now applying for an intern program, and she had a feeling he would do well. The thought reminded her she had received an email from him and needed to write him a letter of recommendation.

Opening her task list, she added the letter and coded it a high priority. She looked at it for a moment, and then she deleted it and opened a blank document. It only took a few minutes to compose the letter, and she sent it to her TA to look it over and put it on letterhead. Brandy usually added a few well thought out points based on the application and other information sent with the recommendation request. The letter would go out today so the kid could get his application in for the intern program quickly. He was a great candidate for the program, and the company was always in need of several English speaking and reading interns, so they would probably scoop him up as soon as his application hit their desk.

Rafe just wished her personal life was going as well. She hadn't seen or heard anything from Jake since the dinner party over a week ago. It worried her some, but she was beginning to think he finally did what she told him. It was so hard to tell if Jake was the only one she was fighting as a rival for Eden's love or if she was really fighting them both for the dream of having the family and life she hoped to save. Eden hadn't mentioned Jake at all, and Rafe hoped it was because there was nothing to mention. Still, there was the note Jake had shown her, and it continued to give her doubts. It seemed like she and Eden were getting closer, and she wanted to believe Eden loved her, but she still hadn't answered any of her questions, and again, the note with those damn intertwined hearts.

36

JAKE THOMPSON PULLED up to the dated industrial building in his black SUV and parked in front of the gray metal man-door. He looked over at Daniel, who had been silent for most of the drive. They both received a text from Mason saying there was a mission review meeting today, and Jake was pissed. Who the hell was this little prick to call him to a review meeting? If he had his hooker in there again, he was taking matters to the reverend, and hopefully, he would ship the brat back home to mommy. If not, then he better stay out of his line of sight because the next time he saw him, Daniel might not be around to stop what he had coming.

"What do you think this is about," asked Jake gruffly.

"I don't know, Jake," said Daniel annoyed. "Maybe the fact you're avoiding the reverend and you haven't made any attempt to rescue the charge."

"Have you seen an opportunity?" asked Jake hotly and waited for Daniel to answer. "No? Well, neither have I! Eden has been keeping a tight rein on Bronte since the last attempt. Unless you want to arrange a riot or a stampede of people to cause confusion so we can take her, there's not much I can do. But even then, you need to get them in an open public place, and they haven't been going to places with her where it would work."

"We need to give him something," insisted Daniel.

"I know!" snapped Jake and hit the steering wheel. "We just have to wait for an opportunity, though. If we have patience, she'll let her guard down, and we can make a move. We just have to make sure it's a move designed to do the most damage."

Daniel looked at Jake with a frown. From his point of view, the move just had to result in a successful mission. "Let's go," he said and opened the door. "Remember to keep your cool."

They entered the gray man-door, walked past the shelves full of equipment to Mason's office, and found the door locked.

"What the hell?" Jake grumbled.

They went over to the conference room then, and Daniel turned the handle and looked at Jake questioningly as he pushed the door open and they walked inside. The conference room, painted to look like the inside of an old church, had textured walls in a terracotta color. On one wall, there was a large silver cross, and on the other, a portrait of Jesus, and one of the founders of their church, Reverend Ezekiel Cazzak.

At the far end of the room, a podium stood in the corner, and a white screen hung from the ceiling. Filling most of the room was a long conference table with chairs to the sides and an imposing executive chair at the end. Sitting in the chair with two silver bowls in front of him and his head bowed in prayer was Mason. He was wearing white regalia with a white beret on his head with a gold cross on the beret denoting his authority.

Jake stopped short and looked at Daniel in confusion but found him looking back with a questioning look. Before either could say anything, Mason stood and looked at both of them in turn, and then lifted his arms. Silently, he made the ritual signs of blessing over the gathering.

"Come forward," said Mason solemnly and looked at Jake and Daniel expectantly. When they stopped in front of him, Mason offered them a bowl with wine and a bowl with ashes. "Christ shed his blood for you. Will you once again take this symbol and pledge to shed your blood for him?"

"I will," they answered and dipped their fingers into the wine.

"Our Great Leader on Earth saw the vision of innocents being burned in the depths of hell so evil could be forged from their ashes. Will you once again take this symbol and pledge to dedicate your life, following God's command to save innocents from such a fate?"

"I will," they answered and dipped their wine covered fingers in the ashes.

"Mark yourselves as soldiers, and may God be with us as we do the work we have pledged before him to accomplish," said Mason and watched as Jake and Daniel wiped the wine and ash across their foreheads. "Please, be seated," he said as he set the bowls aside then sat in his imposing chair at the head of the table.

When they were seated, Mason smiled at both of them and could see their discomfort with the situation. It was exactly his intent. He pushed the sleeves of his official robes of office up his arms and cleared his throat. "As with all mission reviews, this meeting is being recorded on video so, if necessary, it can be watched at a later date by superior members of our order," he said softly. He stood up and went to the podium where he turned on the overhead projection equipment and the laptop and brought up his first screen—*Kingsley Mission*. He looked at the two men and then at Jake, his intended target, and began. "This mission is in danger of failing. I have expressed my concerns, but I am sure, because of the circumstances at the time, they were not taken as seriously as they should have been. This is the reason I have called for an official mission review."

Jake looked up at Mason while clenching his fist under the table. "Are you kidding me?" he said trying to keep his voice calm.

"No," said Mason evenly. "I believe you're putting this mission at risk because you have developed feelings for a secondary subject, the woman Rafe Salvaggio, and this is why you're failing."

"You're fucking ridiculous!" Jake yelled as he stood up and slammed his fist on the table.

Daniel looked at Jake with a frown. "Sit down," he said softly. He didn't know what Jake was doing. They were being recorded. Mason was wearing a gold cross pin on his beret. It meant he had authority over them no matter what they thought of him. It just proved for a fact Mason was the reverend's favorite, and they needed to be careful.

Mason typed on the laptop, pulled up a file on the screen, and began typing again. "I never like to allow simple speculation to leave my department. I've found it's much more satisfying to know my work has integrity, is factual, and the probability factor of error is very low. Look at this," he said looking at Daniel, knowing dismissing Jake would anger him. "This proves I'm right. I ran an algorithm through Jake's reports, and he mentions Rafe at a much higher average than a normal secondary subject." He highlighted the results. "Scores high on sympathy and on commonality." He looked up at Jake. "Interesting."

"What?" Jake demanded angrily.

"Nothing," said Mason and looked knowingly at Daniel. He opened more files and pulled up a report. "Now this is even more interesting," he said looking at the image on the white screen. "I compared every time I notated Jake and Eden having sex and what preceded it," he said hiding his smile.

"What do you mean, *you* notated?" demanded Jake with a threatening growl. "Were you spying on us?"

"Of course I was," said Mason as he turned to look at Jake with a serious face.

"He's been accessing the Stewards confidential database files without authorization," spat Jake angrily.

"Oh, I have authorization," Mason assured him. "It's what I do! Like the reverend says, I watch and I listen so I may speak the truth into the ear of God's Great Leader on Earth." Mason smiled benevolently at Jake. "I tell him truths so he can know the status of his soldiers and their missions from a more objective point of view."

"So," Daniel said trying not to show his annoyance with the game Mason was playing as the reverend's favorite. "Come on, Mason. Let's stop wasting time. What does this have to do with anything?"

"You will respectfully address me as Imperator or Commander in this meeting and whenever I'm in my robes of office or displaying my rank," Mason said, his benevolence suddenly gone and his demeanor now menacing. He looked at the two men until they looked down buckling under his authority. "Oh, and this is not a waste of time, I can assure you," he said, relaxing since they were now compliant. "Jake is a liability. If you want to fix it, you'll shut up and listen." He picked up a remote control and pushed a button. "There," he said softly. "I've turned off the cameras," he lied. "Now, we can work this out today—my way. Or we can take it to the reverend immediately. He'll fail Jake in the mission, and you know what that means." He found his smile again and looked at Jake who was trying to hide the fact he was seething. "What do ya say, Jake? You want to go through reprogramming with the shrink you and Eden went to for your little bedroom problems?" He winked knowingly.

Jake looked hard at Mason, and his blood ran cold. Reprogramming was not a joke. It was usually reserved for those who were too high risk to let loose in the world with what they knew about the Stewards, but who they also couldn't make just disappear without a lot of questions. It was also disturbing how Mason knew about the fact he and Eden went to see the psychiatrist and the issue they discussed.

Daniel didn't like the power play happening now and was getting a new understanding of why the reverend might treat Mason as a favorite. "No one is going to reprogramming," he said calmly and tried to say something more, but Jake cut him off.

"What the hell are you talking about, Mason?" fumed Jake, "I'm not a liability! I'm dealing with things!"

Mason noted Jake's disrespect in not using his title, turned from him, and instead, addressed Daniel. "He's sabotaging himself so he can stay in the mission longer," Mason declared and nodded at their shocked faces. "Look at this comparison. Jake and Eden started going to the shrink because they were having problems in the bedroom," he said and pointed at the document on the large screen. "Then they argue about Rafe and boom! They have sex. Suddenly, they're having a lot of arguments about Rafe and have sex right after." He looked at Daniel. "I don't know about you, but it looks to me like both Eden and Jake have a little something going for Rafe," he surmised with a wink.

"You're sick!" Jake spat angrily clenching his fists.

"Hey, the numbers don't lie," he asserted with a shrug. He began typing on the laptop again. "I'm gonna help you out, Jake," he said as he worked. "I'm gonna tell you the odds of you doing the dirty with Rafe." He hit the enter key and turned to look at Jake. "Your chances are less than point zero six eight seven nine five percent. Not good. You're just not compatible, even if she weren't a lifer," he said with a churlish smile.

Daniel held his hand up in front of Jake. "Don't," he said stopping him from leaving his chair and moving toward Mason, "he's just trying to provoke you." Daniel looked at Mason. "One coincidence means nothing. He's not sabotaging anything, and he's not going to sleep with the woman." He was glad Mason had turned off the cameras for all their sakes.

"Oh, I know," Mason assured him with a soft laugh. "He's definitely not going to sleep with her. The closest he'll ever be able to say he got to her was when he slept with Eden, and he couldn't keep her in his bed even when invoking Rafe." He chuckled and looked at Jake. "Just admit it, Jake. I have all the proof in here," he said and pointed to the laptop. "You weren't upset because of what I was doing when you walked in on me listening to the recording. You were upset because you have a thing for Rafe. You heard her voice, all sexy talking to Eden, and saw me getting off, and you were jealous. You sympathized with Rafe when you were with Eden." He moved around the podium and leaned on the table toward Jake. "I'll bet you thought you and Rafe were cut from the same cloth." He watched as Jake's eyes shifted from him to Daniel and back and knew he hit a nerve. He went back to the laptop. "Then things started going downhill with Eden fast, and you scrambled. Friends, church, therapy, arguments," he paused and smiled, "invoking Rafe." Mason looked at Daniel. "He was so obsessed with Rafe he would make Eden talk about her all the time, and he wonders why she left him." He shook his head and rolled his eyes. "Then this beautiful woman, who you think you've defeated and dominated, comes out of nowhere and challenges you. It had to be such a turn on," he said as he pondered.

Mason looked over at Daniel with sympathy. "Jake thinks he's done so well all these years because he's some kind of a stud," Mason shook his head. "However, if you think about it, there have only been two situations, two," he repeated, "where he had to try to keep a woman in a sexual relationship for more than three months, and he failed at both. His own marriage and his current mission. You want to know why?" he asked Daniel. "I think this will be important for you to know because it may help you on missions when you're finally called up."

"Why?" Daniel asked hesitantly as he looked from Mason to Jake who was still just sitting there looking angry. He didn't understand why Jake didn't stop this whole thing and set the record straight.

"It's simple," said Mason casually. "Jake is a bad fuck. He's a terrible lover. He's shit in bed. He's got no game. He's a bad luck fuck. He's not up for the job. He's got the tool but not the skill. He's a one-pump punk. A woman sees him, and she goes from wet to dry in less than sixty seconds. He's the reason for the spike in double-A battery sales. He can't give no satisfaction," he laughed glibly. "Get the picture?"

"Who cares," said Daniel with dismay. "We aren't here to give good fucks. Just to do what we have to do to get the innocents out."

"What? Wow!" Mason laughed and shook his head. "Well, because Jake can't give a good fuck, he's failing to get an innocent out, now isn't he?" Mason looked at Jake again. "Jake only had one job. One," said Mason firmly. "Keep Eden in the fold to rescue the innocent." He paused to let the words rest in their minds. "But when the mission got prolonged, he couldn't perform. He couldn't keep her interested in sex—hell, he never even went down on her the whole time they were together."

"She didn't want that!" Jake burst in anger, his neck and face red with rage he could no longer hide.

"She's a lesbian, for fuck sake!" Mason laughed condescendingly.

"I would have fucked her any way she wanted it!" Jake yelled.

"You did fuck her how she wanted, but she still left," said Mason enjoying Jake's nosedive. "She left because you couldn't keep it up and keep her interested. Like I said, you're a bad fuck, Jake."

"Eden is a fucking cunt who doesn't know what the hell she wants half the time!" fumed Jake. "She probably won't even stay with Rafe long, so we're actually doing her a favor by splitting them up!"

Mason arched his eyebrows and looked at Daniel for a moment but didn't comment on Jake's last remark. "It was your job, Jake, to tell her what she wanted. You were there to be the Master of the household and guide her. Even with all your successful missions, you failed the task." Mason moved around the podium and sat on the end of the table. "But Rafe..." He chuckled. "Oh, man, now she knows how to give a good fuck. I could tell just by listening to her. She was making Eden cum with just a whisper in her ear. No wonder Eden ran back to her after dealing with mister lame dick," he concluded with another laugh.

Mason calmed his mirth, ignoring Daniel trying to calm Jake at the end of the table, and looked at the laptop again. "I read all your reports after the last surveillance detail I did of them because I couldn't figure out why you were fucking up so bad. It was then I first suspected, but now I'm sure I've confirmed it," he said smugly. "I've watched her," he said and licked his lips. "I've even talked to her several times when she was out shooting photos." Mason smiled at Jake and the dumb look on his face. It was as if Jake thought he was the only one who could have a conversation with Rafe. Having a conversation with her was easy. It was stimulating and enlightening too. "I'm telling you, Jake, you will never, never, ever, be on her level, even with God on your side." He tried to look at Jake with sympathy but ended up laughing again softly.

"Oh, now you're even daring to be sacrilegious?" asked Jake in a low, menacing voice.

"Oh, yes, I dare," confirmed Mason with a scowl. "I told you I'm here to speak the truth. You have to face facts. You aren't cut from the same cloth. She's cut from better cloth. You need to remember who and what you are, Jake. You're a servant. You're a boot licker. You're a failed husband who couldn't keep his own wife in line without the help of the church. You're a failing soldier whose mission is in jeopardy. You're a weak man beaten by a powerful woman. You're living in a delusion if you think you have any kind of sexual prowess or any kind of power. You personally never took or enticed anything away from Rafe. You're just a pawn of the Stewards. You're replaceable," he said pointedly, allowing it to sink in for a moment. "Rafe, on the other hand, has taken everything from you the Stewards asked you to hold. She even warned you she was going to do it, and she did it all by herself. You see the difference, Jake?" Mason stood back up with a confident grin.

"You don't know what you're talking about, you fucking little prick!" Jake seethed, the vein in his neck bulging as he jumped from his chair, fighting the urge to break Mason's neck. "I've got this under control, and she hasn't beaten me! This isn't over, and I'm not a fucking pawn!"

"Whoa, hey guys!" Daniel shouted as he got between the two, pushing Jake into his chair again. "This mission isn't about power or sex! It's about getting this little girl out of an unrighteous life and onto a better path toward God." He looked from one to the other for a moment. "I think you both may have lost sight of why we're here."

"No, just Jake," Mason said as he shook his head slowly. "This is what I've been trying to show you. It's why Jake is failing, and his reactions prove it. Your diagnosis is correct, Daniel. He has lost sight of why we're here. But my analysis is correct as to why. He has feelings for the woman, Rafe, and those feelings are affecting the mission. He's in a power struggle with her, and he wants to dominate her and have sex with her. He must confess it and purge it," said Mason calmly as he crossed his arms. "We have no choice now. We have to report this to the reverend, and he has to be sent to reprogramming. The mission needs to be reassigned."

"You can't do this!" screamed Jake angrily. He could feel his body break out in a sweat caused by fear of just the possibility of going to reprogramming.

"I can," Mason said calmly, "and I have to. I'd be negligent if I didn't. I could lose my job, and I am close to getting a promotion. I'll have my brass wing by this time next year. I'm not risking a promotion for you."

Jake looked at Mason in disbelief. Mason was getting a wing already, and he had only been a soldier for the two years since he got out of college. Jake had been a soldier for almost five years, and he was always told he was one of the best, yet he only had a brass cross. It took him three years to get it. It wasn't fair how this kid sat in an office all day getting blow jobs and got to move up so fast while Jake was out doing all the dirty work.

Daniel could see Jake was either too angry to speak or at a loss for what to do. Since this was his mission too, he needed to try to help save it. "Maybe," Daniel started hesitantly, "maybe you can give us a little time." He looked at Mason who frowned. "Since I know about this now, we can address it and fix it, like you said, Commander."

Mason sat down in the large chair at the head of the table and opened the file, looking at a few of the pages. "I'm not sure," he said with a sigh. He knew it was hard for Daniel to call him Commander, but it felt great it had happened. He would make Jake say it too before he left. "There are a lot of red flags from my perspective. Jake's avoidance of the reverend for one thing." He looked up at Daniel. "You have to understand I wouldn't have called this meeting if I hadn't found so many incriminating facts. It's very disturbing."

"I understand," Daniel assured him hoping to show him he was on his side. "I think we can work together on this."

"There's only one way I can think of to begin, and then whatever plan of action is decided on has to have certain requirements," said Mason thought fully.

"Tell us what you have in mind," said Daniel hopeful this would work out. He looked at Jake who was glaring at Mason.

"To start, Jake must confess," said Mason firmly. "He must unburden himself and then restate his oath."

Daniel looked at Jake. "That sounds okay, doesn't it?" he asked Jake nodding encouragingly.

Before Jake could answer, a soft tone interrupted, and Mason answered his cellular phone while the two men watched. After a moment, he hung up the phone and looked up. "If you'll excuse me a moment. This is a priority task." He got up and left the room, closing the door behind him.

Quickly entering his office, Mason smiled at the dark-haired girl who was sitting quietly making intricate folds to a piece of paper while she sat on the pallet he had put together for her in the corner. He sat down and turned his attention to his computer monitor. The screen showed the video feed from the active cameras recording in the conference room. He planned this moment to give Jake and Daniel a chance to scheme behind his back.

In the conference room, Jake was pacing back and forth angrily as Daniel watched. "I'll destroy him!" Jake vowed and hit a chair making it roll to the side. "How the hell did he make commander?"

"He's a favorite," said Daniel trying to stay calm. "They may have started him out at a much higher rank than where we started."

"Why the hell didn't we know?" asked Jake heatedly.

"There are probably a lot of things we don't know," Daniel guessed. "Who knows what they have him doing. We only really see him when we need something he can handle for us."

"Well, it seems lately, he hasn't been handling much of anything for us," Jake complained. "I wonder if it's something he's been ordered to do."

"Don't get paranoid, Jake. What we should be doing is figuring out what the hell we're going to do about this problem before he gets back," Daniel reminded him. "How the hell did this happen? Is he right? Is this why you don't deny his accusations?"

"Of course not!" scoffed Jake. "I've just been trying to create an opening." He had to turn and pace again because, even though he denied it, Mason had been right about some things. He did feel he and Rafe had similarities and they were in a competition. Battle was a competition. But all the other sex crap was bullshit. It was all Eden's fault, not his. Rafe deserved better than Eden. If he wasn't cut from a good enough cloth, then neither was Eden. Jake realized what he was thinking and forced himself to stop this line of thought because it was too close to Mason's accusation.

Daniel watched him pace and shook his head. "Jake, he's going to make you confess."

"I'm not confessing anything," said Jake evenly. "When he comes back in, we'll tell him we have a plan and we're taking to the reverend to prove none of what he says is true."

"Do we have a plan?"

Jake ran his hand over his head and face. "I don't know," he sighed. "No."

From his office, Mason rolled his eyes at what he was hearing. "Idiots," he said to himself. They couldn't even come up with a plan to save themselves. The more he worked with soldiers like Jake and Daniel, the more he wondered why he ever admired them. He took the page from the desk he had prepared before the meeting and went out of his office locking it behind him.

Entering the meeting room, Mason frowned distractedly at the two men and walked to his seat at the end of the long table. "Sorry for the interruption," he said politely. "There are some people who can't be asked to wait." He looked up at them and took a breath. "So, I think when I left, we had agreed Jake would confess, and we would come up with a plan to fix the problem and salvage the mission."

"I'm not confessing," said Jake flatly.

"What he means is we need time," Daniel said quickly, "to prove all of this was just Jake trying to open an opportunity. It's all just misinterpretation and misunderstanding."

Mason looked from one man to the other sternly. "So you're saying all of my analysis and research was a waste of time? You're saying the numbers and algorithms I've used in countless other cases with perfect results just happened to be wrong on yours?" He gave them a tolerant smile. "I don't think so." He looked at Daniel. "If you would be so good as to step outside. This way there will be no chance of random background noise in the video." He watched as Jake and Daniel looked at each other warily before Daniel got up and left the room.

"I have typed out a simple confession for you to read," Mason said and passed the sheet of paper down the table. "You will look up into the camera to your right and read it. Then you will go to a Soldiers Service and restate your oath." He looked at Jake as he gripped the piece of paper angrily.

Mason looked at Jake, and then he picked up the small remote control and pretended to reactivate the cameras.

Jake looked up at Mason and wanted to kill him. He knew Mason was recording him and this was a direct order from a superior. If he disobeyed, things would be even worse for him. He wished he had never been assigned to this mission. He wanted to kill Eden, Rafe, Daniel, the reverend, the psychiatrist and everyone else who had anything to do with putting this mission in his path. The threat and the fear of reprogramming not forgotten, it was the only thing keeping him in his seat. He was backed into a corner, and he knew he had no choice.

Jake looked down and closed his eyes for a moment then turned to his right and began to read the confession provided to him. "My name is Jake Thompson, Soldier 5th Tier, California Regiment in the organization *Stewards to the Protection of the Innocence and Morals of Youths*. I am speaking to all who see this video documentation freely and out of my own conscience for what I believe is the good of all innocents and mankind. We must root out the evil residing within the Stewards, beginning with the evil within myself. With this in mind, I feel it my obligation to confess the evil corrupting me and, by default, this organization, so it may be purged.

"I have allowed my current mission to be compromised by losing sight of the intent of the vision of our Great Leader on Earth. My mission was to rescue and remove the assigned innocent, Bronte Kingsley, from the unrighteousness she was born into and include the mother, if possible, for the convenience of legal transition to a godly environment chosen by the church. Instead, I allowed evil to fill my mind and heart, and it led me to direct my intent toward my own personal desires for sex and power.

"After reflection, I have come to regret my actions and the harm they have caused. With the understanding justice must be done and with the acceptance punishment must be doled out, I beg for mercy and forgiveness. I hope this confession shows the depth of my sincerity.

"Along with this, video documented evidence will be provided, and you will see it is indisputable. I will cooperate in all ways, to the best of my ability, to put an agreeable end to this dark threat."

Mason put the tips of his fingers together and put his hands to his mouth to help hide the smile forming despite his effort.

"Very good," said Mason softly. He got up, walked toward Jake, took the confession from the table, and folded it in half.

"If you would like, I can call the reverend or another chaplain to lead us in a private prayer." He watched Jake's face turn red again and pushed his luck by putting his hand on his shoulder. "I think, as soldiers, we can handle this matter ourselves." He bowed his head. "Great Lord, make our weaknesses your strengths. Make our failures your successes. Make our troubles your fortunes. We are warriors of the faith, and our hearts and arms are yours. Do as you will with us. Bless our Great Leader on Earth. Amen."

Mason took his hand from Jake's shoulder and went over to open the door. "You can come in," he said to Daniel. He made his way back to his seat and looked at the two lost men at the end of the table again. "Now," he said as if a burden had been lifted from them all, "we can make an outline to get this mission back on track. Of course, there will be certain requirements." He paused dramatically. "First, limit your contact with Rafe to only what is necessary to the mission. Reflect on being certain you aren't making it personal. Second, take back what the Stewards gave you to hold. You must find a way to save the innocent and the mother. It was the original intent of the reverend and the mission. They worked for two years to get what you lost in less than one. Third, you will be required to undergo a full psychological review when this mission is over to be sure you're fit for continued service as a soldier. I will hold your confession and will only give it to the doctor if it becomes important for the reverend to know about this matter. We need our soldiers, and fixing this, and having a successful mission, is what matters." He looked at the two men and nodded his head in satisfaction. "So, Jake, since you're the lead, what are your suggestions to fix things?"

Jake had been sitting in a stunned, angry silence. He didn't understand how Mason had shifted from a shaggy, fucked up geek kid to a perfectly dressed, confession demanding, prayer reciting, and well-spoken commander. He looked over at Daniel, who had nothing to offer except widening his eyes a bit. "I've been trying to come up with something," said Jake evenly. "It takes time. Sometimes, waiting for an opening is the only option."

"You don't have time to wait," Mason stressed. "A court date is on the docket. You need to either find a way to delay it or complete your mission before then."

"Our previous attempts have the mother on alert," said Daniel.

Mason frowned. "She knows about your mission? This is even worse than we thought."

"No!" both men said at the same time.

"No," Jake repeated. "She just thinks I was trying to get her to talk to me. She knows nothing about the Stewards. But since then, I've been acting like the love sick ex-fiancé, and she's a little scared."

"Oh," Mason said thoughtfully, "well, fear can be a powerful tool if used correctly." He let them sit in silence for a while. He already knew everything they could possibly tell him. He needed them to suggest working on the court case angle. "You've looked at all aspects of your mission, and nothing can be done because of the mother?" he asked with disappointment. "I thought you were the best, Jake. I know from my analysis, you're a horrible long-term fuck, but in other cases, where you didn't have to screw anyone for long, you did well. This will have to be added to your file." He wrote a note on the folder next to him. "It always comes back to the woman Jake couldn't keep in his bed." Mason sighed.

Jake clenched his fist under the table because Mason had just turned back into a punk kid again in his eyes. "What the hell do you want me to do, Mason? I can't get near enough to take the kid, and now, going near Rafe is off limits. My hands are tied."

"Why would you need to go near Rafe?" asked Mason with a frown. "Fucking her won't help the mission." He watched Jake try to control his anger once again. Jake really was obsessed with the woman. He hadn't realized it would be so hard to get him to back off her.

Daniel perked up as he realized what they could do to help the mission. "Maybe we could focus all our energy on the court case and get information for our lawyers for now." He looked at Jake. "Mason said we needed to find other ways to find out what's going on because their lawyer has such good security." He looked at Mason hoping this would solve the problem. "Jake and I could use the equipment we checked out and cameras. Jake could do his magic with his graphic design programs as he's done before. We could probably think of a lot of things to do to help the case."

Mason could feel his lip twitch, but he controlled the smile trying to take over his face. "So, you want to focus on the court case," he said thoughtfully. "That might be a good idea since it is approaching quickly."

Jake grasped at the straw Daniel held out. "It's a great idea. We can keep an eye out for other opportunities at the same time. Give us time to come up with a plan. A couple of days."

Mason stood up from his chair. "Fine," he said. "Send me the details. I'm sure the reverend will be calling you, so this will please him." He lifted his arms to perform the ceremonial signals for the end of the meeting. "Soldiers to attention." He watched as both men stood and took the attention position. "This review, executed by Commander Mason Essex, Imperator Technology Western Division, is at an end." Mason walked up to Daniel formally. "Bless you, Soldier, for your sacrifice for our God and our Great Leader on Earth."

Daniel saluted Mason. "Thank you, Commander."

Mason stood in front of Jake. "Bless you, Soldier, for your sacrifice for our God and our Great Leader on Earth."

Jake hesitated but only for a moment. "Thank you, Commander," he said evenly, holding in his desire to choke Mason.

"Don't forget to go to the Soldiers Service," Mason reminded Jake with a small smile before walking out the door and heading happily to his office.

Jake looked at Daniel angrily but didn't say a word as he turned and stormed out of the building. All Daniel could do was follow.

In his office, Mason watched the video feed as Jake and Daniel left the building. When they were outside, he turned to Trouble. "That was fun," he said with a grin. "I think this calls for Chinese food tonight. I have a little video editing job to work on now," he chuckled. "We'll take it to my apartment. I have much better equipment there."

He began to save the video of the meeting to a USB drive, and Trouble began putting away her paper. "Jake really is obsessed with our girl," said Mason as he worked. "Hopefully, he'll back off her now and focus on the court case and his charge. He may be right about her being better off without Eden, but we like them together. Don't we?" He grinned at Trouble and watched as she shrugged her shoulders almost imperceptibly.

He turned back to his work and thought about Rafe. "Jake is an ass if he thinks he could get a woman like her. Even if she were straight, he couldn't. Shit, I couldn't," Mason admitted with a soft laugh.

He looked over his shoulder quickly at Trouble again. For the first time, he wondered why she hardly spoke. He didn't mind, but he could tell she was smart. He wondered what the dumbass pimp Tony had done to her. He decided he would do research on girls in her situation so maybe he could understand why she did the things she did.

He looked at his watch. "Time to go," he said happily. "I don't want to be up too late. I want to surf in the morning."

37

RAFE SALVAGGIO WALKED through the campus and headed back to her office. She was in a good mood today, mostly because of the distraction of her job. Things were going great, and she was starting to enjoy her new academic career. She had just finished her morning special topics lecture, an overview of historic conservation. She would be doing specialized lectures, as well as some technical demonstrations, once the board approved and added the classes to the academic catalog.

She would love to show students how to do something like recreate an ancient paint or varnish or do a project remaking something like an architectural detail, restore period furniture or do a painting with a period theme like she used to do on her restoration projects. It would even be great if they could find a way to do an actual restoration somewhere over the summer. It was an amazing feeling to open up an old building and see time go by, with layer after layer removed, until finally, one makes it to the true intent of the architect. It was incredible, after the research was done, to combine finding the perfect furniture piece or painting for the property and then having the structure look like it would have when it was new.

Her restorations were not just patches, they were repairs done with the same techniques used by the original workers wherever possible. She remembered going out with her father and finding old buildings and historic properties and the deals he would make to buy them or compete to get the bid to restore them. They made great partners, him with *Salvaggio Real Estate*, and her with *Eroina Conservazione e Design*, her construction and restoration business. They always wanted to buy and restore an entire Italian village, but they were never able to accomplish their dream. She missed him and the work she spent so much of her life doing.

Of course, nothing would ever be as satisfying as seeing a grand, historical property perfectly restored or a landmark building reclaimed and retrofitted for modern purpose. But being able to teach even a small part of what she knew to students who wanted to learn it was turning into something she enjoyed more than she thought she might. Teaching was a nice break from her primary work as Dean. There she knew was where she made the most difference. As Dean, she was able to help students find a way to get what they wanted in the way of a career, and it gave her a sense of purpose. There was also the added challenge of raising funds for the department and problem solving for the instructors so they could give the students the best possible experience.

Rafe turned into her office and her TA, Brandy, was there to greet her.

Brandy held up a cup of coffee for Dean Salvaggio along with a handful of messages. "Only one priority call so far," said Brandy.

"Thank you," said Rafe with a smile as she took the mug and messages. "The lecture went well. I'm late because the questions put us over the time limit so we may not be able to skip out early today like we did last Friday."

"We can't win them all," said Brandy with a laugh, "but we can work hard trying."

"I agree." Rafe winked and lifted her coffee cup in agreement.

"I've got the new schedule for you to approve and there are letters on your desk ready for review and signature," Brandy said as Rafe entered her office.

Twenty minutes later, Rafe was finishing with a priority call and had signed or made corrections on about half of the letters on her desk while she was talking. As she was about to hang up and get another cup of coffee, the CCAD's president, Clarice Biggalow, walked in unannounced.

"There you are, Dean Salvaggio," said Clarice happily. "Good morning."

"Good morning, Clarice," said Rafe as she hung up the phone and smiled back at her. "What can I do for you?"

"This is Ms. Aykland," Clarice answered and motioned to the woman with very long blond hair standing behind her. "She's a freelance reporter working for the L.A. Times. She's here to interview you about the school, the Jackson-Goyer Grant, and the celebration coming up at The Kiki Bistro."

Rafe got up, walked around the desk, and shook the beautiful petite blonde's hand. "It's nice to meet you, Ms. Aykland."

Ms. Aykland smiled and held on to Rafe's hand. "You can just call me Melissa," she said warmly. "It's nice to meet you, Dean Salvaggio."

"Melissa, you can call me Rafe," she said and pulled her hand away gently but firmly.

"Well," said Clarice happily, "I'll leave you two to it. Make the school look good, Dean Salvaggio," she called as she walked out the door.

"I'll do my best," Rafe said as she watched her walk away. She turned to Melissa. "Where would you like to start?"

Melissa took out her voice recorder. "We can start with information about the grant, what you do here, your background, and then maybe a tour." She smiled alluringly. "Then, if things go well, maybe a cup of coffee."

38

EDEN KINGSLEY HAD taken the day away from the office and decided to visit Rafe at school to talk about speaking to the film class and to take her to lunch. She was very excited about working with her for the first time. Rafe's teaching assistant told her Rafe was already at *Artful Grind Café,* a little coffee shop on campus. Eden walked the short distance to join her, smiling at the thought of spending time with her again because she had hardly seen Rafe all week.

When she got to the café, she looked into the window and saw Rafe sitting at a small table with a woman. Their heads were very close together, and Rafe's arm was resting on the back of the woman's chair, her long blond hair partially draped over Rafe's arm. They looked very relaxed and very intimate.

The smile and color vanished from Eden's face as Cathcart's words jumped into her mind. *'I know you slept with her, but it doesn't mean she is in an exclusive relationship with you.'*

Eden stood frozen in place watching them together. As Rafe was talking, the woman watched her with a sultry smile, leaning in close—too close. As Eden watched, the woman touched Rafe's arm as if she were familiar with the soft texture of her olive skin. Eden felt her hands begin to shake and a sick feeling in her stomach. She walked inside and stood in front of their table nervously. "What are you doing?" she asked shakily.

Rafe looked up in surprise at the sound of Eden's voice and smiled. "Eden, hi. We're having some coffee," she said happily and motioned to the woman next to her. "This is Melissa Aykland. What brings you here? Sit down with us," she invited her to the chair across from them as her arm rested casually on the back of Melissa's chair.

Eden looked at Rafe then at Melissa, who had leaned back against Rafe and into her arm as flowing strands of her blond hair entangled with Rafe's dark curls. Eden clenched her fists, her heart pounding hard in her chest.

"I guess I forgot about the other rule," Eden said then turned and walked out of the coffee shop.

Rafe watched Eden walk away and then looked at Melissa in astonishment. "I have to go," she said as she quickly stood up. "It was nice talking to you. Thanks for the coffee. Call if you have any other questions for me. If you're going to visit any other historic buildings being restored, let me know, and I can get you some contact names. Just call. You can keep the map of New York," she called back to the blonde as she made her way to the door.

Rafe walked out of the shop quickly and went after Eden. "Eden! Eden wait!" called Rafe. "Eden, what's wrong?" Rafe asked as she caught up with Eden and stood in front of her.

"Oh, I don't know," said Eden angrily. "I guess I just wasn't prepared for you to humiliate me again so quickly!"

"What are you talking about?" asked Rafe confused.

"No, it's okay," she spat. "It's okay because I guess I just forgot the rule I'm supposed to remember—the one where you don't belong to me yet!" She burst into tears then turned her back on Rafe and started to walk away.

Rafe watched her walk away for a moment, unsure what was happening and then followed her. "Eden, wait!" She stepped in front of her again making her stop. "What are you talking about?"

Eden looked up at her as she angrily wiped the tears from her face. "It's fine! I get it! Just because you have sex with me doesn't mean we're in an exclusive relationship! You can screw whoever you want!" she hissed angrily then pushed past her as a new wave of tears fell from her eyes.

Realizing what Eden was thinking, Rafe laughed and went after her again. "Eden," she put her hand on her shoulder to stop her.

Eden shrugged Rafe's hand off and kept walking. "You're fucking laughing at me now? Fuck you!" she yelled, feeling like it sounded ridiculous coming from her mouth, but she really didn't care at the moment.

"Eden," called Rafe as she shook her head, surprised at Eden's words. She tried to explain as she followed, "She's a reporter for the L.A. Times. I was giving her an interview because of the Jackson-Goyer Grant. I wasn't doing anything else with her."

"I saw you. Don't lie to me, Rafe," Eden demanded as she stopped and rounded on her angrily. "You had your arm around her, and you were kissing her, and she was all over you."

"No, I wasn't kissing her," Rafe said emphatically. "I was sitting close," she agreed. "It was a small table. And there wasn't really anywhere else to put my arm. I didn't really have it around her. I was just resting it on the back of her chair. She wasn't all over me."

"I saw her! She was touching you and leaning so close, she might as well have been on top of you," Eden argued heatedly, her heart beating hard.

"We were looking at a map of New York," said Rafe as she threw up her hands. "I was showing her where some buildings were I helped restore. That's all. She was pointing at the map, but she never touched me. I swear," she said putting her hand to her heart and offering an open hand. She waited for Eden to respond, but she wouldn't look at her. "Come on," she said as she took Eden's hand and led her to a bench in a shaded area of the campus. They sat down, and Rafe put her fingers under Eden's chin, lifting her face up. "Eden, I wasn't doing anything wrong."

Eden pulled her face away from Rafe's hand as tears filled her eyes. "Of course, you weren't. You can do anything you want."

"Eden," Rafe sighed, "I'm not sure what you want from me. Do you want me to apologize for something I didn't do?" She reached out and wiped away Eden's tears. "I don't want to do anything to hurt you again. I love you. What do you want me to do or say?"

"I don't know," she whispered then turned away and pulled a tissue from her bag.

"You don't know?" Rafe smiled. "You have to be thinking something," she said and raised her eyebrows.

Eden looked at her with tears flooding her eyes. "I want you to take the rule away," she sniffed and dabbed her eyes.

"Take the rule away?" asked Rafe, not understanding.

"Yes," nodded Eden, "the one about me having to remember you're not mine yet."

"Eden," Rafe started to smile then stopped herself, "are you trying to control me?"

Eden looked up in surprise at the accusation. "No! I'm not... I—"

"Oh, that's too bad," said Rafe and bit her lip. "You were kind of turning me on." She chuckled. "I thought I was getting a little Alpha E." She leaned in and gave her a small kiss.

"Rafe!" Eden huffed, still angry but unable to hold back a small laugh.

"Don't be angry with me," Rafe implored as she stroked Eden's hair. "I really didn't do anything wrong."

"I'm sorry." Eden sniffed and wiped her eyes again. "I just—"

"It's okay" Rafe reassured her. "Do you really want me to take back my rule?"

"Yes," whispered Eden as she looked down at her hands before reaching up to gently dab the tears as they fell. "I want us to only be with each other," she said softly, "just like we used to be."

Rafe sighed and watched Eden wipe more tears away. "Can I think about it?"

"No, you can't freaking think about it. You're mine!" Eden yelled looking at Rafe angrily.

Rafe looked at Eden and thought about the note with the two joined hearts Jake had shown her and wondered just how much depended on her answer. "Okay," she conceded, "I'm yours." She looked into Eden's eyes intently. "Eden, are you mine?"

"Yes," Eden nodded as she wiped her eyes, "I'm yours. I love you," she said softly. "I only want to be with you."

"You okay?" asked Rafe as she took Eden's hand and watched her nod yes. "Okay, I love you too. Let's go," she said and pulled Eden up. She pushed Eden's hair from her eyes. "I have to say I was surprised when you told me to fuck off," she smiled teasingly.

Eden looked up and turned red with embarrassment. "I'm so sorry! Wait, I didn't say that," she protested.

"Oh," Rafe laughed, "that's right. It was 'fuck you.' Still, I'm very impressed," she said smoothly. "It's a big step up from peahen. Soon you'll be able to go Alpha E like a real bad girl!" Rafe grinned at her.

"Stop!" Eden flushed red again and couldn't help laughing.

Rafe smiled playfully then turned and led her down the sidewalk. "Why did you come all the way out here?"

Eden walked close to Rafe and held her arm tight. "I wanted to have lunch with you and talk to you about my lecture," she said pulling herself back together.

"So, they convinced you?" Rafe chuckled trying not to worry and wonder about what had just happened.

"They did," Eden confessed. "They're very persistent."

"They are persistent," Rafe agreed. "I'm glad you're doing it." She stopped and kissed Eden, refocusing on her and on work. "Let's get that lunch."

39

IT HAD BEEN a very good day for Eden Kingsley. She saw where Rafe worked and met many people who worked with her. Then she got a tour of the campus and the building where she would give her lecture. The students she met all had great suggestions for topics and seemed excited about hearing her speak. Rafe did everything she could to help her prepare, not only for the lecture, but also for dealing with the anxiety speaking in public would bring. This was not the first speech Eden had to give, but even after years of working and having to do presentations, Eden had to go through her process to deal with the anxiety they caused her.

At the end of the day, she went to pick up Bronte while Rafe went to pick up dinner from The Kiki Bistro. Eden swore if Rafe's cousin didn't own a restaurant, Rafe would probably starve. Rafe was terrible at keeping food in the house and remembering to grocery shop. She was also almost a danger in the kitchen and would do anything to get out of cooking. It was as if she had picked one thing to be bad at and decided it would be anything food related. Eden still didn't understand it because Rafe loved eating good food and drinking good wine.

After picking up Bronte, Eden drove to Rafe's house, and they had dinner together. The whole time, Eden couldn't stop thinking about how she felt seeing Rafe with the blond woman. She was so relieved Rafe had said she wasn't with her and agreed they would only be with each other. She should have listened to Dr. Cathcart and talked to Rafe about her expectations sooner. If she had, then maybe the whole situation wouldn't have happened.

Eden felt calm again being in a familiar place with the woman she loved. She had been searching for this feeling and knew now she would never find it anywhere else. It felt so good to be in Rafe's house with Bronte and just being together. There was so much she needed to talk with Rafe about, and it was so hard because she didn't want to mess anything up. She was going to wait on some things still, but she had decided there were a couple of big things she needed to try to talk to her about tonight. After what happened this afternoon, she was even more determined to talk to her about them. When they finished eating, Eden helped Rafe clear the table while Bronte sat in her booster seat, finishing her fruit.

Rafe put her dishes in the sink and smiled at Eden. "I'm glad you came out to the school today," she said and kissed her.

"Me too," Eden said happily as she rinsed off the plates and put them in the dishwasher. "I enjoyed the tour and seeing where you work. I never really got to do that much before."

Rafe nodded remembering all the traveling and private meetings she used to have when she owned *Eroina Conservazione e Design*. "By the way," said Rafe, "did you see I found all of your buttons? I didn't want Bronte to pick one up and put it in her mouth. I put them on the dresser a while back, and they're still there."

"I can just picture you crawling around looking for buttons," said Eden laughing at the thought.

"Who said I crawled around?" asked Rafe as she looked at Eden amused.

"So how did you find them? Did you use some geometry to measure trajectory and find each one?" Eden laughed imagining Rafe with a tape measure and a note pad.

"No, I vacuumed," said Rafe with a wink. "I just emptied the vacuum container, and then used it in the room until I had all the buttons, and then I dumped them out. No problem."

"Aren't you smart," said Eden impressed and wrapped her arms around her and kissed her. "I still would have liked to see you crawling around," she said and smiled mirthfully as she watched Rafe walk over to Bronte.

"I'll bet you would," Rafe chuckled as she took Bronte out of her chair. "You said at lunch you wanted to talk to me about something tonight. What's up?"

"Oh, it's nothing," said Eden quickly and took Bronte's plate to the sink. "It's no big deal."

"What? Tell me," Rafe implored as she held Bronte and seeing how Eden's mood had changed. She could tell something was wrong and thought Eden might still upset about what had happened this afternoon. The whole thing was bizarre. At first, Rafe thought it was some kind of joke, but Eden seemed genuinely distressed and angry.

"I just..." Eden hesitated because she wasn't prepared. "I just wanted to ask you something. Can we talk about it later? Let's just spend some family time together."

Rafe looked at Eden with concern but decided not to push the issue. She didn't know what more she could do about what had happened this afternoon. She gave her what she wanted and took away the rule about not being hers yet. The rule didn't matter anyway. It was just a tool to create an extra barrier she needed at the time. The real barrier wouldn't come down until she was sure Eden wasn't going to leave again. She hoped nights like this would show they belonged together as a family. "Okay, let's go build a city with the blocks."

Eden watched as Rafe and Bronte pulled out the large trunk filled with the wooden blocks Rafe had played with as a child. She remembered when Rafe's father had them shipped from Italy. Rafe said he told her he had found them in one of the properties he stored all the things they had left behind when they moved to America. He found the trunk when he was cleaning the place so he could lease it out.

They opened the trunk, and Eden joined them as they played, wishing she had brought a change of clothes so she didn't have to play on the floor in a skirt. Eden had seen the blocks out before when she picked Bronte up but never played with the two of them and was surprised Rafe let her get so many out of the trunk. She was also surprised at how they played with them. Rafe had taught Bronte some interesting stacking techniques. Some even included the furniture and bookshelves. She also apparently taught her a lot about demolition. Soon, blocks were strewn everywhere in different stages of very creative construction and destruction, and Bronte was falling asleep amongst them.

"Do you think I got her way too many blocks out?" asked Rafe as she started picking up some of the blocks close to her. She had hoped Eden would relax again as they played, but she still seemed a little tense.

"You can give her as many blocks as you want," said Eden and smiled as she pushed some blocks toward her, "as long as I don't have to pick them up."

"You played too, so you have to help clean up," countered Rafe as she laughed and picked up Bronte. "I'll go put her to bed first, though."

Eden followed Rafe into the guest bedroom and made a sudden stop. "Where's her crib?"

"It's gone," whispered Rafe. "She has a new bed. It just came yesterday, and I had them set it up since they botched the shipping." She put Bronte down on her new trundle bed. "This way she doesn't have as far to fall if she decides to get up in the night."

"What? When did she start getting up in the night?" Eden asked, extremely worried.

Rafe looked at her with a smile. "When you stayed over with everyone during the big storm, I caught her crawling over the edge. I tried to wake you up, but you took some sleeping pills."

"Oh," said Eden remembering the night, "I thought she was out for the night before I took one."

"It's okay. I can get her a trundle for your apartment if you want," said Rafe as she tucked Bronte in and gave her a kiss. "Eden," she asked cautiously, "is it okay for you to take those with your Xanax?"

"Oh, I'm not taking the Xanax anymore," she said shyly. "I just need help sleeping some times."

"Okay," said Rafe as she affixed the side rail to the bed. "I'm glad you don't need it. Come on," she whispered and led her out of the room.

After picking up all the blocks from around the living room and putting the trunk away, Rafe poured Eden a glass of wine and made a glass of scotch for herself. They took their drinks to the couch in the living room.

Rafe watched Eden as she sipped her wine. She liked how she was sitting on the couch with her legs folded off to the side. Her skirt slid almost up to her mid-thigh so Rafe could see from there all the way down past her shapely calf to her feet. Rafe put her hand on her leg, ran it over her smooth skin, and couldn't help the smile on her face as she thought of a way she could help Eden relax.

"So, why do you need help sleeping at night?" asked Rafe as she sipped her drink and moved her hand back up Eden's leg.

"I don't know," said Eden not wanting to get into the details of all the things she worried about. Feeling Rafe's hand on her was making her heart beat hard, and she wanted to kiss her. "Sometimes, I just have too many things running through my mind." She sat her glass down and then moved so she could lean in on Rafe to kiss her.

"I think," Rafe started as she moved her hands to Eden's hips because her legs were now out of reach, and Eden kissed her again, "I know what," Eden kissed her again, "your problem is."

"You do?" asked Eden breathlessly as she stroked Rafe's hair and face then kissed her deeply.

"Yes," said Rafe as she pulled back and looked at her seriously. "My diagnosis is you suffer from hysteria."

"Hysteria?" Eden shook her head. "Thanks a lot," she said acting insulted and pouting a little.

"You're lucky because I know the cure," Rafe said earnestly, loving the game, and loving how sweet Eden looked with her pout.

"Really?" Eden inquired doubtfully. "What is it?"

"Well, first we have to determine whether or not you want to be cured," she said and took the last sip of her drink then sat the glass down. She pulled Eden to her and began kissing her face and neck. "Do you want to be cured?" she whispered in her ear and slid her hands under her shirt feeling her smooth skin under her hands.

Eden smiled at the familiar taste of scotch in her kiss and the feeling of Rafe's breath against her ear. "Are you a medical doctor now too?"

Rafe raised one eyebrow. "I could be," she purred, "but I definitely know how to cure your hysteria." She looked at her with a glimmer in her eye. "You have to ask for the cure. You have to say 'Rafe, please cure me of my hysteria. Oh, please, please, Rafe.' Then I can give you the cure," Rafe said with a knowing and serious look as she ran her warm hands deftly over Eden's body as she continued to kiss her.

"I'm not saying that!" Eden laughed loving the feeling of Rafe's warm hands on her body and her kisses.

Rafe looked at her sadly. "Then you're doomed to a tormented life living with your hysteria. Too bad." She sighed heavily. "Poor hysterical Eden," said Rafe as she kissed her and pushed her back on the couch.

"Aren't you... afraid you'll... catch it?" asked Eden between her kisses.

"No," said Rafe as she kissed her. "I'm doing an intervention," she whispered. "I will cure you for your own good." She pushed Eden's skirt up and pulled her lace obstruction off in a quick, smooth motion. "Now, this cure," she said as she kissed the inside of her leg, "may feel really good," she looked at Eden with an impish grin, "but don't be misled. It really works," she assured her as she went down to deliver the cure.

Eden could feel Rafe's hands take hold of her hips then move under her to pull her up. "Oh, my god," Eden gasped at the feel of Rafe's tongue moving over her. "I love this cure." She moaned grasping Rafe's hair and head. "I'll definitely be, oh, asking for it," she gasped again, "next time, ah." She breathed and arched against the dizzying attentions of Rafe's tongue and lips. "Oh, Rafe." She exhaled as her heart beat faster. "Yes, yes, Rafe!" she breathlessly consented as Rafe pushed into her further with her tongue. "My freaking god," she cried out in a long moan of rapture. "Oh, I love you!" From that point on, Eden was entrapped in a sensory onslaught that stole her words and left her with only the intricate sounds air could make over her vocal chords.

40

AFTER RECEIVING HER 'cure,' Eden Kingsley held Rafe to herself as she lay back against her, feeling relaxed and loved. Surrounded by Rafe's scent, savoring the feel of her skin and hair and warmth, Eden stroked Rafe's hair and face. She loved this feeling having definitely missed it.

She thought about the time she had been spending with Rafe. It was so different to have their work lives overlap and have a meaningful connection, where before, a connection may have only been a name if the person had anything to do with Eden's industry. But now, Eden was working directly with Rafe, and the studio's human resources department loved the opportunity for recruitment.

It was also a lot of fun having time with just the three of them together. It seemed like Rafe did so many amazing things for Bronte, just like the new bed tonight and the way they played with the blocks. Eden smiled to herself because it was very clear Bronte already had Rafe wrapped around her finger.

Eden felt Rafe take her hand, lace it with her own, and kiss it. She couldn't help thinking about how different but familiar the things were when they had sex. She remembered sex with Rafe as always overwhelming but more careful and gentle. It was still gentle, but there were times when it was as if Rafe was a different person.

"Rafe," she said softly and heard her acknowledge her. "I love how you make love to me," she confessed and felt Rafe's kiss on her hand again. "Why, when we were together before, did you never do some of the things you're doing now?"

Rafe leaned her head back and looked up at Eden who kissed her forehead. "I told you, I've changed," she said with a small smile.

"I don't know," said Eden. "I'm not sure it has to do with you changing."

"Maybe," Rafe conceded. "Maybe I'm just sharing another side of myself now hoping it will make you love me."

"I do love you," she said and ran her hands over Rafe wanting her to feel the love she had for her. "I love all of you."

Rafe sat up and turned, pushing Eden back on the couch, and kissed her deeply. She felt Eden kissing her back and pushing her body into hers as they ran their hands over each other. She could feel her body react to the woman who was her addiction. She couldn't get enough of her but was terrified of being hurt again. Terrified Jake may be right.

After a while, their kisses slowed and gentled, until Rafe was lying with her head on Eden's chest and her hand under her shirt, feeling her skin and taking in the sensation of being in her presence and her embrace.

"Do you want to tell me now?" Rafe whispered.

"What," Eden asked, then smiled as she remembered Rafe telling her she had to ask for her cure. "Oh," she said softly, "thank you, thank you, Rafe, for curing me of my hysteria." She laughed softly and ran her hands over Rafe's hair.

Rafe turned her head, looked up at her, and grinned. "Thank you, but—not what I meant. What did you want to talk to me about earlier? You said it could wait until later." She paused. "It's later.

Eden held tightly to Rafe and started hesitantly. She then spoke very quickly. "I know we've only been really good for about two months, and I know we have a lot to work on," she said anxiously. "I just want to be near you all the time. I know you need your space, but I was just hoping." She paused, hoping her heart would stop pounding so hard. "I know it's not really our home anymore, it's yours." She swallowed and pushed on. "I want it to be ours again." She cleared her throat. "I just want to know if I can come back. I'll stay in the guest room," she promised. "I know you're not ready for me to move back into your room. I don't know," she took a breath. "Maybe it's too soon. I just feel so much better when I'm here."

Rafe looked up at Eden with surprise, and at the same time, she was amused with her rambling. "Is this your way of asking to move back in with me?"

"This is so hard, Rafe." Eden sighed and shook her head as Rafe sat up. She immediately missed the warmth against her. "I don't want to do the wrong thing." She looked into Rafe's eyes. "Yes, it's me asking to move back in with you," she said anxiously.

"I don't know," said Rafe quietly and frowned. "Will you let me think about it?"

"Of course," said Eden quickly, not wanting to push too hard with her request. "You should think about it. It's not like

I'm in a hurry, I just," she paused, "like I said, I just really feel better when I'm here—when I'm near you."

"Let me think about it," Rafe said then leaned down and kissed her. "It'll be okay. You can come over when I'm here as much as you want," she smiled and kissed her again.

Eden sighed into Rafe's kiss. "I love you. I really love you," she whispered, relieved the conversation had gone well.

"I love you too," Rafe whispered and lay with her back against her again.

Eden toyed with Rafe's hair as her troubles and her sessions with Cathcart raced through her mind. "Can I talk to you about something else?"

Rafe looked up at her and smiled. "Sure."

"Rafe," Eden said as she pushed her up so she could really talk to her. "I want to talk to you about my sessions with Bill Cathcart."

"Okay," said Rafe as she sat up again, this time with a little worry.

Eden sat up straight and looked down at her hands. She took a deep breath to prepare herself and began. "Dr. Cathcart helped me realize the reason I was so unsure about my feelings, and was so angry with you all that time. He said it's because," she looked up at Rafe nervously, "because even though I said I was over it," she paused, "what you did, your infidelity," she swallowed, "I wasn't. I'm not."

Rafe stared at Eden in shock for a moment then deliberately turned her body away and put her head in her hands. "*Fottermi,*[9]" she said under her breath as she wondered

---

[9] Fuck me,

how many more times was she going to find out Jake was telling the truth.

Distressed Rafe had turned away, Eden put her hand on her back. She had to get through this as Cathcart had suggested.

"It scared me more than I knew," she said to Rafe's back. "Those fears ran through every feeling and emotion I had for you turning them into," she hesitated, "into this anger I just couldn't get away from. But under it all, I was still in love with you, Rafe. I think knowing I was still in love with you made me even angrier, but at myself. It just, tied me up inside because I was afraid to love you," she paused, "afraid it would happen again."

"I see," Rafe said softly.

"Rafe," Eden said tentatively, "this is one of the things I couldn't tell you when we were fighting about Jake." She felt Rafe's body go rigid. "I was afraid if I told you then—" she swallowed her anxiety. "I think it was the fear I still have that made me react the way I did this afternoon."

"You do love me, don't you?" Rafe asked, worried.

Eden could hear the worry in Rafe's voice and needed to reassure her. "Yes, I do love you," she said softly and touched Rafe's back again. "I'm not afraid to love you anymore. I just still have the fear..." She trailed off.

Rafe took a breath and turned to look at Eden, fighting her emotions as they twisted inside her from white-hot anger to a deep black and painful grief. "Eden, I don't want to ever hurt you again," she said desperately. "What more do you want from me." She threw up her hands. "I've told you I'm sorry. I've tried to prove to you I'm truly sorry." She looked at Eden, fighting the pain flowing through her body and mind. "I don't know what else to do," she said sadly. "Tell me what you want from me."

"I don't know," she said seeing the pain on Rafe's face and in her eyes. "I guess I need to know why," she hesitated, "why did you do it? Why did you have to go to her? What did I do wrong?"

"You didn't do anything wrong." Rafe sighed not wanting to live through it again.

"Did you love her?" asked Eden cautiously dreading what the answer might be.

"No, you know I didn't, Eden," Rafe said in misery. "I love you."

"Then I don't understand," Eden said as she tried to hold back her tears, but she felt some relief Rafe didn't love the other woman. "Why did you do it?"

"Why does it matter?" Rafe asked in dismay. "I did it, and it was wrong. I fucked up, and I can't take it back. It doesn't really matter if there was a reason why. I betrayed you, and I know it. I understand it, Eden." She turned away from her again and put her head in her hands because she didn't have an answer for her. She didn't know why she did it and thinking about it made her head hurt. She could see the blackness beginning at the edge of her mind, warning of the pain to come.

"I need to know why," said Eden touching her back.

Rafe still could not look at Eden "Why do you want to know this? It'll just cause us both pain to relive it again," she said in despair.

"Because," Eden tried to explain, "I think we're both still in pain. I don't think it's really gone. I know it isn't for me."

"So, you think some great excuse is going to take away the pain?" Rafe said softly with disbelief.

"I don't know." Eden sighed. "I just want to know the reason it happened. You told me you lost control." She hesitated. "Why?"

Rafe turned around to face Eden and tried to be calm and push away the threatening headache. "It really doesn't matter what the reason was. It doesn't excuse my actions," she said evenly not wanting to think about that time again and everything she was going through then.

"So, there was a reason," she pressed. "I know I was hard to deal with sometimes, and I said and did some things," she hesitated. She wondered if Rafe knew what had been on her mind and what she had done online. If she did, then it could have been the reason. It would mean the blame for the affair would be hers as much as Rafe's. Maybe it was why she never did the things Jake said she should have done like sending her lawyer or begging her to come back. "I want to know what it was," she said insistently. "I want to know what I could have done to stop it, what I could have said or done differently so you wouldn't have done it."

"Nothing." Rafe shook her head. "You couldn't have said or done anything differently."

"I don't believe it," said Eden sadly. "If I know why, I can make sure it doesn't happen again."

Rafe let out a bitter laugh. "So, you think if it's going to happen again, it'll be for the same reason and happen the same way? You're not being realistic," she said shaking her head.

"Rafe, I'm trying to understand you, and what you were going through," Eden tried to explain. She didn't understand why Rafe wouldn't just answer her questions so they could both work through things.

Rafe took Eden's hand and kissed it. "And I am not going to try to justify my actions or put the blame on you or anyone else," she looked into her eyes, "for my wrong and painful actions," she whispered, "by giving you some excuse. It doesn't matter what I was going through. What I did was wrong. I made a promise to you, and I broke it. It was the pebble that started the avalanche and it's almost swept my life away."

"No, I don't believe that. Cheating isn't a pebble," Eden insisted. "There was something else, and I want to know what it was. I want to—"

"Stop," Rafe cut her off and took a deep breath, not wanting to feel the black painful hell it caused her when she thought about it. "Where are we right now?"

"What?" Eden asked, confused.

"Where are we?" Rafe asked again.

Eden looked around and answered hesitantly, "In your house?"

"Right," said Rafe and tried to smile encouragingly. "What are we doing here?"

"Talking," Eden answered unsteadily, "talking about things."

"Right again. Where is Bronte?"

Eden was even more confused. "In her bed sleeping?"

"Yes," Rafe nodded. "Do you love me?"

"Yes," nodded Eden.

"Don't you think all of this is fucking amazing considering all the pain we've caused each other?" Rafe asked, hoping Eden could just put the past away and be happy with where they were right now.

"I..." Eden stammered, "yes, I guess it is amazing."

"Tell me," Rafe paused treading carefully, "if we get back together," she saw Eden's look of concern, "I mean, really together, where everything is all worked out," she paused, "and I make the mistake of being with someone else, will you leave me again?"

Stunned by the question and the possibility, Eden struggled to answer coherently. "I, I," she stammered.

"You would, and you should," insisted Rafe. "Do you think I know you'll leave me?"

Eden nodded slowly "Yes," she whispered.

"Hell yes, I know it," Rafe exclaimed pointing to herself agitatedly. "I would expect you to. If you didn't, I would have to leave and go somewhere like Siberia or something because I couldn't stand to look into your eyes and see you in pain again."

"But—" Eden tried to speak.

"No, just listen," Rafe cut her off in frustration. "Do you think I don't know how many people I hurt? I know I can be a self-involved asshole, but I'm not totally blind all of the time," Rafe confessed and tried to calm herself. "I caused you pain, I caused our friends pain, I caused myself pain and believe it or not, I caused her," she sighed, "Lauren, I'm sure I caused her pain too."

Rafe rubbed her temples, hoping to stop the pain in her head from growing. "Everyone or anyone who was close to me or involved, I hurt. I don't want to make the same mistake again. I'm not perfect, and I can't see the future, but I am very confident you have no reason to be afraid I'll do it again. I know what I have to lose, and I don't want to lose it again," she said and looked intently into Eden's eyes. "Do you believe me?"

"Believe you? I…"

"Do you believe me?" asked Rafe as she nodded her head. "You're asking me to believe you love me and a lot of other things. I'm asking you to believe what I just told you."

"You're really not going to answer my question," Eden sighed and looked away.

"I think I did answer your question," said Rafe then sat back and crossed her arms.

Eden looked at Rafe and realized she wasn't going to say more about the issue. "Rafe," she hesitated, "I need you to know," she paused, "I need you to know I do still have that fear. It's something in me, and it scares me, and I don't know if getting over it is just a matter of believing you or not." She saw Rafe clench her jaw tighter and forced herself to continue. "I do want us to be together, like you said, with everything all worked out, but if we are going to be together, I will have some expectations of you in our relationship, and I know I'll have to live by those expectations too."

"Just tell me what you want from me," Rafe pleaded with her. "I don't want to live in the past, I want to move forward.

I've caused this fear in you, and I caused myself pain because I failed you. I don't want to fail you again."

"This isn't really about you, Rafe," Eden tried to explain. "It's about me not being able to get over my fear you'll do it again." She sighed, feeling like she wasn't really explaining things well. "There's so much more I need to tell you," she paused considering if she should talk to her now about when she was having feelings about men and her reasons for leaving her for Jake, but she decided to wait, "but I need time."

"Please, don't tell me this isn't really about me," said Rafe with a frown because it was clear this was about her actions just like Jake said.

Eden smiled sadly and touched Rafe's face. "You're right," she said softly. "It's about us."

Rafe looked at Eden wondering if all this really was just going to be about punishment. "And trust," Rafe said softly, wary of giving it to her again. She let Eden pull her close again but knew she would need to find a way to send her home with Bronte. Her headache was coming back, and it didn't look like this would be a good night for them to stay the night.

41

IT WAS A beautiful Sunday afternoon, and Eden Kingsley was spending it in the park next to her apartment complex with Bronte, getting some exercise. She had run several laps around the path, and now she was letting Bronte out of her stroller to play in the grass with her yellow ball. Eden sat on a bench watching Bronte and helping her when she needed it as she drank from her water bottle. She was thinking about calling Rafe so she could come take photos of all the cuteness happening. But Rafe said she needed some time to do a few things for work and run some errands today. Eden knew she was probably busy or just needed space after their talk on Friday. Going home Friday night was hard, but Eden could tell Rafe was troubled, though she tried to downplay everything. All Eden could do was reassure Rafe she loved her and keep her promise not to push her. Eden smiled down at Bronte playing and took a few pictures with her phone to show Rafe later.

In the parking lot, a black SUV pulled into a space and the engine cut off. The two men inside looked out through the tinted windshield, surveying the park and all the people around. They had followed Eden as she walked from her apartment building to the park and watched her run laps around the park path while pushing a runner's stroller. Since she was stationary, they were ready to put their plan into action.

Jake Thompson looked over at Daniel and handed him a camera. "Okay, Daniel, here's the camera. Whenever Hunter or me are near her, take lots of shots. It's a digital camera so go crazy. Just let me fix the settings," he said and took the camera back to make some adjustments. "I'll try to get close. I may even get a kiss," he said with a cocky grin.

"Well, it's a good thing your lip doesn't look bad anymore," observed Daniel as he laughed. "I can't believe Rafe actually punched you."

"Just pay attention, and don't miss the shot," snapped Jake, hating the reminder of his encounter with Rafe. He looked up at Eden and knew it would be much easier dealing with her. "I should have brought a video camera," he said regretfully.

"I've used a camera before," said Daniel annoyed. "You just make sure this works. The reverend isn't happy about how things are going with this charge. He wants to see you again, and he doesn't like waiting."

"I know, I know," said Jake nervously. "Just let me get something I can take him, and I'll go."

"He thinks you're losing your touch," Daniel informed him.

"I'm not losing my touch!" said Jake, unable to hold back his anger.

"What if Mason changes his mind and decides to talk to the reverend and tell him all the stuff about you having feelings for Rafe and hurting the mission?" Daniel asked, not liking Jake's outburst.

"Mason is a punk!" seethed Jake. "He sits in his office getting off all day and thinks he knows everything, but he has no idea what he's talking about."

"Maybe," Daniel said calmly, "but you heard what he said, and he's a commander. The reverend listens to him, and everyone knows he's a favorite. You can't beat the kid up just because he says something you don't like. Plus," he paused and looked at Jake, "you confessed."

"I had no choice!" Jake barked out angrily. He looked down at the camera in his hands and loosened his grip on it. He knew he was only angry with Mason because he was a disrespectful punk. He looked up at Eden and knew he didn't have feelings for Rafe. What they had was more of just a shared understanding of the frustrations of dealing with Eden. But Mason couldn't understand this kind of connection. There had to be respect between them like all opponents had for each other. It was all it was. "Things were going perfectly until the bitch got horny, and Rafe challenged me."

"You should have tried harder to stay with Eden so this wouldn't be happening," said Daniel matter-of-factly.

"Thanks. You don't think I realize that?" Jake shot back sarcastically. "I just have to be able to give the reverend something to show Rafe is unfit and the injunction might be saved. I think a picture of Eden with me will set Rafe back and make her rethink the relationship part."

Daniel looked over at Jake and wondered if, despite their review with Mason, he had become too focused on doing things to Rafe and not focused enough on rescuing the child who was the center of their mission. "You're supposed to stay away from her," he reminded him.

Jake snapped his head up and looked at Daniel through narrowed eyes. "I don't give a shit what Mason said. I've been doing this a long time, and I know how to get results. I don't even give a shit about the confession. After we do what I have planned, I'll be able to show Mason's wrong and his little computer program doesn't know everything."

Daniel looked out at Eden as she played with her little girl. "We could just take the kid. She's alone."

Jake looked at Daniel and shook his head. "We can't take her," he said in frustration. "Look around. Think! There are too many witnesses, and since she's back with Rafe, the police know exactly who to go after if we take her. Talk about the fastest way to go to reprogramming and kicked out of the soldiers. If the police arrest us, we're on our own. Is that what you want?" he asked angrily.

"No," said Daniel sheepishly. "What are you going to do about the injunction?" he asked as he watched Eden. He knew if he looked at Jake, the doubt would show on his face. He was beginning to think he should report everything to Mason to save his own skin. It wasn't what he wanted to do. He wanted to be loyal to Jake as a fellow soldier, but if Jake failed, things wouldn't go well for either one of them.

"I asked for Melissa's help." Jake gave him a twisted smile. "She's already been to interview Rafe. I'll give Melissa time to write her article and get it published so our lawyers can file another amendment. Then Rafe will get these." He tapped the camera. "A photo never lies. No relationship, unfit applicant, injunction stands, no adoption." He ticked each one off on his fingers. "I'm an asset, not a liability," he said confidently. "The best part is Mason will be proven wrong—because he is wrong," he added firmly. "I'll not only get what I want, but it will also take care of Mason's little requirement to take everything back."

"Let's get this over with," said Daniel as he shook his head—because the first requirement was to stay away from Rafe. Jake really was obsessed with her. He took the camera from Jake and focused it on Eden. "I'm ready."

Jake got out of the SUV and went to the back passenger door. He opened it and reached inside. "Come on, Hunter," he said as he unbuckled the car seat. "You want to see Bronte again?"

Hunter smiled and reached out for his dad. "Yes," he said happily.

"Well, let's go see her," he said as he picked up Hunter and started walking toward Eden. "You can see Eden too. You should give Eden a big hug, okay?"

"Okay," said the little boy as he smiled.

As Jake approached, he could see Eden and Bronte were playing with a yellow ball in the grass. When he got close, he put Hunter down. "There they are," he said and pointed to them. "Go say hi," he encouraged Hunter.

Hunter ran up to Eden and Bronte. "Hi, Eden," he said sweetly. "Remember me? I'm Hunter." He smiled and went over to Bronte to play with her and the yellow ball.

Eden looked at Hunter then looked around to see who was with him. She went over and bent down in front of Hunter. "Hi, Hunter." She smiled at the little boy. "Where's your mommy?"

"I'm with daddy," he said as he picked up the yellow ball. "He's coming," he said pointing over Eden's shoulder.

Jake walked over quickly and picked up Hunter. "There you are," he said and kissed Hunter on the cheek.

Hunter reached for Eden from his father's arms, still holding the yellow ball. "I want to give Eden a hug," he said shyly.

Jake smiled at Eden, looking embarrassed. "You don't mind, do you?" He looked at Hunter then back at her. "He doesn't understand."

In shock at the situation and not sure what to do, Eden looked around and then down at Bronte. She picked her up, afraid Jake was going to try to take her again. "Look, Bronte. It's Hunter," she said nervously.

"Can I have a hug?" Hunter asked again sweetly.

Jake looked at Eden and shrugged. "Can he?"

Eden hesitated and looked at Hunter as he smiled expectantly at her. She gave him a small smile back because she didn't want to hurt his feelings. It upset her Jake would use his own son like this. "Okay," she agreed reluctantly and hugged Hunter. Suddenly, she felt Jake's arm around her, and he kissed her on the lips before she knew what was happening. "What are you doing?" she shouted as she pushed Jake back. "Get away from us!" she yelled as she backed away.

"I'm sorry." Jake smiled and let out a soft laugh. "It was just too hard to resist. Hunter and I love you so much. Don't we, Hunter?"

"I love Bronte," Hunter said with a big smile holding out the yellow ball to Bronte.

"See, Eden," said Jake, "Hunter misses you and Bronte." He looked at Eden sadly. "I wish you would reconsider and be a family with us again."

"We're a family," said Hunter. "A mommy, a daddy, a little boy, and a baby girl. I'm the little boy." Hunter pointed at himself and smiled at Eden as Bronte held onto her yellow ball.

"I'm sorry, Hunter," Eden said as she looked from Hunter to Jake and then back to Hunter. "Bronte and I aren't in your family." She looked at Jake horrified. "We have to go. Please, stop doing this. I've gone back to Rafe. I love her. Like I told you before, I'm not coming back to you!" she said frantically then grabbed Bronte's stroller and walked quickly toward her apartment.

"Eden, you're making a mistake," Jake called after her. "She's not the right kind of person to have around your daughter." He watched her walk away without looking back. "Well," he said to Hunter, "at least you got your hug."

"I got my hug." Hunter smiled. "Can I have some ice cream?"

"Yes, you can," Jake cooed and chuckled at his son. "Let's go see if Uncle Danny did good enough to get ice cream too."

"Okay. I want chocolate," Hunter exclaimed in his small voice.

42

WALKING QUICKLY TOWARD her apartment complex, Eden Kingsley went straight to her car, wanting to get as far away from Jake as possible and as fast as she could. She drove away quickly, watching to see if they were following them. Finally, she pulled into the parking lot across from The Kiki Bistro and sat there with the car running until she stopped shaking. When she had calmed, she turned off the car and got Bronte and her stroller out and headed into the bistro. She was hot and flustered from her stress and the short walk but relieved by the air conditioning once she was inside.

She pushed Bronte in her stroller over to the order counter and ordered a drink and a snack for her and Bronte. She looked around and saw Letty. "Letty! Letty, have you seen Rafe today?" she asked anxiously.

"Hi, Eden," said Letty as she walked over. "No, I haven't seen her. She's probably out taking pictures if she isn't grading papers." She bent down to talk to Bronte. "Hey, little B, you having a good day out with Mommy today?"

The server behind the counter handed Eden her tray, and Letty helped her get Bronte to a table. They got settled, and Eden gave Bronte her drink. "I went by Rafe's house, and she wasn't there. Do you know where she went to take pictures?"

"I stopped asking," said Letty as she gave Bronte a french fry. "She goes to some very unusual places. But she usually stops in here to pick up dinner on her way home. Do you want me to tell her you're looking for her?"

"Oh, no," said Eden anxiously. "It's okay."

"Is something wrong?" asked Letty. "Are you okay?"

Eden was adjusting her clothes and fixing her hair to hide her anxiety. "I'm fine," Eden said. "I'm fine. Nothing's wrong. I just wanted to talk to her."

Flynn walked into the bistro and saw Eden sitting with Bronte and Letty. He went to the counter to place an order, got a drink, and then went to talk with Eden. "Hi, Eden," he said as he sat down. "Hey, Letty."

"Hey, Flynn," said Letty. "Eden, I've got to get back to work. I'll tell Rafe you're looking for her if she comes in," she said as she walked away.

"Flynn," Eden grabbed his arm as soon as Letty left. "I'm so glad to see you," she said relieved.

"What's wrong?" Flynn asked. He was concerned at how upset Eden looked.

Eden started shaking, "Jake showed up at the park today. I was so scared."

"Jesus, Eden. You should have called me," he said alarmed. "You should always have someone with you."

"I just—" Eden fought back her tears. "Everything was going so great with Rafe. I just forgot about him."

"You can't forget about him," insisted Flynn. "What if he finds out you know all this stuff about him? We need to tell Rafe. You need to talk to your lawyer and have her tell Rafe," he said. He was upset he wasn't there to protect her.

"Telling Rafe won't keep him away," Eden reasoned with him. "The hearing is so close. I want to make sure they throw the injunction out, and then I can tell her. If I tell her now, it could mess everything up with us. I have so many things I have to tell her." Her voice trembled. "We can't tell her about this right now. I'll tell you whenever I go somewhere from now on, okay? I won't do things alone, I promise. Please, Flynn," she begged him.

"I don't know," Flynn said uncertainly. "I want to keep helping you, but I'm not sure if agreeing with you is helping or not."

"Please, Flynn," she said desperately. "The court date is so close."

"Do you promise to tell her after the court date?" asked Flynn anxiously.

"Yes, yes, I promise," Eden assured him and wiped the tears away quickly. "I just need to wait until then. Please, promise me you'll keep the secret until then."

"Okay, I promise," Flynn agreed hesitantly. The waiter brought his food order over and sat it on the table. "I have to get this home," said Flynn. "It's for Stacey. She's sculpting a new alien and needs some food. Are you going to be okay? Do you want to come with me?"

"No, I think I should just go home," Eden said anxiously, not wanting to deal with Stacey. "I'll be okay. I need to let Bronte take a nap, and I have some things to do for work."

Flynn looked at his watch then back at Eden. "Okay, I'll wait for you to finish and then walk you to your car," he offered protectively.

43

FLYNN OGDEN WENT home after he made sure Eden got to her car safely and drove away. He had delivered Stacey her food, and while she ate in the kitchen, Flynn went into his bedroom. He closed the door, locked it, and walked over to the mirror. He reached behind his back and pulled his gun out. He looked in the mirror and into his own eyes and pointed the gun at the mirror.

"Bang, you're dead," he whispered.

He looked at the gun, pulled out the clip, and checked the bullets, and then snapped the clip back in place and pulled back the loading arm, loading a bullet into the chamber. He then checked the safety. He pointed the gun at the mirror again.

"I've been practicing, Jake," Flynn said in a low voice. "I know you're still out there. If you hurt her, I'll kill you. The one person I can't talk to about this has helped me learn what I have to do. I have to be patient, be watchful, and never hesitate. I'll do it for her. I'll do it for Eden. I won't let you do to them what you've done to all of those other people."

Flynn put the gun down and lay across his bed. His mind raced through all the things about war he and Rafe had talked about over the past months. He wished desperately Eden would tell Rafe everything.

But he could understand, in a way, why she wanted to wait until after the court date to tell her. She wanted Rafe to love her again. She didn't want anything to get in the way of it, and she thought if Rafe knew the first person Eden got involved with was the one responsible for the injunction and all of these problems, Rafe would blame Eden and never want to be with her. Eden felt responsible for everything and wanted to fix the problem herself. She wanted to show Rafe how she could be there and take care of her when she needed it. She wanted to make up to her for leaving her in the first place. She wanted to protect Rafe from Jake and from her mistake in being with him.

But still... he was sure if Rafe knew right now, it would be better. However, it didn't matter what he thought. He made a promise not to tell and he wouldn't. He made a vow to himself to protect Eden from herself and to help Eden protect Rafe. Tomorrow, he would ask for some time off work. He needed to be where Eden was to watch over her since Jake was trying to get near her again. He would be patient and watch, and he would not hesitate to take action if needed.

44

MONDAY MORNING, THE sky was a clear blue and free of clouds. Rafe Salvaggio was stopping by The Kiki Bistro to pick up coffee and breakfast to take to the office. She meant to stop by last night to see Letty but was engrossed in her night photography project and had stayed out later than planned. She was excited about the photography project and couldn't wait to see how the 35mm film images she took would come out. She loved using the film rather than digital. It felt more like an art form to her, though some of the students would argue digital art was better.

Rafe walked inside to find Letty behind the counter helping the cashier and server. "Good morning, Letty," Rafe said happily. She looked at the cashier. "Coffee and one of those." She pointed to a pastry in the case. "To go, please."

"Mornin'," Letty smiled. "Did you see Eden yesterday? She was looking for you."

"No, did she say what she wanted?" asked Rafe concerned. "Was something wrong? Why didn't she call me?"

"She said it was nothing," said Letty waving Rafe's concern away. "She probably just wanted to eat with you or have you do something with her and B. Where were you? You didn't stop by."

"I drove out to get away from all the lights to take some long-exposure night landscape pictures," Rafe said with a smile. I hope they turn out the way I envision them."

"If I know you and your perfectionism, they will." Letty laughed.

"Perfect?" Rafe chuckled. "No one's perfect, Letty, especially me," she said wryly.

"Yeah, right." Letty scoffed, knowing Rafe's propensity for being a perfectionist.

"Anyway, I didn't get back until late." Rafe watched the cashier put her pastry into a small bag then put the bag on the counter. "I kind of got sidetracked."

"Do tell," queried Letty as she got a lid for Rafe's coffee and put it on the cup. "Don't tell me you've got something else going on!" she challenged.

"No," said Rafe annoyed. "Why does everyone always assume the worst of me?" she asked disgruntled. "If you must know, I met with a kid I helped out by writing a letter of recommendation for a job internship."

"Oh, one of your star students?" asked Letty brushing away Rafe's annoyance with her.

"No," she said with a smirk, "just a kid I met. We got to talking, and things took longer than we planned last night."

"That's my girl," said Letty and laughed as she sat her coffee on the counter. "Saving all the kids of the world now, even if they aren't going to her school!"

"I'll see you later," said Rafe, giving her a cheeky smile as she took her coffee and pastry. She walked out and made her way to her car. As she sat her coffee on the car to open the door, she heard a voice call out her name and ice ran through her veins.

"Rafe!" Jake called again as he jogged up to her. "Rafe, I need to talk to you."

Rafe turned and steeled herself for the confrontation she knew was coming. "Jake," she said icily. "I told you to disappear."

"I need to talk to you," Jake said catching his breath. "I gave you a chance, so you can give me one."

Rafe just stared back at him coldly.

"You have to stop this," Jake pleaded. "I talked with Eden yesterday, and she was so pleased with herself. I can't convince her to leave now, and it's your fault," he complained doing his best to seem upset.

Rafe could feel the anger building in her and fought to keep it from her expression. "I'm glad you can't convince her, Jake. It gives me more time." She smiled at him coldly. "You know, I read a book called *The Art of War by Sun-Tzu*, a Chinese General, and his advice is to keep your friends close, and your enemies closer. And it's just what I intend to do."

Jake was up to her challenge and was confident he would win and, at the same time, wouldn't fail his mission. All he had to do was set everything up, and then he could sit back and watch. Once the dust cleared, he would be back in good with the reverend and have time to see what he could do about the thorn in his side—Mason.

"Why are you doing this?" Jake asked acting exasperated. "I was trying to do you a favor by telling you all this."

Rafe opened her car door and looked back at Jake. "Because, Jake, I'm convinced she won't leave with you because she is falling in love with me again. I don't need your favors. I think you're lying to me. I don't think she talked to you."

"You're so fucking stubborn!" he yelled angrily. "What possible reason would I have to lie? You're hurting everyone by doing this!" He clenched his fists and spoke with a broken voice. "She would only give me a kiss yesterday! I know you're sleeping with her, aren't you? How could you do this to her?"

"It's none of your business anymore," Rafe said as she gave him a cold stare. "She loves me. If you touch her, I'll kill you."

"I will touch her, and you can't stop me!" Jake declared angrily. "She doesn't love you! You think you're in control, but she's using your arrogance against you."

"I can be very arrogant." Rafe smirked disdainfully. "Maybe you're right, and it's why it's so easy for her to stay with me." She looked at him condescendingly. "Whatever the reason, I suggest you take my advice and don't talk to her again," she paused, controlling her temper, "if you really did talk to her. I told you I didn't want you to see her or talk to her."

"She called me," he seethed pointing to himself. "If I didn't go, she would know we talked. She and Bronte wanted to see Hunter. How could I tell her no?" Jake looked at Rafe and could tell he had her convinced of his anger and enough of his story to give her doubts.

"Think of a way," Rafe said evenly. "If you don't, I'll tell her you're talking to me and then we both may lose her. This is your last chance. Goodbye, Jake," she said as she picked up her coffee from the top of her car and got inside. Through her rearview mirror, she could see Jake still yelling at her as she drove away.

45

USING HER DRIVE to school to cool her temper, Rafe Salvaggio's mind flooded with scenarios of what she should do about the Eden and Jake situation. She knew the only way to verify anything was to talk to Eden. Eden knew she didn't want her to see Jake. So, Rafe reasoned, if she had seen him, she would tell her so they could keep the trust they were supposed to be building.

She also knew if Eden were keeping her meetings with Jake a secret, she wouldn't admit anything. If Eden lied about it, then Rafe would need to rethink everything. She made her way to her office, distracted by her problems.

"Brandy, get me Eden Kingsley on the line, please," Rafe said to her TA shortly.

"Good morning," said the Brandy even though she saw the Dean was too distracted to notice. "I'll put the call through as soon as we're connected." She dialed and connected with Eden within a few minutes. She pressed the intercom button. "Dean Salvaggio, I have Ms. Kingsley on line one."

"Thank you," Rafe replied and snatched up her head set and punched line one. "Eden? Good morning," she said trying to sound happy. "How are you?"

"Hi, Rafe. I'm fine. What's up?" Eden's voice came over the phone.

"I saw Letty this morning. She said you were looking for me yesterday. Is everything okay?" Rafe asked her with concern.

"Everything's fine," Eden said reassuringly. "I just wanted to spend some time with you."

"Oh," replied Rafe. "Okay. What did you and Bronte do all day?"

There was a hesitation on the line.

"We didn't do much," Eden finally answered. "We just had a lazy day at home," she hesitated again, "and we went to the park. What did you do? Where did you go?"

Rafe ignored her questions but noted her hesitations. "I'd like it if you and Bronte would come over tonight for dinner," she said calmly. "Will you come?"

"Sure, we'd love to come see you."

"Okay." Rafe wondered if she should press her for more information. She decided against it. "I'll see you tonight. Bye."

After Eden had said her goodbye, Rafe hung up and leaned forward on her desk, putting her head in her hands. "She loves me," she said with intention. "She loves me." She punched line one and dialed. "Is Katheryn available? Rafe Salvaggio. No, I won't hold. Put me through." Almost immediately, Katheryn was on the line. "Hello, Katheryn. I'm fine. I need your advice on something."

46

AFTER LEAVING WORK, Rafe Salvaggio picked up food, set the table for dinner, and changed her clothes. Then she waited for Eden and Bronte. She paced the floor because they were running late. She had already called and left one voicemail and was on the verge of leaving another, as scenarios of what Eden was doing ran through her mind. She heard a car pull into the driveway. She went out, seeing it was Eden, and quickly walked out to her car.

"Hi, let me help you," she offered then kissed Eden and took the bags she was holding. "What's all this? What took you so long?"

I wanted to go home to shower and change," she said and could not help her smile, "and I thought I'd bring a change of clothes just in case you let us spend the night."

"Spend the night?" Rafe pretended confusion. "Did I mention anything about spending the night? I thought we were just having dinner." She winked as she turned with the bags and walked to the house and went inside.

Eden unbuckled Bronte and got her out of the car. "I think your mama is in the mood for games tonight," she said as she closed the car door. "Let's go see, shall we?" She walked into the house with Bronte. "Rafe? Where are you?"

"I'm here," said Rafe as she walked out of the guest bedroom where she had deposited the bags she had carried inside. "Dinner is on the table. Let's sit," she said then ushered them to the dining room. She sat down and put her napkin in her lap.

"Thank you for inviting us to dinner," said Eden as she put Bronte in her booster chair and then sat in her own chair. "This looks good. Did you cook?"

"No, I didn't cook it," Rafe admitted. "This was done by a professional. Only the best for my guests." She smiled and started putting food on Bronte's plate.

Eden looked at Rafe and could see she was in a strange mood. She was acting very formal and silly. "Rafe?"

"Yes, Ms. Kingsley," said Rafe giving Eden her full attention.

"So formal tonight," Eden observed with a smiled. "You look very beautiful tonight."

Rafe raised her eyebrows. "Ms. Kingsley, you are very forward, and the compliment is mine to pay," she said as she took a sip of her wine. She looked over at Bronte. "Your daughter has excellent table manners for one so young."

"Rafe?" Eden said softly, seeing she was playing a game they had played before. 'Properly improper people.' Rafe and her father made it up after they came to America and sat through some excruciatingly proper dinners with some New York elite.

"Yes," said Rafe after wiping the corners of her mouth.

"I'd like to touch your hand," said Eden pushing the improper side of the game.

"Touching is very inappropriate at the dinner table," Rafe said stoically. She was happy Eden remembered the game and was playing along. "Talking about touching is just as inappropriate."

Eden looked down at her plate and smiled at Rafe's imitation of her father. "I'm very sorry."

"Guests need never apologize," said Rafe as she waved her hand. "I would remove the temptation if it were possible."

"Please don't," Eden said, trying not to laugh and end the game. She took a sip of wine. "Rafe?"

"Yes," said Rafe then took a bite of her food.

"The wine is excellent," Eden said, raising her glass and taking a sip.

"Thank you," said Rafe as she picked up her glass of wine and looked at it. "I chose this golden wine because it reminded me of your hair," she said and smiled. "And the taste reminds me of," she paused and raised her eyebrow, "well, it would be inappropriate to talk about at the table too."

"Then we definitely shouldn't talk about it," said Eden as she covered her mouth to grin and felt a tingling sensation run through her body.

"No," said Rafe then looked at her and Bronte with a serious face. "Would you like to know what I have planned for us after dinner?"

"Please," said Eden as she helped Bronte with her food.

"First," said Rafe looking from Eden to Bronte, "I thought we would build a castle for the lovely Bronte."

"A castle?" asked Eden wiping her hands on a napkin. "Aren't they cold and drafty? I don't know if she would like it."

Rafe sat back in her chair and took a sip of wine. "What do you suggest then?"

"A small cottage just big enough for all of her friends and is warm and cozy all of the time," answered Eden then picked up her fork to eat.

Rafe took a little time to think about the matter. "It would take less time to build," she said, considering the option.

"It means there will be more time to live in it," said Eden warmly.

"True," agreed Rafe

"And more time we can spend together," added Eden sweetly.

"Bronte," Rafe said as she handed her the water cup, "your mother is *brillante*." Bronte laughed at Rafe and babbled. "A cottage it is," she declared and returned her attention to her food.

"Rafe?" Eden said and looked at her with a glint in her eye.

Rafe picked up her glass of golden wine. "Yes," she said in acknowledgment.

"What else do you have planned for us?" asked Eden curiously.

Rafe looked at her and took a sip of wine. "This too would be inappropriate to discuss at the dinner table," she said resigned.

"I see." Eden nodded, and her heart skipped a beat. She smiled at Rafe in anticipation of whatever inappropriate things she had planned. "You're doing very well at controlling yourself tonight."

Rafe looked very seriously at Eden. "I thought it would be a nice change," she said thoughtfully.

"Yes," she said as she speared a vegetable. "Finishing a meal is a nice change."

"Courtesy is never unappreciated." Rafe gave a small polite smile and then picked up the wine bottle. "More wine?"

"Yes, please," said Eden and watched as Rafe poured some wine into her glass. "Only half a glass?" she asked surprised.

"Everything in moderation tonight," Rafe said and poured wine for herself and filled her glass halfway. "We must have our wits about us for a discussion we need to have."

Eden picked up her half-filled glass and swirled the wine. "It sounds like you expect to have a very serious discussion," she said and took a sip.

Rafe looked somberly into Eden's eyes. "I do."

"May I ask what the discussion will be about?" asked Eden curiously.

"You may," nodded Rafe as she sipped her wine.

Eden looked at Rafe and cleared her throat. "What is it we need to discuss tonight, Rafe?"

Rafe looked at Eden with an even, probing stare. "Our future together," she said chivalrously.

Eden stopped in mid-bite and looked at Rafe's serious face. "Our future together?" she asked surprised.

"Yes." Rafe nodded once.

"This is serious," said Eden as she put down her fork.

"Yes, it is, Ms. Kingsley," said Rafe softly.

"Rafe?" Eden said looking at her with a small smile.

"Yes," Rafe answered calmly though she was not calm inside.

"What game are you playing tonight?" Eden asked nervously.

Rafe looked at her intensely. "Eden, I'm not playing a game tonight. After playtime with Bronte, we will be having a very serious conversation."

"Oh," said Eden anxiously. "Okay." She looked at Rafe, unsure if this was part of the game or if something was wrong.

47

IN THE DINING room, Rafe Salvaggio cleaned up Bronte and took her out of her chair as Eden took care of the dishes in the kitchen. Rafe carried Bronte into the guest room, and they got a small storage box of toys and a couple of sheets from the linen closet. Bronte followed Rafe through the house and back into the dining room. They saw Eden had cleared the table, so Rafe put the toy box on the floor. She took a sheet from the toy box and flung it out over Bronte, letting the force of air rush over her and stir the toddler's dark curls into a dance. Bronte reached out and laughed as the silk fabric floated down onto her and tickled her with its softness.

Bronte was giggling at the sensation of the air and sheet flowing over her. Rafe flung the sheet up again, and this time, she rushed under to join Bronte as the sheet floated down gently on top of them. Rafe reached out to tickle Bronte and kissed her when she jumped into her arms.

"We're in the clouds again, B Girl!" Rafe said as they played.

Bronte jumped up and stood in Rafe's lap, raising her small hands. Rafe took her cue, lifted the sheet, and shook it, making it billow around them. The air washed over them in little bursts.

"Kiss me in the clouds, B Girl!"

Bronte laughed and kissed Rafe's cheek as the air whipped around them. Rafe kissed her back.

Rafe let her arms down slowly, and the sheet fell limp around them. "We're back on the ground," Rafe said playfully. "Now it's time to build our house."

Bronte grabbed Rafe's neck and hugged her excitedly, feeling the smoothness of the fabric as it ran over her as Rafe pulled the sheet off them.

"What are you guys doing?" Eden asked as she walked into the dining room.

Rafe smiled up at Eden with disheveled hair. "We're playing with our cottage construction materials," she answered with a laugh.

"You're using your silk sheets to make a cottage?" asked Eden in astonishment.

"If she can't have a castle, she should have other luxuries," said Rafe as she ran her hand through her hair to fix it.

"Okay," said Eden shaking her head. "How are you going to build a cottage with a silk sheet?"

"First of all," Rafe began with a smile as she got up off the floor, "we have two." She handed Eden the end of the sheet. "Second, we just put them over the table so they hang to the floor." They put the sheets on the table, and then Bronte started to pull out a chair.

"Whoa," Eden cried out as she grabbed the chair and held onto the sheets. "Wait, babe. You're going to pull off the sheets."

"Here. Put these books on the sheets," said Rafe. "I'll help Bronte make the door." She helped Bronte carefully move out two chairs to make a doorway. "There we go," said Rafe then stood back to look at their work. "Now we just have to move in. Get inside, you two, and I'll bring in the box."

"We're all going?" asked Eden as she watched Bronte climb under the table.

"Yes, we're all going." Rafe's eyes twinkled as she smiled. She bent down and picked up the box of toys. "Get down there."

"Rafe, I'm in a skirt!" Eden complained. Rafe just looked at her and pointed to the table with her chin as she carried the box over. Eden laughed as she got down on her hands and knees and crawled under the table. "It's kind of dark under here," she said from under the table.

Crawling in behind Eden and pushing the box in front of her, Rafe made her way under the table. "Not to worry. Bronte and I have thought of everything." She helped Bronte dig through the box and pulled out a big flashlight. "See?" Rafe said as she turned on the light, lighting up the whole area.

"Much better," said Eden as she watched Bronte start taking more things out of the box. A small pillow and blanket, some stuffed animals, a dish towel, which she handed to Rafe, and more small toys. "What's with the dish towel?"

"It's a tea towel," said Rafe like it was something she should know, "and it's our table cloth. It's my job to set out the tea things." Rafe reached into the box, pulled out a little glass tea set, and set it up on the tea towel. "Okay, B Girl. The table is set. Would you like to serve?"

Bronte crawled over, sat in front of the tea set, picked up the little teapot, and pretended to pour into a cup. She handed one to Rafe then looked at Eden and poured another, handing it to Eden.

Eden took the teacup from Bronte. "Thank you," she said as she pretended to take a sip. Bronte looked at her then looked at Rafe and took the cup away from Eden. "What's wrong?"

Rafe covered her smile with her hand. "You're supposed to wait for the hostess to pour her cup before you drink," said Rafe. "I guess you're in trouble."

"I didn't know I was supposed to wait." Eden sighed and watched as Bronte pretended to pour a third cup.

"It's okay," said Rafe. Bronte looked up at Rafe and took a pretend sip and so did Rafe. "This is very good tea, Bronte. Can Mommy have another cup now?"

Bronte looked at Eden, smiled, poured her another cup of tea, and handed it to her.

"Thank you," she said to Bronte then looked at Rafe. "Can I drink it now?"

"Of course," Rafe chuckled. She watched Bronte as she pretended to stretch and yawn and began to do the same herself. "Oh, my!" she said. "It's getting late. We have to go to bed now so B Girl can get up early and go to work. Come on, Eden." She pulled Eden to the far end of the table and lay down with her as Bronte went and laid on her little pillow and blanket. "Good night," said Rafe and turned off the flash light.

"How long do we have to lay down here?" Eden whispered in Rafe's ear.

Rafe found Eden's lips in the dark and kissed her. "Not long." She sat up and turned on the flash light then watched as Bronte came over and kissed her good morning. "Good morning, B Girl," Rafe said then kissed Eden as she sat up. "Good morning, Mommy."

Bronte kissed Eden.

"Good morning," said Eden as she kissed Bronte then watched her as she looked from her to Rafe. "Oh, sorry," she said then leaned over and kissed Rafe. "Good morning." She smiled at Rafe.

Rafe lay back down. "B Girl, I just don't want to get up this morning. You have to convince me," said Rafe playfully.

Bronte looked at Rafe, shook her head, and signed no, no, no. She climbed on Rafe and started kissing her face, and Rafe pretended to complain.

"No, no," she groaned. "I don't want to get up."

Bronte looked over at Eden.

Eden grinned at Bronte. "Let's get her!"

Bronte smiled and started kissing Rafe and patting her on the face as Eden started kissing her and tickling her too.

"No fair!" Rafe was laughing. "Two against one! I'll get you both down!" Rafe grabbed them, turned so she was over both of them, and began kissing one and then the other. "B Girl, I think we should get Mommy now, don't you?"

Bronte rolled over and gave Eden her wet kisses on her cheek and face, and Rafe held Eden down, kissing and tickling her back.

"Revenge, my sweet!"

"Stop!" cried Eden laughing hard. "Stop, I can't take it anymore! St... Stop!"

Rafe looked at Bronte. "She surrenders!" She cheered.

Bronte clapped and gave Eden another kiss.

Rafe looked down at Eden, kissed her on the lips and face, and put her lips near her ear. "I want this," she whispered. "I want this all the time. I want us to play together and laugh together. It's all I've ever wanted," she whispered and kissed her again. "My family." She lifted away from Eden and kissed Bronte when she jumped into her arms. "It's time for you to go to work now," she told her playfully then released her from their hug. She watched as Bronte went back to the box and pulled out her little purse.

Eden sat up and leaned close to Rafe. "I want this too," she whispered. She looked over at Bronte. "Is that your Prada purse," she asked Rafe as she looked at her with surprise then back at Bronte, "the one you bought while we were in Italy?"

"Yes," said Rafe with a nod. "She has good taste."

Eden looked at Rafe bewildered. "Didn't it cost like six-hundred dollars?"

"I don't remember," said Rafe then looked at Eden's face and laughed. "Don't worry. She takes good care of it."

Bronte made her way out from under the table leaving her parents behind.

"Bye, see you tonight," called Rafe as Bronte waved goodbye.

"Where's she going? Should we follow her?" asked Eden worried.

"No. She's going to work," Rafe said as she lay back down. "She brings back some very interesting things when she comes home."

"Really?" Eden laughed.

"Yes, really," Rafe said, happy she could show Eden a game she and Bronte liked to play. "Once she brought back a jewelry box full of jewels. I forgot and left it sitting out on the bed," she said with a grimace. "Another time she brought back a very interesting briefcase full of papers. I wonder what she'll bring back tonight." She leaned over and kissed Eden then snapped off the flashlight. "While we're waiting, I've thought of something we can do," she said then took hold of Eden to kiss her face and neck.

"You want to make out with me under the table?" asked Eden as she laughed softly.

"No," said Rafe seductively, "I want to make out with you in our cozy cottage." She found Eden's lips in the dark and kissed her deeply. "You taste so good," she said. "I may feel you up a little while we're here too," she teased and started moving her hand under her shirt and over her breasts.

After a little while, they heard Bronte returning, and Rafe switched the flashlight back on as Eden fixed her shirt. "Welcome home, B Girl!"

Bronte crawled in, and then she hugged and kissed Rafe and Eden.

"Did you bring me something?" asked Rafe.

Bronte held up Eden's purse.

"Wow! Treasure!"

Bronte opened the purse and started to dump it out, and Rafe stopped her.

"Hold on," she said. "We should ask Mommy first if it's okay." She looked at Eden. "Anything in there she shouldn't have or see?"

"No, it's okay," said Eden and smiled.

"Are you sure? She's very thorough," Rafe warned her.

"It's fine," Eden assured her. "There's not much in there."

"Okay." Rafe gave the purse back to Bronte and let her dump the contents onto the floor. She put the flashlight next to Bronte so she could see everything.

Bronte picked up the sunglasses and put them on Eden.

"She knows where those go," Rafe said with a grin.

Bronte went back and picked up Eden's wallet then sat in Rafe's lap with it and opened it up. She took out the cash and set it aside.

"We're working on understanding the value of cash," Rafe informed Eden with a laugh.

"I'm in no real hurry for her to learn about cash," said Eden not looking forward to dealing with the topic in the future.

Bronte pulled out the credit cards, looked through the pictures, and held them up for Rafe to see. She showed her a picture of Hunter.

Rafe looked at Eden and frowned. "Isn't that Jake's son?"

"Oh," said Eden surprised. "Yes, I guess I just never took it out. It's a pre-school picture." She looked at Rafe with apprehension. "I really need to clean it out."

Rafe looked away from Eden, remembering her conversation this morning with Jake. "Do you miss him?"

"Hunter? He's a cute kid, but no," she said looking down at Bronte in Rafe's lap. "I don't really miss him. I didn't really see him much. He was with his mom a lot of the time."

Rafe looked over Bronte's shoulder, dreading having to look through Eden's wallet pictures. "Hey, B Girl, you want to go sit with Mommy to look through those?"

Bronte flipped the pictures, revealing a picture of Jake as Rafe handed Bronte to Eden.

Eden looked over at Rafe, feeling guilty. "I'm sorry, Rafe. Like I said, I just," she hesitated, "I just never cleaned it out."

"You would tell me if you've seen him, wouldn't you?" asked Rafe as she looked into her widened eyes. "No," she stopped her from speaking, "don't answer that. I don't want you to have to lie to me."

"Rafe," Eden looked away from her, "I don't want to see him. It's just," she hesitated, "I forgot the pictures were even there. I really am sorry."

"It's okay." Rafe tried to smile reassuringly. "I mean," she sighed and lowered her head, "I have pictures of Greer, and you aren't upset with me." She rubbed Eden's shoulder. "I should look into getting you a picture of me to put in there again."

"Sure, I'd like that," she nodded anxiously. She watched Rafe begin to refill the purse. "It's not really the same though, is it?"

"What do you mean?" Rafe asked as she put the purse in front of Eden.

"I mean, Greer didn't hurt me like Jake hurt you," explained Eden as Rafe just looked at her. "Your pictures of Greer are public, and these were in my wallet. So, it is different.

I really am sorry," she said as she took the pictures out of her wallet, wadded them up, and put them in her pocket. "I'll throw them away later."

"Eden, you really don't have to throw them away," said Rafe somberly. "You can have pictures of anyone you want. You love me, right?"

"Yes, I do love you and I think this just hurt you," said Eden, worried Rafe was upset.

"Really, I didn't feel a thing," said Rafe hardening herself so her words would be true.

Bronte had made her way back to the purse and pulled Eden's phone from the side pocket. She handed it up to her mommy and climbed into her lap.

"She wants to see the pictures on my phone," said Eden softly. She unlocked it and got into the photo gallery, so the pictures opened. "These were from yesterday when we spent a lazy day in the park," she said and turned the phone so Rafe could see the photos. "She was so cute with her yellow ball. I was going to call you to come and take her pictures, but you were busy."

Rafe looked at the photos as Eden swiped through them, remembering Jake had said he met her in the park with Hunter. "You look good, Bronte," said Rafe but was unsure what to say to Eden. "That's a nice ball."

Bronte made the sign for *ball* and pointed at the photo. She got up, went to the toy box, got out a small blue ball, and took it back to Rafe.

"Are we going to play ball before we go to work again? Okay," Rafe said and rolled the ball to the other side of the table.

Bronte went after it and rolled it back to her. Then, as Eden watched them play, Rafe rolled the ball over to her.

"Come on, Mommy," said Rafe and smiled at her. "You have to play too."

48

CAREFULLY DRAGGING BRONTE out from under the table, Rafe Salvaggio picked her up and handed her to Eden. After playing house, rolling the ball and going to work several more times, Bronte finally fell asleep while pretending to go to sleep under the table. Eden took her to the bedroom while Rafe picked up all of the toys and folded the sheets and put them away. Rafe went into the living room and sat down with her camera, cleaning the lens and dusting it while she waited for Eden to finish with Bronte.

Eden saw Rafe on the couch, walked over, and started rubbing her shoulders from the back of the couch. "She's all tucked in," Eden whispered in her ear." She ran her hands down the front of Rafe, kissing her neck and feeling her breasts. "I love you," she whispered. "I want you."

Rafe looked back and smiled at Eden, then pulled her around. "Come around here," she said as she placed her camera on the table.

Eden went around the couch and crawled onto it, kissing Rafe.

"Eden," said Rafe as she gently pushed her back, "I really want to have the serious discussion I told you about at dinner."

"We will," Eden said between her kisses. "We will. I want you..." she whispered, "I want you to make love to me."

Rafe tried to push her back gently. "I need to talk to you first," she said firmly.

Eden took Rafe's hand and pressed it against herself. "How can I convince you?" she whispered. "I'm so hot and wet. It's for you," she breathed into Rafe's ear.

Rafe closed her eyes against the warm sensation she felt under Eden's skirt. "Eden," Rafe whispered, "you don't have to convince me. I want to but," she said softly, "we really should talk first." She felt Eden's kiss. "You may change your mind." She pushed Eden back again gently and looked into her eyes. "I'm serious."

"So we can't have sex when I want to?" Eden pouted. "Just when you want to?"

"What?" Rafe laughed and quirked her lips. "Eden, you know that's not true. I'm glad you want to have sex, and I do want to make love to you," she said and kissed her. "It's just what I want to talk to you about is important, and I don't want to make love to you and then possibly make you angry."

"If it may possibly make me angry, it means we probably won't be having sex," said Eden with a frown.

"It could be true," said Rafe cautiously, "but I might be wrong." She looked at Eden's downcast face. "Do you want me to make love to you knowing the possibility is out there? What would you think of me if I did that to you?"

"Real nice, Rafe!" Eden said in frustration. "You got me all worked up with your innuendo over dinner and then the things you were doing to me when we were making out under the table." She sat back on the couch in frustration. "You should have just kept going." She closed her eyes and shook her head to calm herself. "I'm sorry. You're probably right. If you had, I would have probably been more pissed off if whatever you want to talk with me about may make me angry."

"You know," Rafe said as she lifted Eden's head and looked mischievously into her eyes, "I could watch, and maybe take some pictures of you while you fuck yourself." She looked over at her camera then back at Eden. "You'd have to promise to think about me, though." She kissed her softly. "Then you'd get some satisfaction and maybe I can too, just a little." She kissed her again. "Just by thinking about it." She looked at Eden again and smiled as she nodded her head toward her camera.

"No way." Eden huffed then laughed. "I'm not doing that for you." She gave her a smirk. "Not right now, anyway."

Rafe raised her eyebrows and frowned. "I don't have any film for the camera anyway."

"What?" said Eden vexed. "What would you have done if I said yes?"

Rafe smiled impishly and kissed her. "I would have pretended I had film."

"You drive me mad, you know," Eden said and then kissed her back.

"*Ti voglio da impazzire*,"[10] Rafe purred in Italian as she kissed Eden over face and neck playfully.

"Yes," Eden said softly, enjoying when she knew what Rafe was saying in Italian and the attention she was giving her. "You do drive me crazy," she said as Rafe kissed her again. She looked into Rafe's beautiful eyes as she pulled away. She then sat back and took a deep breath. "Okay, let's talk. Let's talk about our future together."

"Okay, good." Rafe took her hand. "I've been thinking about you moving in with me like you asked."

Eden looked up with wide eyes and hopeful. "And?"

"I think it's a big commitment," Rafe said evenly. "There are a lot of issues to take into consideration. First, there's Bronte, then our relationship, then money. We have to know how things stand before we jump into things."

"So, you're saying no?" Eden said deflated.

Rafe hesitated then picked up a manila envelope off the table and handed it to Eden. "I'm not saying no." She paused and looked at Eden intently. "I'm saying yes, with conditions."

Looking at the envelope with uncertainty, Eden opened it and took out the papers. "A co-habitation agreement?" She skimmed through it. "Why do we need this?"

"Because," said Rafe cautiously, "if things don't work out for some reason, we're both entitled to some protection."

"Protection?" asked Eden confused.

"Eden," Rafe sighed, "when we split, you had nothing. You moved in with," she hesitated, "Jake," she sighed, hating she had to even say his name, "and really, you just had the clothes

---

[10] I drive you crazy,

on your back. Then you moved out of his place into your own and had almost nothing. It was hard for you, even with what I was giving you to help with Bronte. As the social worker said, your apartment was sparse. I don't want you to go through the same thing again if this doesn't work out. I want you, both of us, to have options."

"What makes you think things won't work out?" Eden asked worriedly.

"I don't think that," Rafe stopped herself and sighed. "I hope things do work out. But, like you pointed out, we've only been good for a couple of months, and we still have a lot to work on."

"But we were together for over four years before we really completely split, and we've known each other for six," argued Eden in frustration. She looked down and began to read the papers. "So, according to this, we both have to be gainfully employed or self-sufficient financially." She looked at Rafe. "I don't want to quit my job."

"Good to know," said Rafe. "You need to keep your job. You're great at it, and, even though you hate it sometimes, most of the time, you enjoy it. Abby told me about your need for autonomy, and the way to keep it is to keep your job."

"I have to install my own phone line if I need it and pay rent equal to one-half of the mortgage plus taxes and insurance," Eden read then looked up at Rafe, "and half the utility bills less any storage costs for my things from the apartment."

"Then you have a utility in your name for credit," Rafe explained, "and you don't have to pay double rent if you have things in storage."

"This is crazy, Rafe! You have my whole life micromanaged and on paper!" said Eden pissed as she waved the paper around. "Look at this," she read from the agreement. "This agreement in no way implies a marriage, common law, or otherwise—nor any other relationship emotional or physical." She looked up at Rafe. "What the heck does that mean?"

"It means we don't have to fuck each other just because we live in the same house," said Rafe calmly. "It means you're not my wife or my partner yet because we still have a lot to work on," she said softly.

"So... what?" Eden burst out upset. "I'll just be your roommate?"

"Yes," said Rafe and nodded, "I guess it's one way to look at it." She looked at Eden earnestly. "Eden, we aren't kids anymore who can just jump in and out of things. We have responsibilities and a child's emotional state to think about. If you two move in, it will be a big deal, and if you decide you want to leave again, it will affect her. By having this agreement, it makes us take everything very seriously."

"I won't want to leave again," Eden promised as she looked at the papers again. "It says I have to live in the guest room."

"Yes," confirmed Rafe. "You need part of the house you can call yours. Where you can go, and I can't come in without permission so you can have privacy."

"Will I ever get to come into your room again?" she asked gravely.

Rafe looked into her eyes trying to hide the pain she was feeling. "I don't know."

"Why didn't you just say no?" asked Eden with tears forming in her eyes.

"I don't know," said Rafe as she sighed and sat back, feeling like maybe she had let Jake's words force her hand and maybe she should be saying no. "Maybe I should have. I just thought since you asked me, and you wanted to move in, maybe things could move forward faster if you did," she said soberly. Maybe this would tell her faster if Eden was going to leave her for Jake. She looked into Eden's eyes again. "I want to make sure we're serious," she said firmly.

Eden fought back the tears as she looked through the papers more. "What's this dissolution of agreement?"

"It's there for you," Rafe explained, "in case you have to move out."

"It's a freaking pay off!" yelled Eden in anger. "If I move out in the first six months, you pay twenty thousand dollars for moving expenses and, after six months, an additional five thousand dollars per month up to forty thousand dollars." She looked up at Rafe in shock. "You've already put all this money in an account?"

"It's so you can get a nice place right away for you and Bronte if things don't work out," Rafe explained. "I don't want you to have to move just anywhere or into the first thing you see," she hesitated, "or with the first person."

"You've already got me moving out," Eden cried, unable to hold the tears back any longer. "It looks like you don't think things will work out."

"It might seem like it if you just look at those few parts," said Rafe as she took the papers from her and scanned through it. "Look," she pointed to a section, "this agreement is null and void if there is a legally binding marriage between the parties or other such agreement binding them is formed." She looked at Eden. "So, if we get married, or if we get a palimony agreement, or something similar, this agreement goes away." She handed the agreement back to Eden.

Eden flipped through the pages with tears running down her cheeks. "I'm not sure what to do."

"You should take your time to look it over," insisted Rafe. "Make sure there's nothing you think needs added or anything you can't live with. You can have a lawyer look it over if you want," she encouraged her. "Take your time, and if you want to do it, then we can sign and have it notarized and give it to Katheryn. Then all the rent payments will be sent to her, so you don't have to give me any money directly."

"So now it's up to me?" she asked as she wiped her tears with the back of her hand.

"I guess," Rafe said with a sad smile. "We don't have to do this now. We can wait until we've been together and seeing each other longer," she paused and looked into her eyes, "but if you want to move in now, I think it's best we have this agreement."

"What about Bronte?" Eden asked. "You said there would be issues with her."

"There will be," she paused and ran her hand through her hair, "if the adoption goes through. If you move in with me and we stay together, everything will be fine. But, if you move out, what will happen to my relationship with Bronte? I know I'll be her other parent, but you're still her mother and..." She stopped letting Eden finish the rest in her head. "Then there's the possibility the adoption never goes through," said Rafe softly. "If things go bad between us again, what happens then? Will I still get my visitation time and get to be part of her life?"

"Rafe," Eden said as she touched Rafe's sad face, "I've said and done everything I can think of to let you know, no matter what, you will still be in Bronte's life—nothing will change my mind."

"It's always nice to hear you say that," Rafe said as she smiled sadly at Eden. "But I think it's best for both of us if there is some sort of official agreement."

Eden sat back in frustration. "I just don't understand why you don't believe me and everyone questions me about it," she complained.

"Because," Rafe said cautiously, "you said you had a lot more to tell me. Unless you're ready to tell me everything tonight," she paused, "I'll have doubts."

"I don't want you to have doubts," Eden insisted. "I want to tell you things." She tried not to cry again. "I just need a little more time."

"I know," said Rafe. "It's something we both need right now." She looked away from Eden's tears. "I just hope we have enough," she said under her breath.

"I want you to love me. I don't want you to stop," Eden said, wanting to reassure Rafe of her feelings. "I'm talking to Cathcart and working through things so I can get it together, so

I can tell you everything. Please," she pleaded. "Just have patience with me."

"I will," said Rafe as she reached out and pulled Eden to her. "I love you, and I want you too. I want to be here for you and give you whatever you want," she sighed, "but I also want to make sure everything is right, and we aren't making a mistake in getting back into a relationship."

"A mistake?" asked Eden as she pulled back. "We're not making a mistake, Rafe. We're fixing our mistakes."

"Okay," said Rafe hoping it was true. "You look at the agreement, and if you want to, we can sign it. Then we can try living together again." She pulled Eden back to her and stroked her hair.

Eden breathed in Rafe's calming scent and soaked in her warmth. "Rafe?"

"Yes, Ede," she said softly.

"I need to tell you something," she said as she felt Rafe kiss her head. "You—" she took a ragged breath, "you make me feel safe." She felt Rafe hold her tighter. "Rafe?"

"Hmm," Rafe breathed.

"I think we both want the same things," Eden said hopefully. Then she closed her eyes as Rafe held her.

"I'm sure we do," whispered Rafe reassuringly, hoping it was true.

After a long silence, and listening to Rafe's calming heartbeat, Eden opened her eyes. "Rafe?"

"Yes," Rafe answered softly.

"Will you tell me about the inappropriate things you mentioned at dinner now?" Eden smiled against Rafe's chest.

"No," said Rafe as she raised an eyebrow. "I don't think so Ms. Kingsley." She spoke most properly as she had at dinner.

Eden heard Rafe's heart rate quicken. She lifted up and caressed her face. "No?" she said softly.

Rafe pulled her close. "No, I think I'll have to show you," she whispered then kissed her deeply and ran her hands over her body. "Do you want to get back under the table?" she asked playfully.

"Rafe!" Eden laughed. "Stop playing with me and fuck me," Eden moaned.

"Hmm," purred Rafe between her kisses. "Alpha E is back," she teased. "I guess we'll have to see who's in control tonight."

To be continued in Book Five — Sowers of Discord...

NOTES

Translations: For translations of Italian, French and Spanish use: www.Babblefish.com

The chapters in this book were arranged with the intent of saving paper. This chapter style saved 9 pages. Original Total Book Pages 330 — Final Pages 321.

Music mentioned in this book.
No financial incentive was given for the mention of the following artists in this work. The author is a fan and felt mentioning them worked in the story. For the use of their name, credit is given, and links to their work are below.

Enjoy!

Jen Foster
Website: http://jenfoster.com
Facebook: https://www.facebook.com/jenfostermusic
Twitter: https://twitter.com/jenkfoster
Instagram: https://instagram.com/jenkfoster
YouTube: https://www.youtube.com/user/JenFosterOfficial
Tumbler: http://jenfostermusic.tumblr.com

ABOUT THE AUTHOR

C.L. CATTANO LIVES in the Midwestern U.S. with her partner and their dog somewhere between the city and the forest. With a joy for traveling, she and her partner have visited many countries and have a love for meeting people and learning about the places they visit. When possible, she likes to include references in her work about the things she has learned, the places she has been and people she has met while on her travels and in her everyday life.

Cattano has a variety of creative interests including, but not limited to, creating fine art, writing, photography, and supporting women in the arts. She considers herself a 'Jack of All Trades' dabbling in what she terms the 'whimsies of her soul' that pull her toward happiness and fulfillment.

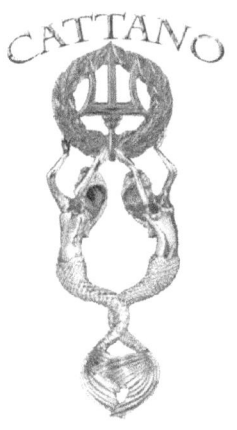

OTHER BOOKS

By C. L. Cattano

Cursed Hearts is a love story transcending time and gender. Separated from by a gift from a bored demon on All Hallows Eve two souls connected by the power of love have been searching through time for each other and incarnated as both men and women.

Over time, the gift became a curse and a game for the demons.

Now the souls have finally met again, and they must fight for a life together.

Will love prevail? Will they finally be able to live together again for a lifetime? They have one night to figure out the riddle and get it right to break the curse.

NOTE: 18+ Lesbian Romance. Some light erotic moments.

Cursed Hearts

Salvaggio's Light Series

Shattered Paradise – Book One
Blue Inferno – Book Two
Secrets & Rivalry – Book Three
Wildling's Claim – Book Four

REQUEST FOR REVIEW

Thank you for reading **Salvaggio's Light** — *An Epic Contemporary Romance Serial.*

I hope you enjoyed book four, **Wildling's Claim**, and will consider leaving an honest review. It only takes a few minutes, so I encourage you to go now and leave a review!

Check out the Salvaggio's Light Facebook page to join in the discussions and fun!
www.facebook.com/pg/SalvaggiosLight

Join the CL Cattano Mailing List www.clcattano.com

I love getting fan mail, and you can contact me at
clc@clcattano.com

www.ingramcontent.com/pod-product-compliance
Lightning Source LLC
Chambersburg PA
CBHW070630260626
47161CB00007B/2653